D1524582

The End of Lies

By
Andrew Barrett

Copyright © 2017 Andrew Barrett

The right of Andrew Barrett to be identified as the Author of the Work has been asserted by him in accordance Copyright, Designs and Patents Act 1988.

First published in 2017 by Bloodhound Books

Apart from any use permitted under UK copyright law, this publication may only be reproduced, stored, or transmitted, in any form, or by any means, with prior permission in writing of the publisher or, in the case of reprographic production, in accordance with the terms of licences issued by the Copyright Licensing Agency.

All characters in this publication are fictitious and any resemblance to real persons, living or dead, is purely coincidental.

www.bloodhoundbooks.com

Print ISBN 978-1-912175-83-3

This book is dedicated to my wonderful fiancée, Sarah Jowitt. I simply couldn't wish for a more tolerant and selfless lady who is always there for me as I chase my dream. Sarah, this is for you.

Chapter One

How can you tell if you're lying to yourself? I always thought I was in charge of my own destiny. Everybody does.

Turns out that I was no more in charge of my own destiny, or even my own thoughts, than I was in charge of the weather.

I hopped over the low wall surrounding our back garden and walked towards the house, watching my feet parting the long grass and driving tiny white moths airborne. My mind grappled with all the possibilities of leaving behind a dead life and all the fears of beginning a new one. I'm not good with change, and something as enormous as this…

The back door was open.

I stood there like a drooling fool with my hands hanging by my sides staring at something I'd never seen before. The door was open. I never left the door open. Chris never left the door open. The only time that door was open, or even unlocked, was when we were going through it. I wanted to call out but something made me keep my mouth shut.

I tried to swallow but it caught in my throat; I felt vulnerable. I turned a quick three-sixty but everything looked in order, just as it had when I left home this morning. Now my mind was nowhere near thoughts of the future; my mind was stuck here in the present wondering what the fuck was going on, and it was telling me to get the hell away from here right now. But I couldn't do that. Where would I go? And what would I do once I got there, except worry? And where was Chris?

Chris was in there making plans for us. "We each walk from here with a single bag," he'd said. "In that bag is our new life. It's very precious. You're to tell no one we're going. When the day comes, don't even hand in your notice; you come home as normal and wake up in Milan the next day."

My hand touched the door, pushed it all the way open, and I crept into the hallway, clutching my shoulder bag so hard that my nails turned white. I listened but heard nothing. I took a few hesitant paces toward the full-length mirror at the far end of the hall, wondering if this was a practical joke. If so, it wasn't the slightest bit funny and I'd leave Chris in no doubt of that. The woman creeping closer to me, hitching her bag up again, had white knuckles and wide eyes. Coming up on my right was the lounge, but it was the under-stairs cupboard door to my left that caught my attention. It, too, was open. I stared at it, confusion tickling my mind.

I almost called out but just then I heard a noise from the bathroom.

"Fuckwit," I whispered. He *had* left the door open after all; my hand relaxed on the bag, and the tension seeped out of my stiff shoulders. Wait till I get... And then I was walking forward again, slowly, *creeping* – in my own house! But *I* hadn't closed the back door either, and that realisation struck me like a brick to the head. Why hadn't I closed it?

I peered into the lounge. The curtains were still drawn, but I had no trouble seeing the body lying on the floor. I tried to remain quiet, but I'm sure I gasped as my hand gripped the doorframe and my heart kicked me in the chest. The tension was back and for a moment I was immobile, unable to move even if I'd wanted to.

Chris lay on the floor only half a dozen yards away, but they were the longest six yards in history. He was on his back, head twisted to the side facing me like he was waiting for me to scream before laughing his nuts off. Only he didn't blink. And his chest was completely still. And even from here I could see the blood on his shirt glistening in the light from the curtained windows as it dried and crusted over at the edges.

I didn't scream. I didn't do anything because I was holding onto the doorframe to stop myself sinking to the floor and vomiting.

I took long deep breaths but I found myself going light-headed, so I stopped trying to prepare myself and just walked to him. My Chris. I could see his hands, the ring on his finger, could see the stubble on his cheek, the shirt collar frayed where those whiskers had eaten away at it. I felt a cold wave of dread flood through me from the centre outwards, and then my eyes began to sting as my vision rippled. I blinked and my tears fell onto him, but still I made no sound. I wonder if it was some kind of subconscious self-preservation mechanism. I pictured myself screaming, pulling at my hair and running around in jagged little circles as the pain of his death tore me apart until there was nothing left of me.

I bent down to him, ran the backs of my fingers against his cool face, and could feel my nose blocking up as I choked on a ball of sorrow the size of a fist. He looked strange without his spectacles. They were next to his right shoulder, and there was a tiny indent on either side of the bridge of his nose where they used to rest. Details I hadn't really noticed before.

Inside, I was still screaming when a noise from the bathroom shattered my turgid thoughts like a window exploding in the dead of night. I was back, blinking, breathing so hard that anyone would have thought I'd been sprinting. My eyes were everywhere at once, and I could feel the tendrils of panic spreading through my mind, and like hot bile I could feel a scream crawling up my throat. I opened my mouth to make it audible, but then I saw it.

There, by the doorframe.

I looked back at Chris, knowing this would be the last time I'd see my husband.

The knife was over there by the door. I should pick it up, I should walk out through the back door and call the police.

Who was upstairs? Who was in the bathroom? Why had they murdered my Chris?

I stretched over and picked up the knife by its blue handle. It had a thin smear of redness and glistening traces of fat on its blade. My husband's blood.

Someone upstairs shouted something; sounded to me like, 'Pink!' The bathroom echoed like someone was moving furniture, and I listened for more noises so hard that I almost ignored the squeal of the front gate as it opened. Panic stabbed me and anchored me to the spot.

I heard footsteps on the path outside to my left. And now someone was coming down the stairs to my right, the wood creaking under their weight. Still I stood there like an idiot with a knife in my hand staring into space, wondering what flavour of nightmare was to come next.

Chapter Two

Chris stared at me over the rim of his coffee cup. "What?" I said.

"Nothing." He looked away.

Normally I would have pursued it, but there was something strange about him today that said I'd be wise to keep my mouth shut. Actually, there'd been something strange about him for weeks. And when I'd tried to get it out of him before, he'd smiled and said there was nothing wrong, that his mind had wandered and he was just silently enjoying wherever it took him. And that excuse was fine to begin with; I could understand it, had been there myself, so I let it go. But recently these fugues had been more frequent, more intense.

The last time I questioned him about it, he damned near bit my fucking head off.

And that wasn't like my Chris at all.

My Chris was a gentleman, and I loved him so much that it hurt. Even after all these years together, the blaze of love was still so bright you had to wear sunglasses, the feelings so pure that time without him was painful. Life outside of our marriage was pale, insipid, lukewarm, and dull.

Life only became intense and vivid when we were together.

And that was true for both of us. I know, not only because he told me, but because I could see it in his eyes. And I know eyes. I know what a person is thinking before they even open their mouth.

But these days I didn't know what was wrong with Chris. He stared at me again, and I dared to be unwise. "Chris." I shuffled closer, rubbed his leg and smiled at him. "Come on, talk to me."

I waited, kept quiet for a while, and when it was clear he wasn't going to speak, I said, "It's work, isn't it?"

He blinked and then looked away.

"What about it? What's happened?"

He sighed and put down the cup as though he meant to speak. But he kept quiet.

My toes were beginning to curl, and I was struggling to keep my temper. "Is it someone at work?" I swallowed, thinking the worst.

He shot me a look. "You think I'm seeing someone from work?"

"Oh, come on! You're not exactly overloading me with information; allow me to speculate."

"Speculate in a different direction, Becky. Christ's sake."

Thank God, I thought. I couldn't bear it if he were… nope, not going to say it. "So what, then?"

And still he said nothing. He was sitting there wringing his hands together like he was about to shit a brick, staring at the floor.

"If you don't spit it out soon," I whispered, "I'm going to get a frying pan and smash your face in."

He smiled then, and it was good to see. "You want a whisky?"

"No. I want you to tell—"

"I'm having one."

I could hear the bottle clinking against the glass, and he was back in the lounge pacing around like an expectant father, rubbing his neck, back bent almost double. He was going to tell me, I think he was just searching for the right *way* to tell me. I sat forward; a feeling of foreboding hitched a ride on my speeding thoughts. "Blurt it out, Chris. Go on, don't choose your words carefully, just hit me with it."

He stopped pacing and looked at me.

I grabbed a cushion and clutched it to my chest. "I haven't been this nervous since I had colonic irrigation, now do me the courtesy—"

"I'm a criminal." His nostrils flared, and he stood bolt upright, chest out.

"'Scuse me?"

"I am a criminal. There."

"What kind of criminal? Have you walked out of Sainsbury's without paying for a sandwich again, or have you finally killed your boss?"

"Neither." And then he looked up in thought. "At least, I think I paid—"

"Chris! Fuck's sake!"

"Okay, okay. Just the outline though. No details."

I gripped the cushion tighter. "Fair enough."

He downed the whisky. "I've watched criminals get away with murder for years. I've seen the criminal justice system wait for a chance to get a strong prosecution case."

I stared at him, hoping he'd start to make sense sometime soon.

"Sometimes that strong case just doesn't materialise. So they go on, the criminals, to get richer, more powerful. And we clean up after them, and we sit on our thumbs just waiting…"

I blinked. I'd never seen him like this before; so animated, punctuating each clause with a pointed – and very angry – finger.

"I'm sick of seeing them get away with it. Year after year they get fatter, their cars get bigger, their holidays get more exotic, while year after year you and I struggle just to get by from one month to the next." He swallowed. "You and I," he said, "we work ourselves silly and we're left with nothing."

"We have our house. We have each other." That feeling of foreboding grew less translucent.

"I want more."

"We can sleep at night."

"I want more. For us, Becky. I want a holiday, I want a new car. I want to fill the tank without worrying about the price of diesel."

This dream of his was turning into my nightmare. "You want some criminal following you around waiting for a chance to double-tap you?"

"Double-tap?"

"Bang-bang. To the head. Execution style."

"How the hell—"

"I read, alright. I work in a fucking library. I read."

"Why must you swear all the time?"

"Because I'm a librarian, and I hate clichés."

He sighed, padded at the carpet with a tartan slipper. "I'm bored."

That got my attention. "Bored? With us?"

"No! You're not listening to me. I'm bored shitless at work. I collate intelligence against organised criminals. I process intelligence from informants, I rate that intelligence and decide how to action it, whether to action it or just to ignore it. I watch those bastards dicking around in their Range Rovers, I see them come home from trips to Monaco, I read the intel on them, and I know they're worth a fortune. *They* sleep well at night, Becky."

"They sleep well because they have gorillas with guns outside their doors protecting them. It's like a luxury prison for them. And so what anyway?" I shrugged, confused. "What, you're going to muscle in on their operations? With all due respect, Chris…"

His slack mouth tightened into a thin pink strip. He looked away, and I thought that was an end to the conversation. But he said, "The less you know, the better."

I laughed. "And how do you arrive at that conclusion?"

It was his turn to look confused.

"You can't just say that kind of shit without having the reason to back it up." I threw the cushion. "How is me not knowing any of the details better? Exactly how?"

He folded his arms, looked at me down the length of his nose like I wasn't worthy.

I stood up and he flinched. "Are you saying you can't trust me?"

"Can I?" he blurted out.

"I'm your wife."

He said nothing.

"Fuck you, Chris. I've been through everything with you for the last twenty-two years. I'm forty-bloody-six years old. If I haven't earned your trust in all that time then maybe you haven't earned the right to stay married to me." I glared at him. "I mean it. Trust me or we're through."

He stared at me, thinking, considering. And yes, even that hurt, because he shouldn't have needed to think. This is the man whose piles I've inspected; this is the man whose testicles I've had in my hand!

Damn it, I should've squeezed.

"Okay," he said. "Sit down and grab your cushion."

Chapter Three

I moved!

I kept quiet even though my heart was banging at my ribcage as though the bastard thing wanted out. I was breathing so hard and so fast that I thought it would give me away as sure as standing in the hallway and shouting, 'Come and get me!'

I'd left the door to the under-stairs cupboard open behind me. They were obviously searching our house for something, and had already searched in here. If I'd closed it, even to offer me more protection from discovery, I risked someone else searching again. I hid behind a shoe rack full of winter boots and wellies, of carrier bags full of carrier bags – folded neatly – hanging from nails above my head. I curled into the tightest ball I could and stopped thinking about Chris almost instantly. I had to survive.

Instead, I thought about the spider's web I'd brushed aside as I hid here, I thought about the spiders crawling in my hair, and down to my neck. Anything to keep my mind away from my dead husband and focused on the business of staying alive.

I wanted to vomit; it was clambering up my throat, I was sweating, my mouth watering, and every part of me trembled. I gripped the knife so tightly that my hand ached. It was all cramming in on me until I wanted to scream. I wanted to run out of the house and never come back, I wanted to kill myself to get rid of this terror. I looked at the knife and closed my eyes again.

Who the hell were they? What did they want? Surely they'd made a mistake?

Within seconds of me coming to rest, the footsteps from outside thudded past the cupboard doorway. I couldn't see who it was because I was so far behind the shoe rack and just daren't move. But they belonged to a heavy man; they were slow, and they were determined. And the owner of those big feet shouted, "Anything?"

From upstairs someone replied, "No."

Directly over my head, more feet beat down the stairs, making the wood creak. I knew once they were at the fifth step, the wood would crack loudly. It cracked, and I jumped, smacked a hand over my mouth, eyes wide, shivering. I had to clamp my jaw closed for fear of my trembling teeth giving me away.

"Pinky, give me a leg up," someone called.

"I'm bringing a chair," the man on the stairs shouted back.

"Fuck the chair! Give me a leg up!"

I had never been so close to the edge as I was now. My head throbbed, heart hammered even faster, and then my vision began to cloud. Now I had something else to be afraid of. I daren't blackout. They'd find me for sure, and then they'd kill me too, wouldn't they? I reached up and found a nail holding carrier bags in place. I dug it under my fingernail – a sharp intense pain that cleared my vision, and brought me back round enough to feel the fear again and keep still and quiet.

From above me I heard a tut, and Pinky creaked up the stairs again. The fifth stair cracked, and then it cracked again. My breath came out in a rush and without even thinking about it, I shuffled away from the spider's web, around the shoe rack and paused, hand against the doorframe.

More shouting from upstairs, more heavy footsteps.

I'm not a brave person, but I simply couldn't stand being under there any longer – it really was a case of now or never, and going now was the lesser of two evils. I clambered out into the hallway, eyes on the open back door and freedom. As I stood, someone said, "Hello, darling."

I screamed as they grabbed me by the hair and pulled.

"Pinky, get your arse down here!"

All the horrors that my imagination could produce stuttered across my petrified eyes, and left me with little time to think of my next move. Another scream tried to break loose but was hammered to death by a further yank on my hair that almost toppled me backwards. I stared up into the close-together eyes of a bald man with a fat face, a thin moustache, and bad breath. He began to speak again, but I swung the blade behind me and prayed it would make contact.

It did; it penetrated and hit something solid. His hand let go of me and I fell to the ground, watching spots of his blood spatter to the floor not a foot away. His feet danced, and I could even see the tremble in his baggy trousers. As he collapsed to the floor, spewing his rank breath over me, I gained my feet and gawped, afraid I'd really injured him, and held out my hand as though in apology; my other against my mouth to stifle the vomit and the gasp and the scream.

He was crouched now, chubby fingertips propping him against the laminate floor. His breath was as ragged as my own, and when he looked up, his face was crimson, eyes buried deep inside, veins standing out on his forehead. "I'll fucking have you."

The fifth step cracked again.

I turned and ran for my life, slamming the back door and clearing the low wall at the foot of our garden.

Chapter Four

C hris cupped a fresh whisky, had kicked off his slippers, and deemed me trustworthy enough to sit beside. He cleared his throat and said, "I wondered how to get on level terms with these men."

"The gangsters?"

"Yes, the— No, they're not gangsters; don't credit them with a grandiose title, Becky. They're vile people."

"Bastards?"

"Yes, they're… If you're not going to take this seriously, I'm going to bed." He checked his watch; it was almost ten-thirty.

"I'm sorry. Go on. We're getting on level terms. With the vile people." I hid the smile; it was unfair of me. But I could tell this was going to be some fantastical story that was ill-conceived, implausible, impossible, irresponsible, and likely to end either in tears or bloodshed. And probably both. But, I humoured him; he needed to get this out.

"I have at my disposal all the information that these men crave. I have information that they would pay handsomely for."

My smile committed suicide.

"I've been targeting one particular individual for two months. I know how much money he's making, and can hazard a guess at the amount he's got in the three accounts we've marked. There will be others no doubt, but we've only found three so far. Still need to work out how he's laundering it, though."

His fingers tapped against his knees. "I have a list of informants; people who each know bits and pieces about him, things that collectively could lock him up for a few years—"

"Then why don't you use it? Why *don't* you lock him up?"

He looked at me like I was stupid. But since this was the first time he'd ever opened up to me about any aspect of his work, I suppose my ignorance was understandable. "No use buying two litres of petrol when, with a little bit more work, and a little bit more luck, you can have the entire tanker full. See what I mean?

"We want to shut down the entire operation. No good putting him away for a few years for petty crime. We want the entire outfit, the entire crew, and we want them for the murders we suspect they've had a hand in, not so much for the burglaries they've done, or the red lights they've jumped. We want to end him."

"Murders!" Wow. I've often felt proud of my Chris, but right then, I couldn't have been prouder if I'd found out he was playing the lead role in the next Jason Bourne movie. All he needed was a bit of stubble, ditch the spectacles, and he'd have had me round his little finger in no time. Twenty-odd years on, and the flame was still burning. It just needed a bit of a blow now and then. He saw my eyes – dreamy – and he tutted.

"I'm going to bed. You're not taking this seriously."

"No. I am, I am, sorry. Go on, Chris. Please."

He eyed me, and I found it strangely arousing. But he carried on with his tall tale. "I have a list of informants – among them men he trusts, and others he knows nothing of, but who got their information from those men he trusts."

I gasped, I knew what was coming. "If you give that information to him, a lot of people will die."

He pulled in a long breath through his nose, and simply nodded at me.

"You're happy about that? You don't mind?"

He shrugged. "They know what they got into."

"No they don't. Not all of them. They're giving information to the police to help with their enquiries in the strictest confidence, surely."

I could see he was holding back a laugh, but managed to get his point across by allowing a snort to escape. "They're being paid for that information. Good money."

"Wait a minute." I raised my hand. "Just… I don't understand. The police *pay* these people to give information about Mr Bastard, and it might or might not be true?"

"Sort of."

"Wow," I said, more confused than ever. "Then why don't we all give up work and make up stories about Mr Bastard?"

"Because it's risky for them. They could die if he found out. Like I said, they know what they're getting themselves into. They're prepared to take the risk and take the money."

I stopped thinking all this was funny. I stopped pretty abruptly. I knew what Chris did for a living: he was an intelligence analyst and coordinator. Now I understood what it involved. Now I understood the importance of that role. And now I understood what an enormous responsibility it was.

I looked across at him, this mild-mannered man wearing spectacles, clean-shaven, respectable. And I think I had some inkling of the pressure he was under; I certainly had an inkling as to why he felt so under-valued. He earned eighteen hundred a month. I wouldn't mind betting that Mr Bastard earned that in a morning.

It really wasn't funny any more. In fact, I began to think it wasn't at all ill-conceived, implausible, or impossible. I still thought it was irresponsible, though; and I knew for a fact it would end in tears and bloodshed. What I found most startling was the amount of time he'd given this. A couple of months, he'd said. He was way past just being curious about it; he was well inside being determined to make it happen.

"Becky?"

I mean, he was working out the details.

"Becky?"

I jumped. Smiled. "Sorry," I said, "I was miles away." I pulled my cushion tighter still.

"Can I still trust you?"

What the hell do you say to a question like that after such a bombshell? "Of course you can." It was the easiest way to buy time, to mull it over and give it proper consideration. I looked at him, and I smiled in reassurance, but I had the feeling he knew it was insincere.

"I'm ready to go with it," he said. "But if *you* can't go along with it, and live with its consequences, you have to tell me."

"What?" I laughed. "Come on, this is me you're preaching to." I was shitting myself.

"I mean, if you think it's too immoral for you, and you'd consider turning me in, then I'll forget the idea. I can't risk losing you."

That brought tears to my eyes. I loved that he said, 'I can't risk losing you,' when I thought he was going to say, 'I can't risk going to prison.' That was the kind of love we had: pure.

"What consequences?"

"Well—" he began.

"Wait." I swallowed hard. "Can I have that whisky now?"

Chapter Five

I ran. I ran blindly, my mind and vision a blur; just getting away from there was my priority. Fear propelled me. I had never been so afraid in my entire life – I was screaming as I ran, but soon my breath was gone and all I could do was whimper as my lungs began to burn. As I ran by people, they turned and stared at me. Some asked if I was alright as the tears tracked down my red cheeks, arms pumping, numb legs working like they never had before. Fear. Impending doom.

Still I had no plan in mind except distance.

Then I heard something that scared a shriek out of me and forced the tears to come quicker as I approached Main Street up ahead.

"Thief! Stop her, she's a thief!"

As I ran I pulled my bag across my chest, and sacrificed speed as I reached inside, fumbling around for my mobile phone. But who was I going to call? The police? I'd just killed someone! And I'd just killed someone with the same knife used to kill my husband – things looked worse by the second.

"Thief," he called again.

"I'm not," I shouted to the people who now stood to watch the spectacle. I know how pathetic that sounds, but really, I wasn't thinking straight. I was already protesting my innocence to people who couldn't care less, to people who only wanted to watch a scene, a show to brighten up their shitty day. Trust me, their day was nowhere near as bad as mine.

People now stood still and watched, and I could see one, an elderly man, change his course on the wide footpath, choosing a collision course with me, and I knew he was a wanna-be fucking hero, and I knew I was going to knock the old guy off his feet.

Fear.

I grabbed the mobile and pulled it out of the bag just as a young lad stepped into my path. First thing I noticed was the look of stolen thunder on the old guy's face. Second thing I noticed was the pavement coming up to meet my face at an astonishing speed. I felt the sickly taste of blood as my front teeth went through my lip, and gravel buried itself under the skin of my outstretched hands. The phone skittered into the road where a passing car smashed it to dust.

I didn't stop, I didn't cower there on the pavement waiting for the bastard to haul me to my feet and kill me in front of a crowd of bored shoppers. I was still running as I hit the pavement, and my legs didn't stop for a second even when I got back onto my feet; I was off and running again, sprinting. And then the old guy was ten yards in front of me.

"Stop, lass," he shouted, palms out.

"He's trying to rape me!" I screamed, and suddenly the old man's milky eyes swivelled from me to my pursuer. I ran by him and saw the confusion on his face, the conflict in his mind. "Help me!" I called back.

He hesitated – a charging bull was a different prospect to a fleeing chick. I made it to the road where the traffic was stopped at a red light.

I barged through a throng of people crossing the road, and I don't know where I was going – just putting distance between us again. And then I saw a phone box on the footpath opposite. My shredded mind worked hard, and I wondered if I'd at least have enough time to dial three-nines before the kiosk door opened and that murdering bastard pulled me out.

I snatched a glance back over my shoulder and he was just pushing the old man into a group of women and kids. Forty yards.

I was gagging; my legs were on fire, and my lungs threatened to leave town. It was the phone box or nothing. I pulled the door open as the crossing emptied and the lights turned green again.

I got a dial tone and punched the buttons, air scraping down my frayed throat. "Please, please, please!" I closed my eyes, face crumpling with despair and then—

"Which service do you require?"

I stared through the glass, and backed into the corner. He was approaching the road, looking straight at me – eyes narrow with hatred. And he wasn't even out of breath. He hardly broke his stride as he rushed across the road. He even had the audacity to point at me as he ran, perhaps hoping to intimidate me further. He wore latex gloves.

"Police." My hands trembled on the mouthpiece. I was ready to collapse.

"What is the nature of your emergency?"

What do I say? My mind played with words that I didn't recognise. "They... they killed my husband." And just that sentence took any remaining fight right out of me, and I began to slump against the window.

I knew he had me. So, this was my last day; I missed my Chris so much. I cried.

I opened my eyes and he was there, just a few yards away, almost reaching for me when the van ploughed straight through him. As the tyres screeched down the road, leaving a plume of grey smoke in the air, I saw him cartwheel, saw his face smash into the windscreen. Delicate slivers of glass sprayed into the sunlight, along with teeth that pattered against the kiosk window and a slender fountain of blood that trickled down the window frame.

I could see the crowd of motionless people staring, out of focus. I saw him slap into the road, limp, flaccid, limbs in all the wrong positions. And then the screaming started.

And all I could see clearly were the little rivulets of his blood trickling down the glass.

"Hello? Hello, madam?"

I heard the door squeak open and I closed my eyes. Hands clamped around my shoulders, and I screamed.

"It's me! It's me... Sienna."

Chapter Six

I could smell baking. Chris used to sing that old Ultravox song, *Vienna*, every time he saw her.

Sienna. Just the sight of her face set me off crying again as soon as I opened my eyes. This was as close to safety as I could get right now, and nothing makes me shed emotion more than feeling cosseted and warm and secure.

"Let it out, love."

She stroked my hair, and I felt snot leaking down my face again. My eyes stung like I'd had a pepper facemask. I looked up at her, and the tears I saw in her eyes made me cry all over again. I always thought that if anything so dramatic ever happened in my life, I'd be able to shrug it off and function at near-normal capacity until time blunted the wound in a week or two. Then I'd be back to my old self but with a little added melancholy.

Turns out I was pretty fucking naïve.

I've been lucky; I've only ever had my parents pass away. That was bad enough, but I was in my twenties when they did, and I think at that age you're still made of rubber. I loved them, of course I did, but I was selfish; I spent all my time with my friends– Sienna being one of them – and out partying. So, their deaths had minimal impact on me – or so I thought. Actually, their deaths were an emotional time bomb.

I only really grieved for them after a few weeks when I was at a loose end and decided it would be a good idea to spend the day with the wrinklies. Except the wrinklies weren't there any more, and they never would be again. That's when their deaths hit me for the first time. I had lost my chance. And I'd never have them at my side ever again.

Sometimes I lie to myself. I did just then.

That's not the only time I've had to deal with grief in my life. I lost a child in my mid-thirties. Stillborn. Thirty-two weeks of being a mum-in-waiting, only to walk out of the hospital with a smudge of a handprint and a plastic wristband. I smashed the nursery up – it's now Chris's office – *was* Chris's office. We never found the words to discuss it.

It just went away; there were no tears, just a mental adjustment, and a new way of living, born out of still being two people, instead of three people. I got used to it, and we always said we'd try again, and we did – unsuccessfully. Eventually, I decided that I had a choice – become obsessed with having a family, or carry on as though nothing had happened.

I chose the latter, and my shrink said it was the lesser of two evils, but still not the right choice. She went on about the five stages of grief, and I stopped listening. The drugs crushed the pain's sharp edges until there was no pain any more. There – grief and longing effectively by-passed. And life went on.

Chris was always there, scared that I hadn't wept. He was my punch bag and my nursemaid and, when I'd pissed off the real deal, my would-be shrink. Me and Chris. Nothing else mattered.

As I stared at Sienna's ceiling, I realised that I'd lied to myself all these years. I'd always known that if something happened to Chris I'd collapse into a heap and never get up again. He was my bones; and without him, I was nothing. Without him I lost all my self-confidence, and all my bravado. I loved him.

Starting a new life without him was a prospect that had only just dawned on me, and it frightened me. If truth be told, I don't think I wanted a life without him anyway. I didn't want to bludgeon my way through an almost impenetrable wall of grief, I didn't want to know what waited for me on the other side.

Did I really want to go through the rest of my life alone? Or worse, did I really want to start over again with dating and small talk, and disappointment? And then the guilt at just thinking that so soon hit me like a sledgehammer, and I found myself sinking into a cold blackness of despair that I'd only ever been close to once before. It hurt, and I curled up on Sienna's sofa, wailing into my shaking hands. I prayed to die.

Sienna continued to stroke my face and pass me tissues. "Want some tea?" She was in tears too, and I loved her then for sharing my despair, for loving us enough to suffer with me.

I nodded, tried to sniff but my nose was still blocked solid. I had a headache, and I couldn't stop shaking. I think I might have been in shock.

"How 'bout some cake? I just made a Victoria sponge."

She busied herself in her tiny kitchen, and I wondered if she'd really just offered me a piece of fucking cake. Sienna was my age, and she'd never married. Never even had a proper man in her life, so far as I knew. We used to joke that her fanny would have healed up by now, and then giggle about it like a couple of silly teenagers.

She lived here, in this small flat, in the east end of Garforth, and had done ever since her mum died there ten or twelve years ago. She had tasselled rugs on the wall, dream catchers dangling from the kitchen ceiling, crystals on the small tables, and a bass note of joss sticks lay beneath the warm sugary smell of the cake. There was a small flat-screen TV in the corner, but the pile of books in front of it suggested she never used it. There were three bulging bookcases along the back wall.

I had no idea how she made ends meet.

I heard the doorbell, and saw Sienna walk past me to answer it, but I faded into blackness for a short time. And then she was back, stroking my hair and dabbing at the blood on my swollen lip.

"Was that someone at the door?"

"Just the girl from next door. She has CCTV and saw us come home. She wondered if we were okay."

"Sweet of her," I whispered.

"Who were they, do you know?"

I shrugged.

"Well, what did they look like?"

"Leave it, Sienna." I closed my eyes.

"I'm only trying to help."

"Well, you're not. Leave me alone."

She sighed the words, "You need to remember, that's all. Don't blot it out. I mean, what were they even looking for?"

I opened my eyes.

"You said they were tearing the house apart. Sounds like a thorough search to me. Did Chris say anything? I mean, has he told you where he's hidden something?"

I turned my head to stare at her full on.

"What? I'm only trying to get to the bottom of it."

"My husband has been knifed to death, I've been chased from my house by a murdering gang, scared out of my wits, and then witnessed a man get killed." I sucked in a deep breath and sat up. "So, leave the bottom of it alone. For now."

The tea was strong and sweet. I nodded my thanks, and she retreated to a chair by the window. She looked at me, kept a sorrowful smile in place for my benefit. "You've got to call them back, Becky."

I sipped.

"Becky?"

"I'm not ready."

"Then it's the perfect time to call them." She sat up straight. "I don't want to trivialise this, but now, while you're in such a state over Chris's… well, it looks better for you."

"Looks better for me?"

She nodded.

"You don't think I did it, do you?"

"Of course I bloody don't! But look at it from their point of view; you're distressed, as any grieving widow would be. It's the right time, it sends the right message. And you were witness to a fatal road accident. Pretty sure you have to come forward."

Widow. I was a widow. My chin began to tremble again and I had to focus on the cup in my hand to keep me from sinking. She was right. I had to consider how this looked; I knew that most murders were carried out by a spouse. And the tears – the genuine tears – would help my case.

I looked at her through fogged up eyes, and nodded.

"Will you drive me to Main Street?"

"Yeah, course I will. But why—"

"My phone. It smashed. I need the SIM card or else I've lost all my contact numbers."

"I wouldn't worry about—"

"Please."

She shrugged. "Sure. But you'll be lucky—"

"Well let's hope I'm lucky."

Chapter Seven

Chris stood there holding out a whisky glass towards me. I was staring at the wall, and all the things running through my head were comprised of scenes from *Goodfellas* or, more accurately, *The Sopranos*.

Everyone carried a gun, everyone talked street-wise, had their hair slicked back, and didn't say 'mate' as they did here in Yorkshire as an endearment, they said 'dude,' or they said 'bitch.'

"Consequences."

I returned from my reverie, looked up at him, confused.

"You wanted to know about the consequences?"

"Yes, yes, I did. I do." I took the glass, held it beneath my nose, and let its aroma sting my eyes the same way onions did.

He sat next to me, a fresh glass in his hand. "I can be caught by two organisations," he said. "One will play hard but by the rules, and the other will play hard with no rules at all. Dealing with them brings its own set of dangers.

"But anyway." He sipped. "The police first. If I'm caught giving out sensitive information like this, I'll lose my job. It'll mean a custodial sentence, probably ten years plus. I'm breaking a multitude of laws, not least Data Protection and The Official Secrets Act. There are others, of course, but they're the main ones.

"The thing about betraying the police is they, understandably, despise you. You were in their loop, you were trusted, you were part of the crew, in the fold—"

"I get you, Chris."

"Yes, well, I'm trying to illustrate that the acts here are a by-product of that hatred of duplicity. In other words, they'll throw the book at me, and they'll go all out to make sure they have enough evidence to sail a conviction through CPS without a question being raised – they'll work very hard. Part of the reason they'll work so hard is because I'll have screwed up at least two years' hard work getting to grips with… this individual. Once PSD gets a hold—"

"PSD?"

"Professional Standards Department. They'll assign a detective inspector – or even a chief inspector – to a case like this, and they'll carry out a thorough audit. They'll probably come here and they'll go through my sock drawer."

I looked at him quizzically.

"They're *very* thorough, Becky. They'll probably question you too. They will freeze our accounts and get a forensic accountant to scrutinise them. Every asset we have will be confiscated and searched. They won't leave anything to chance; they can't afford to. If you look at it from their point of view, they have to get every piece of evidence they can because they want a water-tight case, and they'll want the harshest sentence they can get for me. And they'll want it like that to act as a deterrent so that other would-be miscreants don't feel tempted to go down the same road.

"Of course, they'll also want to know how I got away with it – assuming we *do* get away with it – in order to prevent it from happening again. They'll formulate new policies, new procedures, new safeguards…"

We? I tapped my finger against the empty glass, stared at the fireplace, eyes unfocused. I was totally absorbed by his voice. It was mellow, smooth, and calming – just like the whisky I'd downed. But I was lost among the words too, their meaning. And I was growing more and more nervous at each passing sentence. I was thinking, "This isn't such a good idea after all, is it?" I looked at him.

He was smiling.

"What?"

"That was the best bit," he said.

"There's a *worse* bit?"

"If I go to prison, they'll have a duty to segregate me, because I work – *worked* – for the police. But segregation is remarkably flimsy."

"Flimsy?"

"Well, I'm only surmising, really. I mean, I've heard tales of coppers in jail, the usual stuff, and I suspect some of those tales are fairly accurate—"

"I have to say, Chris, you're not exactly selling the fucker to me!"

"I'm only trying to give you the facts. And please cut down on the swearing."

"Trust me, I already have." This was looking worse with each passing second. What possessed him to come up with such a shit idea? Eighteen hundred a month looked great right about now! "And thank you for the facts," I sneered, "it's very considerate of you. Most gangsters would hide that level of detail from their molls."

"You'd rather know what to expect if it all goes wrong, wouldn't you?"

"Of course I would," I lied. Did I really want to know that he'd be returned to me after ten years with an arsehole so stretched that you could use it as carry-on luggage?

"We need to be careful," he continued, "because I'd rather not end up in jail if you don't mind."

"I get it."

"We'll have a large amount of cash and no way of banking it, and no realistic way of making large purchases. It would need to be well hidden, perhaps for years. And if we did get away with it, we'd always wonder if they were watching us. We'd always jump at a knock at the door."

"Will there be a handout later?" I flicked the glass, heart racing because of the booze and because of the subject matter. Without realising it, we'd both slipped into whispers, moved that little bit closer to one another. It all reeked of subterfuge.

I found it both exciting and scary as hell. Mostly scary. But when you've lived a life so mundane, so fucking boring, for as long as we had, then a little danger seemed to fill the hole where passion had once resided. That sounds cruel, but I don't mean it to. We have a very good relationship – in and out of the bedroom – actually, in any room you can think of.

But a little danger to us was the bacon and eggs fried in lard, it was cruising through a red light, it was walking out of Sainsbury's with a chicken and sweetcorn sandwich and no receipt. In short, it made your arse twitch and brought a giddy smile to your otherwise downcast lips. But it didn't send you to jail for ten years.

"So, if there's no way of enjoying being nouveau riche, what's the point of having the money?" I couldn't believe I just asked that.

He raised his finger. "Ah, that's how we'd have to live if we stayed here. We'd have to squirrel it away, spending it in small amounts. We'd still have to go to work, and complain we didn't have enough money for a weekend away in the Lakes, or that the washer had broken down again."

"I feel a 'but' coming on."

"But. We're not going to do that."

"We're not?"

"We're going to bail out straight away."

"Italy," I said. "I've always wanted to live in Italy."

He hadn't heard me, or chose to ignore me. "They'll know I've done something illegal, and when they find us both gone, they'll do that audit, and that's when we become felons."

Felons. Persons outside the law. Images of Bonnie and Clyde ripped the importance of the moment to shreds, and all I saw now were gunfights and a painful death. I swallowed, looked across at him. But still I wanted the whole picture because I couldn't make up my mind based on only half of the information. Of course, I had already made up my mind, but the more he gave me, the more harrowing the future could be, the easier it would be to dissuade him from this lunacy.

Playing cops and robbers inside your own head was fun, but it probably lost the appeal when professional people began hunting you for real. "Now, that's the police side of things aired. Tell me about the baddies."

"More whisky?"

"No," I said. "Lots more whisky."

Chapter Eight

The local police station in Garforth was less than a mile from Sienna's front door. It was a steady ten-minute walk, and she stopped abruptly in the front car park as though she'd run out of fuel. I was five paces in front of her before I realised I was alone. I turned, a questioning look on my face.

"I'd rather not. If you don't mind."

"I mind," I said.

"I've been in there once or twice. On first name terms with some of the coppers."

She smiled at me but I didn't smile back. I walked to her. "What's happened?"

"Oh, nothing really." She studied her boots, and then sighed. "I do a bit of cannabis every now and then." She looked up into my eyes, resolute, defences raised, ready for combat. "Sometimes coke."

There was no need for any bravado – there'd be no combat from me today. I nodded at her, and headed for the blue-painted front door.

"Becky?"

I turned.

"Good luck." Her smile was lost on me. I waved as I walked away.

* * *

They arrested me.

I stood at the front counter for a couple of minutes while a police officer dealt with paperwork from a motorist. When the motorist left we were alone. He looked up at me, and I saw him grow more and more concerned. I suspect my face was blotchy, eyes red-rimmed, fresh blood seeping from my punctured lip, and I still couldn't stop shaking. His concern made me burst into tears again.

Ten minutes later I was in an interview room. It had a red band around the wall and a tape recorder in the corner. And opposite me was a young man in shirt sleeves, pen in hand, ready to begin scraping all the details from inside my perplexed mind.

He peered at me and I went blank. Where the hell do you start when you're telling a complete stranger that you found your husband stabbed to death on your lounge floor? Only days before we were due to run away. I felt sick. Light-headed.

And then how do you go about telling him that you killed someone in order to escape? Words pissed off and left me to stutter to the youth.

"Take your time," he said.

I did take my time. Almost two hours of it.

And after languishing in that room for so long, pouring my emotions across the scratched table, hoping he would catch them as they rolled off the edge – the way all the best shrinks could– I found myself in the back of a plain police car, being driven through spike-topped gates into the sealed compound of a large police station. It was all a blur. I was in cuffs because he was alone, he said. Short staffed, he said.

Yet this was the time when I needed to stay sharp and focused. Try as I might, all that came to me was blunt and fuzzy.

He led me into a custody area. All the while the young detective smiled at me as though he was leading me to an ice cream van, making small talk like I was a date. He seemed more nervous than I was.

I stood before an old sergeant who, speaking over the shouts and curses coming from the next booth along – probably from some youth high on drugs – asked if I was a danger to myself, whether I was on any medication.

My feet ached. They photographed me, took my clothes and gave me a plain grey tracksuit. They put me in a dry cell with a paper cup of pissed-in bathwater that they dared tell me was tea. My brief time with Sienna seemed like weeks ago. And, if truth be told, everything that happened this afternoon seemed like a lifetime ago.

Chapter Nine

I sat alone at a desk, still feeling groggy from an uncomfortable night, and a boring day, in police custody – my first ever.

When you watch cop shows on TV, you're apt to think that all the cells and the interview rooms are from the sixties, all painted cream with bare bulbs overhead, and a WPC standing in the corner with her hands folded in front of her crotch. And some quirky old gent wearing tweed will bimble his way in, and play tough guy as he wrangles truth from lies.

It's not like that. Well it wasn't like that here. The room was spacious, painted a pleasant shade of magnolia, and there was carpet on the floor – tiles, I grant you, but tasteful, like we had in the library. There was no WPC because they don't exist any more – they are police officers, same as the men are. And I was alone anyway. No cameras, no cuffs, no harsh lamp blinding me.

Inside my head I was busy. I tried to imagine the questions they'd ask, and I tried to formulate answers that were meaningful, and not some stream of drivel conjured up by a mind in pain. I found it difficult to stay tuned; my mind wandered at everything in here, but mostly it went off of its own accord and found memories of Chris to play with. And something quite odd struck me: how I was apt to feel guilty even when I was innocent. I imagined that just my face or my overreaction to some mundane question could land me in the dock, and there was a judge in full court dress, pounding his gavel before placing a black cap on his wig. I have no idea how long this idle train of thoughts chugged along.

The door opened and a man and a woman entered. They smiled at me, shook hands with me, and introduced themselves.

"Hi, Becky, I'm Detective Inspector Steve Hughes." He had a single eyebrow. It reached from one side of his forehead right across to the other, like a furry caterpillar. I have no idea how I avoided staring at it. "And this is Detective Sergeant Alison Merchant."

"You want a tea, Becky?" Alison asked. She had a flat chest. Completely flat! And no other curves either; she was just straight up and down all the way, like a pipe-cleaner with shoes.

"Depends."

She laughed. "Proper tea, honestly."

I nodded. "Thanks, white, no sugar."

"Be right back." She left and Steve took a seat opposite me.

"I'm sorry we kept you waiting so long," he said. "We like to be thorough."

I waved his apology aside, but noted how they both read me as they came in. Would I be a tear-soaked mound of jelly wobbling in my chair, unable to lift my head because of the rope of snot linking it with the desk? Or would I be bubbly, all smiles and giggles, able to take them easily on a magical journey into my newly-acquired widowhood while keeping the atmosphere light and bouncy? I was neither, thankfully. I was just me: quick-to-tears because of Chris's death, but not so wrapped up in my own grief that I couldn't acknowledge their presence.

"And I'd like to extend my sincere condolences at your loss."

I welled up – that was the quick-to-tears part. Couldn't help it. Despite Chris always moaning because of his boring low-paid job, the police service was a great big family. Oh sure, the family had some unpleasant members, just like any other family, I suppose, but every member took care of their own when the shit hit the fan. And right now, my pac-a-mac was heavily soiled.

Chris had told me to expect this if ever I was brought in. Of course, he couldn't know the circumstances under which I'd ever be brought in, but he assured me that if his plan went tits up, I'd be treated well. He didn't know how tits up it could possibly go.

"Thank you," I tried to say. But it was a vowel-loaded croak that came out, and then I sobbed. I have no idea where that came from; I think when you're braced against your emotion, and someone is kind to you, that kindness dissolves the wall. you . Alison came back in with proper cups of proper tea. I dragged a box of tissues towards me, cleaned myself up a little, and eventually looked up at them, embarrassed.

"You okay?"

I nodded. "Sorry." I mopped at my nose, dabbed at my eyes.

"I have to ask again if you would like a solicitor to represent you. We can supply one if you'd prefer?"

"No. I have nothing to hide."

"It's not about hiding anything, Becky," Alison said, "it's so that you're aware of your rights and of your legal standing."

"I know. I appreciate it, really, I do. But I will not be party to lining some lawyer's pockets as he tells me to 'no comment' each question you ask. You're trying to find out who did this to Chris, and why. And I want to know too!" I was shocked at my own vehemence. My eyes were wide, and so were theirs. I was suddenly furious that Chris was gone. I had been angry and upset all day, but now I was furious that someone could do this to us. To me! "I'm sorry. I just want to help you. I want them behind bars."

Despite my earlier fears of the consequences of overreacting to a simple question or situation, I would like to say that I was acting, especially that last little outburst, but I honestly wasn't – it was heartfelt. And I was heartbroken.

All that planning, and finally Chris comes up with a wonderful plan to get us out of humdrum and into a decent quality of life, and someone shattered our dream and left me with a mountain to climb in nothing but a pair of flip-flops and a shit-covered pac-a-mac. Alongside the obvious and genuine remorse, I also felt badly cheated, and that's partly why I was so furious; I suppose that's a very selfish way to behave.

I would have loved to express that fury by smashing the place up or stabbing the murderer through the eye with a billhook.

But since I didn't have a billhook, and since I couldn't know who had killed Chris and ended our dream and cheated me out of a wonderful future, I was left with only the option of smashing the place up. But I chose to stay seated and weep instead.

I looked at Alison and Steve, at their pitying smiles, and I just folded up, crying into the crook of my arm like a kid whose pet rabbit had died.

I spent the next few hours going over with them the whole story of yesterday's events. I left nothing out; I even declared that I'd stabbed a man with what I'd assumed was Chris's murder weapon. When I mentioned that, I saw them glance at each other – I had no idea what that glance meant, but I figured it was something crucial to their case. I even described him, as best as I could, bearing in mind I was almost upside down at the time. Later, I wondered if the description I had given was accurate. I couldn't actually remember him; the only person I could clearly remember was the man who chased me. His face as he sneered at me moments before that van hit him kept obliterating all other images. I was pretty sure his face would stay with me till the day I died.

"All I know is that he was called Pinky."

The eyebrow wrote it all down, eyes flicking between me and his note pad.

They took me into their trust. I know, I've seen a lot of cop shows on the TV, and one of their ploys is to side with the offender, with the person sitting on the other side of that table – with me – and gain their trust so they wouldn't be quite so reluctant to talk. But I had no reluctance, I'd proved that by waiving my right to a solicitor, and I'd been more than forthcoming. The only thing I didn't go anywhere near was Chris's plan.

"Pinky is Dominic Pinkman."

'Dominic', I thought. It was strange name for a gangster. You'd expect a Dominic to have a glass of Pimm's at his lips, not a sneer as he chased down a fleeing woman.

"But as far as we can tell, he's not associated with anyone your description fits."

Because they trusted me, they told me about the knife – I *knew* it was crucial. They said the blade had been wiped. Of course, traces of Chris remained, but there were no traces of anyone else, no splashes of blood on the hall floor, just an odour of bleach. And yes, my fingerprints were in Chris's blood, and that had made me a prime suspect. But everything else I'd told them fitted together perfectly with what they were getting back from the crime scene.

It seemed that Pinkman had worn latex gloves when he'd stolen Chris's phone – which the police had never found – and searched the house. Pinkman had chased me; CCTV and witnesses verified that, as well as his unfortunate ending. It all fitted together perfectly, and had this been a sixties cop show, the tweed-wearing detective would have stamped the file's cover with 'No Further Action' and guided me to the door.

I'd told myself repeatedly, like mumbling a mantra, that I was innocent. But even though I told myself that I was innocent, and I'd been chased and almost caught by this gang of men, I still had a nagging feeling that the police didn't believe me. I was worried about that, of course, because you hear of stories where they had found the suspect innocent after serving twenty years in prison. But now I felt comfortable that they were on my side. They believed me. I could see it in their eyes.

There was one thing I couldn't get from them though. And that's whether I'd killed a man or not. I assume not, since there was no mention of him, or of any blood – even though I'd seen it spatter onto the floor. I didn't understand it, I'd swung that blade like Steven Seagal, and I'd definitely connected.

"So, we're just about done," Alison said. "Just one more thing. Why do you think someone would kill Chris and search your house? What were they looking for?"

I swallowed but made sure I kept my gaze on them. I looked from one detective to the other, my face blank, my eyes squinted slightly as if giving the question some deep consideration. "I've thought about nothing else since it happened. And I have no idea why. Mistaken identity, perhaps," I said, "or maybe they knew who Chris worked for, and it was some kind of retribution."

Alison looked across at Steve. I knew she was finished; just the DI to go.

Steve cleared his throat. "Do you know if Chris ever brought any of his work home?"

"As in paperwork?"

He shrugged and his eyebrow crawled up his forehead. "Anything."

I took my time, and thought it through. "Chris wasn't a homework kind of man. He was far too keen on *X Factor* and *Coronation Street* to be bothered by work." I smiled at him. "Sorry, not much help, am I?"

"We have another department here called PSD. The Professional Standards Department. It's customary for them to run a separate investigation whenever anyone from the police family is... is killed." Palms out, he said, "It's just routine, but if they deem it necessary, they might pay you a visit over the next few days just to make sure everything's in order, you know, when you've moved back into your house. Then again, they might be content with letting us conclude things."

I hadn't thought of it, moving back in.

My chest felt tight again, and I put my fingertips over my mouth. "I can't... I can't go back there," I said. "I could never live there again." Each time I thought of the lounge, all I ever saw was Chris lying on the floor. Dead.

But I couldn't burden Sienna either, not for much longer, it wouldn't be fair. "What do I do?"

"They can speak with you wherever you choose."

"No, I mean where am I going to stay? Where am I going to live? I can't live there any more."

Ten minutes later, after a lot of shrugging from them, I stepped out of the interview room into a wide carpeted corridor, a glass-ceiling two storeys above us, with large motivational pictures on the walls, drinking fountains arranged every forty yards or so.

Steve and his eyebrow disappeared, and I walked slowly beside Alison through it all as she guided me to the exit. We'd gone less than twenty yards when I heard my name. I turned, and a short man with a bald head raised his arm to me. "Becky," he called again. Alison looked too.

Eventually he caught us up, and he held out his hand to me "I'm so very sorry, Becky."

The ID on his lanyard said *P. Ingram, Police Staff*. "Peter," he said as though he knew I found remembering names and faces a hard task. "I worked with Chris."

I shook hands with Peter, and Alison patted me on the shoulder and said, "If you two want to catch up, I'll leave you in peace. Would you mind showing Mrs Rose out?" She looked at Peter, a warm smile on her face specifically for him. This family was a lot friendlier than I'd first thought.

"Yes, yes, of course I will, yes."

Alison and I shook hands, and then like an aroma in a gust of wind she was gone.

Chapter Ten

"They let me out." I rubbed a knuckle into the corner of my eye. I don't know if was trying to get rid of the incessant stinging that comes from crying enough water to fill up a small paddling pool, or whether I was trying to get the sleepiness to piss off and leave me alone.

My life had become complicated recently, and I was in a shitload of danger. It didn't take a genius to work out that the motley crew turning my house upside down had been, and possibly were still, looking for something – even Sienna had said as much. But my guess was that they hadn't the time to find whatever they were looking for. And I knew that what they were looking for was a list of names. Simple as that.

If they didn't find it in my house, and Chris hadn't given it up to them before they killed him, they would probably think I had it hidden in my bra or somewhere equally obscure.

They would come for me.

The questions that flitted around my over-stressed mind were these: what had gone wrong with the deal for them to kill Chris? Had they reneged on the final million, and Chris had stood his ground? Was it a rival gang that had learned of the list and wanted it for themselves?

Sienna asked, "Where are you ringing from?"

"The police station. Elland Road. They moved me from Garforth last night."

"Look over the road. Is the park-and-ride full?"

"What?" I snorted a tired laugh. "Why? No one's watching me."

"Is it full?"

I turned and looked over the busy road, and all I could see was a sea of car roofs. "Yes," I said, "it's full—"

"Walk to the far end of it, near the train tracks. I'll see you there."

"I don't understand—"

The line had died. I listened to it hum, and hung up the receiver.

What the hell was going on?

They say if your body has no time to fully experience grief, then it never leaves you. It dogs your waking life until you die. And I could understand that right now. It was there all the time like a fog, no, like a headache bubbling away in the back of my head and stopping me from thinking clearly, incessantly threatening to come to the fore and claim me. The wobbling chin and the tears were sure signs that it was there, waiting patiently.

For the time being, I had no choice but to put up with the headache. I hoped it wouldn't be too long before I could actually think about my poor husband and how cruelly he was taken from me. I *needed* to think of him; I needed to make sure he was alright, and that *we* were alright. Only then could I think of other things.

I sighed, let the phone box door close behind me and crossed the road, eyes fixed on the pavement, ears replaying my hurried breath from the last time I'd been in a phone box – and even that seemed a month ago, not just a few hours.

I was just a passenger hovering through the sea of cars, and without any conscious thought at all I made it to the far edge just as the lamp there lit up. Dusk arrived and a thin mist faded the bright lights from the police station a couple of hundred yards away, and I was able to sink into my mind and listen to the voices in there.

Half an hour or more passed before I saw a set of headlights coming in my direction. I licked my lips, felt my palms sweating even though it was growing cold out. I found myself holding my breath, not daring to blink as it approached. And then it swung around and I saw it was Sienna's little blue Corsa. I puffed out my breath and climbed aboard.

There was no talking as she drove from the car park, turned right, and headed on the outer Ring Road up towards Beeston. She didn't even mention my change of clothes. We'd got as far as the White Rose Shopping Centre before I broke the tepid silence. "Thanks. For coming to get me."

"What the hell's going on, Becky?"

I looked at her, confused, could see the tendons in her forearms protruding as she clamped her hands on the wheel. "Apart from being arrested for Chris's murder, you mean? Other than that, it's been fairly quiet; looking forward to *Coronation Street*, a glass of red, and maybe a pizza. With extra peppers."

She snatched a glance at me, eyes screaming.

"And I might get some garlic bread too. Push the boat out." Chris always loves garlic bread. And that thought caught in my mind like a barb in my throat. Was it the same as setting a place at the table for a dead loved one? Was this how the headache intended on letting me know it was still there? Was I slowly going mad?

"*Did* you kill him?"

I blinked as though slapped, unsure I'd heard her right. It amazed me that she seemed able to say that without moving her lips, like she was a dummy, and the real Sienna was in the back pulling the levers. I felt my heart gallop and then it grew hot. "Pull over. I'll walk."

"I'm shitting myself."

"Pull the fuck over!"

She didn't pull over, but she slowed so she could look over at me, and I saw something in Sienna's calm eyes that I hadn't seen before. I saw fear.

"He's sent me a text," she whispered.

My anger assuaged only slightly, I shouted, "Who?"

"Savage. Well, one of his men."

I turned front again. I watched the tail-lights of the other cars ahead of us as we joined the motorway, how hypnotic they were. I think I sounded convincing when I said, "Who the hell is Savage?" I wished I could trust my own mind; chaos reigned in there and clinging to a single thought was like trying to catch smoke with a sieve. I dug my nails into the seat and closed my eyes, clinging onto something physical, real. And I found it difficult. "Talk to me."

"When we get home. I'm liable to crash right now."

* * *

"Cake?"

I folded into a chair, exhausted, and grabbed a cushion to my chest. "Just tell me."

"I need sugar," she said.

For someone who was shitting herself, she'd done a bloody good job of calming down, and I wondered if she'd had help in the form of a little white tablet or two.

Why couldn't I be that calm? I almost asked if she had anything that might alleviate my anxiety, but was afraid of what she might offer me.

I was a cumbersome, unwieldy character where my emotions were concerned; trying to change my mood felt like trying to perform a handbrake turn in a supertanker. I could spend days in a sulk for no real reason. I put it down to intermittent bouts of depression, and everything I'd read on the subject seemed to confirm it. Chris would give me a wide berth and proffer flowers at every opportunity. He was a good man…

And just that single innocent thought brought the tears again. And when they came, I grew angry because I didn't have the luxury of time to deal with them or my collapsing mental strength. I couldn't afford to be weak now.

I scrubbed the cushion across my face, gritted my teeth, and squeezed the skin under my armpit. The pain refocused my wayward mind.

"Here," she said, holding the plate out. "Having a piece of cake doesn't make you a bad person. And it doesn't mean you're suffering any less, okay?"

"No, I don't—"

"It doesn't mean you're enjoying yourself when you should be grieving, Becky."

We looked at each other for a moment, and I realised for the first time since this day began how lucky I was to have her as a friend. "Thanks." I ate voraciously.

It was fully dark when we'd finished our second slice, and Sienna put the kettle on again. I drew the curtains, and sank back into the sofa waiting for my own personal soap opera to recommence.

"Did Chris seem a little strange to you in the weeks leading up to his death?"

I shook my head, shrugged. "No. Why?"

"Think, Becky. Anything at all. Was he secretive, quieter than usual?"

"You sound like the police. They asked all these questions too. But I have no idea what either of you are searching for. Chris was… Chris was just Chris. He was always quiet, reserved. It's what I loved about him."

"Did he confide in you? Something to do with work, maybe?"

I stared, blank-faced. *Tell no one, Becky.*

"Those goons in your house. They were sent by a man called Savage. He thinks Chris has… had something of his."

"Who's Savage?" I asked.

"A villain. A nasty villain too."

I laughed. "What would Chris have that could possibly belong to him?" I looked away; I didn't need to see her response because I knew she was fishing blindfolded. I'd done it when the police questioned me, nipped my armpits hard and thought of other things. I thought of how Chris's jaw clicked whenever he ate. I thought of his blood on the shirt I'd ironed a hundred times, never suspecting it would end up being the final thing he'd ever wear .

And I kept quiet because he told me to. 'No matter who asks you,' he'd said. 'Tell no one.' And I was good for my word, irrespective of how close a friend Sienna was, irrespective of how much the police wanted to help. If Chris said say nothing, that's exactly what I did.

"I mentioned that I do cocaine every now and then."

"None of my business."

"It is now." She sat in the armchair opposite, hiding behind a mug of coffee. "I needed a hit today," she said, "after what's happened."

I was about to ask for a blow or needle, or whatever it is they use to get high, but thought better of it.

"My dealer." She looked away, embarrassed.

"It's okay, just tell me."

"I've heard that Savage is a nasty bastard. He runs south-east Leeds. He *owns* it." She swallowed. "He's put the word out that he wants *you*."

My blood ran cold, and my remaining strength deserted me. "What do you mean he wants me? Why would he want *me*? How does he even know who I am?"

"He found out who lived at your house. He says you have something he wants."

I stared at the wall, heart shrivelled to rigid fist. "Jesus, Sienna. What do I do?"

"That's why I asked if you had anything from Chris."

I almost spat out my tea. She said those words not in a threatening tone, but it wasn't far from it; it was as though *she* was the one in danger. "Is there something you're not telling me?" I watched as her fingers began to fidget, and added, "Do you want me to leave? I don't want to put you in any danger."

She took a mouthful of coffee and appraised me. "You're my best friend—"

"Who you can't trust."

"Of course I trust you."

"Then why didn't you tell me about your addiction?"

She laughed the same way I had earlier, a derisive snort. "I trust you with my life, you daft cow. I just didn't want you being disappointed in me."

I felt like a shit right there and then. My guard was up, everyone was a suspect, and everyone had a gun zeroed in on me until I was satisfied otherwise. I'd successfully built a high wall all around me. There was only me in there. All alone. Just as Chris had told me to.

"And I don't want you to leave. Silly." There was a flicker in her eye caught by the lamp at her side, and it turned out to be a tear. It spilled over her lashes and cascaded down her cheek. "You stay as long as you're comfortable."

The police reckoned they'd have my house under cordon for about a week, and no matter what happened they wouldn't allow me back inside. I had some Prozac in there, but I could get more from my doctor in the morning – if I remembered. Clothing… well, I had my credit card. But right now, I didn't ever want to go back there.

As far as I was concerned I didn't live there any more. I would always see Chris lying on the lounge floor. I would forever see him as dead. And I wondered, when I finally came out the other side of grief, how much of me would have died with him.

I tapped my cup. "This Mr Savage. How do I find him?"

Chapter Eleven

It was after midnight, and Chris and I had to be up for work in the morning.But we'd hit upon a subject that seemed to grow in pressure the more we poked at it. It became more interesting the more we talked, but it also became more serious the more we explored. And despite our needing to be up in a few hours, we'd given ourselves a special pass because of the severity and gravity of the topic.

"*Buona sera*," I whispered.

"What?" A fresh glass of whisky in his hand, Chris swayed by the fireplace and looked down at me.

"Just practising," I said. I breathed into my glass and the predicted tears came. "Go on then, tell me about the baddy."

Chris raised his eyebrows. "Ah, the baddy," he said. "Right. The baddy in question is one Dougie Savage—"

I snorted.

Chris pointed a finger. "Name is hilarious, isn't it?" He wasn't smiling.

"Sorry. Do go on."

"I wonder if we should leave this for another night when we're a bit more sober."

"Go fuck yourself, this is the best bit!"

"Best bit? This is the bit that you need to pay particular attention to, Becky. This is the bit that could save your skin. This guy is an A-list baddy; NCA is taking a great interest in him too."

That wiped the silly grin off my face pretty quickly; it sounded bad. "What's NCA?"

"National Crime Agency. Used to be SOCA – Serious and Organised Crime Agency. The big boys."

I cleared my throat. This had just become very silly indeed, into a whole new league. And any hope I had of this being a walk-over curled its toes up and died a horrible death. "I'm not sure this is such a great idea any more." I was always good with understatement.

I really should have pulled on the handbrake there and then, bringing this whole ridiculous idea to a halt. But I couldn't. I was enthralled.

"We suspect Savage of being party – a distant party – to eleven murders across Leeds, into North Yorkshire, and even into Greater Manchester over the past three years. Again, you can treble that number when you take into account all the missing persons that have tenuous links to him and his organisation.

"His business ranges from internet fraud, to trafficking, to drugs distribution, to chop shops, and recently to legitimate property deals. His assets, the ones we know of, run somewhere along the lines of fifty to sixty million. We think you can easily double that though. He's very rich, and so he's very powerful. We think he has links to politicians and to law enforcement."

"Links?"

"Fingers in pies."

"Proper Richard Branson, isn't he?"

"This is why it was important for us to get the whole crew, and gain a better understanding of what buttons he pushes before we pull him in."

It made sense. I eyed Chris, my meek and mild man, and felt even more in awe of him than I did only an hour ago. The highlight of *my* day was fining people for bringing books back late, or confiscating cans of booze from the kids who'd congregate in our foyer.

"Our investigation…" He paused there for almost a minute. And I didn't want to interrupt him because he'd gone inside himself somewhere, probably fighting some internal war of right versus wrong. He blinked as if coming back into the room, and continued as though nothing had happened. "The police investigation is coming to an end, and we think in a few more months, as plans fall into place, they'll have enough to end him and his entire network." He stuck his chest out then, but only for a second or two before I saw it deflate. "That's why I chose him." Chris stared at me.

"Because he knows?"

He nodded. "Like I said, he has contacts within the force, I'm sure he does."

"If he has contacts, why would he be bothered about a list?"

He smiled. "Because only I have access to the full list, within our office, I mean. No way could anyone else present him with the amount of info we have on him. He's in a dark place—"

"I feel so sorry for him."

"He knows it's likely to come crashing down around his ears, and this list might mitigate some of the fallout. Get rid of the witnesses before they can testify."

"You're giving him everything?"

"No, no. God, no. Just a list of informants. It'll weaken us – the police – and some of those names might bite a bullet, but it's still valuable to him. I checked."

My jaw had dropped open a little bit, and Chris smiled down at me. He came to sit beside me and draped an arm over my shoulder.

"Don't worry. It's all systems go. We have details to work out first, but it won't be long now, another couple of weeks."

"I thought you were going to discuss it with me before going ahead?"

"I was. I did. I mean, I will have; I haven't given him any information yet. I just wanted to get a feel for the situation; I had to know that he trusted me, and that I had an assurance from him that he wouldn't kill me or do anything stupid."

"Wait. You got an assurance from a man who's already killed eleven people?"

"He might be a scruffy tramp, but he's switched on. He's a businessman, and he knows a good deal when he sees one. I'll get a call. When it comes, he'll want that list within the hour. It's worth a couple of million to him. Easy."

"Two million? You're getting two million for this info?"

He finished his whisky, gasped at the sting in his throat, and with a smile, nodded at me. "Think we could live off that?"

I did think, for some considerable time. In fact, that was the end of the conversation, and we went to bed. But I didn't sleep. Inside my head I had the weighing scales out, and in one cup I had two million big ones stacked up precariously. In the other cup I had Savage and eleven headstones. I had the police and the PDS or whatever Chris had called them. I also had a little box on which I'd scribbled 'morality' and 'integrity.' I'd drawn a red line through both. I like things I can 'see,' it helps me understand them.

So far, the two million was heavier, but not by much. I should have taken out the two million quid and replaced it with a beach view, with a small cottage in the country, with a car that worked properly. I also had a box in there too; on it I'd drawn a ball and chain, and I'd scribbled a red line through it: 'freedom.'

As I finally began to drift off to sleep, I pulled back, widening the view, and realised the scales were part of something much larger. 'Lady Justice,' sword in her right hand, and my scales in her left. She glared at me and then turned away.

Chapter Twelve

I wondered if I'd just made life easy for my husband's killer and much more difficult for myself. Yes and yes. I also wondered if today would be my last; I wondered if I was happy with the way my life had gone, or with the legacy I'd leave behind. No and no. Sometimes I could be so gullible that I surprised myself.

I waited on the corner of Church Street and Main Street, the morning sun skimming off the library windows opposite. I hoped to hell that no one inside there who could see me; there was a group of lads smoking in the foyer. Sienna lit a cigarette and offered me the packet. "Fifteen years," I said.

"Now's a really great time to start again."

I was tempted, but I turned away. "How much longer?"

"Not long," she said.

"I should have bought a gun."

"You ever used a gun?"

I hadn't. Not a real one. I'd used an air pistol before though; only once, and even then, I only managed to fire it into the ground – hardly Bruce Willis, was I? If I did have a gun, I'd probably end up dropping it or pointing it in the wrong direction. "Well, a knife then."

"Not one of your better ideas." She breathed smoke at me. "Becky, you'd better get real for a minute. This isn't one of the books you read; this is real. This is dangerous. This man is a killer."

"Oh, that's it," I said, "cheer me up!"

"I'm just… I just want you to know what—"

"You do realise we look like a couple of prostitutes, don't you?"

She never answered me. I nodded across the road to a large car that had just pulled up at the roadside. "Is that him?" I asked, already knowing the answer. I turned around, and Sienna was already fifty yards away from me, walking quickly, a plume of cigarette smoke in her wake.

The man behind the wheel looked at me and gave the briefest of nods – it was like being at an auction. I hurried across the road, clutching my bag against my chest and wishing I'd taken that cigarette. The back door opened and I climbed in.

I didn't even get my seat belt on before we set off. There was a fat man sitting next to me. He wore a suit of sorts; it looked as old as me and just as worn out. He had a thin grey moustache and a skinhead, a bristle of white hair beginning to sprout on his pate like a velour mat. He looked at me with close, squinting eyes, surrounded by wrinkles, and said, "Hello, darling." Then stared forward.

He was the man I'd stabbed!

I suddenly felt like defecating and vomiting all at once. This was much, much worse than I had ever imagined. Just what the fuck was I thinking when I'd agreed to this meeting? "Can you stop the car, please?"

No one made a reply. It was as though I hadn't said a word. "Hello? Driver? Can you stop the car?"

The fat man turned to me and growled, "No." He turned front again.

I stared forward too, praying this would be painless. The nerves I felt were killing me; I was so on edge that a single word could send me toppling over. Really, I was just one more word away from screaming. I tried to regain some control by beginning my introduction. "Are you Mr Savage?"

His big head swivelled again, and for a moment I thought he was going to smile. He said, "Shut up, and put this on." He threw a black woollen hat at me. But as I pulled at it, I realised it wasn't a hat at all, it was a balaclava. But there were no holes for the eyes. So it wasn't even a balaclava. It was a hood.

I felt sick as I slid it on and the lights went out. All I had coming to me was sound and smell. The engine and road noise as the tyres whooshed over the road's surface, and the smell of leather and cigarette smoke. I clutched my bag, breathed through my mouth, and even though it was dark under the hood, closed my eyes and let my tongue play along the bulge of my injured lip.

I swallowed, nostrils flared, and I felt the tears coming. But I held my breath, kept the tears in check. I would show no weakness today. Today, I was in charge.

* * *

I felt the car slowing. I banged my head against the side window as we mounted the kerb, and the tyre sound was different, coarser, and I heard other noises that seemed familiar to me, and I smelled petrol and diesel.

The car took us away from the noises but the smells lingered. I felt momentum pushing me constantly to the right, so we were making a series of left turns. And then we stopped. I licked my lips; they were as dry as chalk but my hands were soaked with sweat. The fat man pulled off the hood.

I cowered against the brightness of the light, but eventually I saw that we'd parked alongside a Portakabin with wire grilles across the grubby windows and weeds growing from the gutters; not the most salubrious office I'd ever seen. It seemed joined to something like a large hangar with two rusty and battered shutter doors. I was in a concrete-floored arena. Around its periphery I saw mounds of crumpled cars, dead machinery, oil drums, and tyres.

The driver shut off the engine and climbed out. He stared at me for a moment, then opened the door. The fat man next to me just nodded. I swallowed and climbed out, my legs ill-prepared to accept my weight, and I almost stumbled. My mouth watered again like it had the first time they put the hood on me, and I thought I would throw up, but the driver pushed me in the back towards the office. It was quiet; I couldn't hear any noises coming from inside the hangar, and I couldn't even hear any road noise. Where the hell was I?

He shoved me in the back again, and when I got to the Portakabin the fat man from the car was standing at the open door. He held out his hand and nodded at my shoulder bag. "What?" I said.

"Bag."

I was about to protest when he just snatched it from me.

"Inside," the driver said, and pushed me up the steps.

There was a desk, and a tatty chair behind it. The floor was scratched lino, torn in places to reveal oil-stained wood, and the walls were fake wooden panels. To my right was a door that led, I guessed, into another office, and then probably into the hangar. I wondered if Mr Savage was sitting in there polishing his gun, filling it with bullets.

It was dark in here and it smelled of oil and cigarette smoke. Above me was a single fluorescent strip light that blinked and buzzed as though afraid to come fully to life. Surrounding it was a net of dusty cobwebs and nicotine stains.

The door slammed behind me and I jumped.

Now we relied solely on the blinking tube and the dirty window for light. The driver stood behind me but I dare not turn around – I knew he was holding a blade at neck height ready to skewer me through the throat. I swallowed again and my stupid eyes started watering.

I gasped when he turned off the light, and a thick gloom swallowed everything in the office. There was no buzzing from the ceiling light any more, nothing to fill the stark silence. I could hear his nose whistling as he breathed. It all became very real, and I didn't even have my bag to hug. I flinched as he walked around me – with no blade in sight, thankfully. He sat at the desk, and I could see he was balding, yet his remaining hair was long, straggly, greasy. He turned a dusty computer monitor around to face me, and then opened up a laptop.

The monitor powered up and glowed a bright white, obscuring him; it dazzled me, its glare hid everything else in the room from me. His long nails tapped at the keyboard. Words appeared on the screen.

Becky Rose?

I nodded. "Yes."

The driver typed some more. *Take off your clothes.*

I leaned forward to make sure I'd read the screen correctly. "I'm not taking off my clothes!"

Take them off. Now.

"Fuck off." I couldn't believe I was telling this guy to fuck off when he basically could do with me whatever he wanted, and no one knew where I was. But sometimes—

I have men who will rip off your clothes in seconds. Or you can take them off. Your choice.

"But why?"

He typed. *Take them off.*

"Why can't you talk to me? I want to see Mr Savage."

Last chance. Take off your clothes. Now.

I swallowed, stared into the darkness, and caught a glimpse of him sitting there behind his laptop. I turned and reached for the door handle. Locked. Now I felt like crying. I pictured Chris shaking his head at the mess I'd landed myself in. What would he do?

Did he have to do this when he met Savage? Did he take his clothes off?

I turned around, fists at my sides. "I am here to talk with—"

In one fluid movement, the driver stood and slapped me across the face so hard that it almost knocked me off my feet. My head buzzed and the pain in my lip – the one I'd almost forgotten about .

"You're him, aren't you? You're Mr Savage."

He took to his chair again. *You'd like a punch instead of a slap next time?*

I bit into the small bulge on the inside of my lip, and I reached around and turned on the light. It flickered and it buzzed, but it was enough. Fury rose in my chest as I strode around the desk, not giving him the time to stand, and I slapped his face just as fucking hard as I could. I was beyond petrified, but this man had ruined my life, and I'd be hanged before I'd let him belittle me.

He took the slap; his greasy hair flicked around his face and without hesitation he punched me in the gut. I doubled up, unable to breathe, the air purged from me, and I presented him with the perfect chance to slap me again. Before I knew it, I was on my knees in the corner of the office with blood in my mouth. The heat in my chest was now a hot glow in my stomach; I pulled my knees up, spat blood at the wall, and began crying. I felt like the whole world was against me, that despite trying my best not to let this creature intimidate me, I had failed, and that I was completely at his mercy.

The interconnecting door opened and the fat man from the car walked in, said nothing, just hauled me to my feet. He dragged me back around the desk, back to my own piece of wall, and turned off the light. I stared at Savage as the door closed behind the fat man. "You bastard."

Stop talking. Take your clothes off.

Though I was shaking, I slipped off Sienna's jacket, dropped it on the floor. Then I pulled the t-shirt over my head. "You're a pervert. You know that?" I kicked off my trainers, unbuttoned my jeans and slid them down trembling legs. I stood before him in my bra and pants, hoping I'd done enough to appease him. Ridiculously, I felt glad I hadn't shaved my legs in a while. Maybe that would put him off.

All of them.

"You're not serious? Come on!"

All of them!

I couldn't stop myself from shaking, and I stuttered, "Are you going to rape me?"

No.

I heard myself sob. I didn't want to let this bastard demean me any further, but I feared that's exactly what was about to happen. I bit my injured lip again and allowed silent tears to roll down my face as I took off the bra, slid off my pants, and threw them onto the heap of clothes on the floor. This time I didn't even try to see him; I looked straight ahead at the wired window. A new word blinked onto the screen.

Socks.

"Fuck's sake!" I pulled those off too, and blood dripped from my lip. "Happy now?"

The door to the adjoining office opened. The fat man walked in wearing blue latex gloves, and I recoiled. "I want to complain that—" He stared at me, and I knew that I'd better shut the hell up. Even in such poor light, I could see he was not the man to deal with any complaint; he was just a wall of muscle and fat with no room left over for thinking. Without an acknowledgement, he threw my bag onto the desk, said, "Clean," and turned back to face me, his eyes making their way slowly up and down my body. I felt violated, outraged and helpless.

He struggled to bend, picked up all my clothes, exhaling like a marathon runner as he straightened, had another good look at my breasts, and left the room, closing the door behind him. I remember seeing the sweat inside his latex gloves, and a bandage around his right wrist.

"What's... What are you doing with my clothes?"

"They'll be returned to you."

He spoke!

Like a metronome, I leapt between petrified and furious, and I think he got that from my pointing finger and my hyperventilating.

He palmed away my attempted outburst. "It's a precaution," he said, smiling. What sort of twisted fucker smiled at a time like this? "Slap me again, though, and I'll pull your finger nails out."

His voice was low, too calm by far, and that in itself was unnerving. I was waiting for the explosion, or the rush of mechanics who'd just heard there was a naked woman on the premises. I glanced down; not *much* of a naked woman, I had to admit, but despite the stretch marks and the cellulite, I was still female meat.

I put an arm across my breasts and covered my crotch, and backed into the wall by the door. "Do you treat everyone like this?" My top lip curled; I felt nothing but revulsion for this man. "Your boss is going to hear of this!"

He stood up, no smile on his face now, and for the first time I was able to take proper notice of him. In the dim light from the wired windows and the computer screen, I saw he was a lot older than I'd first thought; hunched over slightly as though he'd spent a long time at a desk. His hair was long, shoulder length, and what little of it was left was flashed through with light grey. He was just as Chris had described him. This was Savage.

His cheeks writhed as though his tongue was always trying to get that last scrap of food from between his teeth. I tried to avert my eyes because it was nauseating to see, but I felt compelled to stare.

His eyes swam over me as he approached. They were narrow, black, hidden beneath a large brow and drooping eyelids, and he had a bent Roman nose that rode over a growing sneer.

"I *am* the boss." He stood before me and slapped me again, hard enough to drive me to my knees. I was panicking already, getting ready to release it with a scream, when he was all over me. He had my ponytail in his hand and jerked my head back. "Who the fuck do you think you're talking to?"

I couldn't speak. I tried, but my throat was stretched and it was blocked too, and all I felt now was a fear so pungent it blocked my airway.

A part of my mind remembered that I'd been to the police station, that I'd given a statement and a very bad description of the fat man, accused him of killing Chris. And that part of my mind cringed and gave up the fight. I panted as he pulled my hair tighter, and in the light of the monitor I saw a blade at my face; one of those craft knives, a Stanley knife.

The scream forced its way out, and my fingernails dug into the floor. I tensed up, waiting to die.

Chapter Thirteen

"Is today your last? Has your clock ticked all the way down to zero?" His lips were right up against my ear. I closed my eyes, breathed short breaths through bloodied teeth. I'd like to say that I was thinking all this time, but in truth nothing went through my mind except 'I'm going to die!'

"Where is the list?"

My abdomen hitched and for an awful moment I thought again that I was going to throw up. "I don't know what you're talking about."

"I want that list!"

"I don't know anything about a list!"

He smacked my head into the edge of the desk and a white pain shot through me.

"Where is it?"

"Please, please, I don't know of a list." And I felt ashamed of the tears but I really wasn't in control at all. My body was succumbing to fear and humiliation, and this was the end result. If I'd known for one minute that Chris's plan would turn out this way, I would have had nothing to do with it. But I'd hoped for the best, saw only positives, and went along with it because I was greedy. I admit it, I was fucking greedy; I'd seen a carefree life, an easy way out of the rat race, and I'd grabbed it with both hands.

He stood on those hands now and ground them into the floor.

"No list?" His words were a whisper in my ear and a stench across my wet face.

I tried to shake my head but he still had a tight hold of my hair; it was pulling the skin on my face and narrowing my eyes. "No," I said.

He tugged at my hair, and then I felt him release my head. He took his feet off my hands, and stepped away. The light came on. I was on all-fours, my hands throbbing, a string of red saliva hanging from my bottom lip. My nose was blocked and my eyes were full of tears. I wanted to scream again, wanted to cry for help, and most of all I wanted to beg for mercy.

I noticed a draught coming from my right and my neck felt unusually cold. I glanced up to see the fat man standing there with my clothes bundled in his arms. He was smiling as he threw them at me.

"Get dressed," Savage said.

The fat man turned and left us alone again.

As I got to my feet he threw something at me; I caught only a glimpse and I shrieked, thinking it was a rat or something. But it was my hair, still held together at one end by a cheap plastic clip. The bastard had cut off my hair.

He winked at me. "Be thankful that's all I cut off." He sat in the seat, watched me dress, and his tongue got to work on his teeth again. "Before we go any further," he said, "I want you to know one thing. I can do anything I want with you." He stared at me, slapped the desk. "Anything!"

And that was the thing. If I knew where the list was and I gave it to him, I really would never see another day. But he seemed to have that base covered.

"But I don't kill for a giggle, Becky. I only kill out of necessity, okay?"

Like you killed my fucking husband!

I nodded, as I pulled my jacket on, and zipped it up to the collar. I stood there flexing my bruised fingers. "So why did you find it necessary to kill my husband?" I felt my chest expand with the fire inside, I wanted to leap over that desk and rip his filthy fucking head off. I wanted to—

"I didn't kill your husband." He folded his arms as though waiting for the game to commence.

"You expect me to believe that?"

"I don't give a flying fuck what you believe. I don't have to lie. Remember that. I don't have to lie at all; you're here." He waved an arm. "In my domain. I can do anything I want with you. So why would I lie? He was already dead, see?"

"Is that supposed to be cryptic, or metaphorical?"

"Speak in English if you want straight answers."

"'He was already dead?' Is that supposed to mean you were going to kill him anyway?"

Savage laughed at me. "Stupid cow. It means that he was, get this, already fucking dead. When we got there, to your house. Dead. He was dead, love. Not sure how else I can put it."

"You didn't kill him?"

He folded his arms again.

"Then who did?"

"Go ask the coppers, that's what they're there for."

"I don't believe you."

He shrugged. "Like I give a shit."

"But your man, the one who chased me."

"What about him?"

"He proves you were there, at my house?"

Savage, arms resting on his desk, blew out a long sigh while looking at me through the corner of his eye. Eventually, he said, "Okay, this is the official version of events. This is how the fucker played out, okay? Dominic Pinkman was a friend of mine. He must have been there under his own compulsion, or validation, or whatever the fucking word is. He wasn't working for me and never has worked for me.

"Though now I'm led to believe he used to be a burglar, and if I'd known that, I would have had nothing to do with him." Savage looked at my incomprehension, and seemed to revel in it. "I wonder, therefore, if Mr Pinkman broke into your house and while he was there, he and Mr Rose had a set-to..." He shrugged again, placed a finger against his bottom lip. "I wonder if Mr Pinkman killed your husband, and then, as you claim, chased you out of you house." He lit another cigarette. "Will that do for you?"

"Pinkman. He's the man who chased me."

"I don't know nothing about any chase. But if you say so."

"Pinkman's dead. I saw him die in a road accident."

"There you go then. We'll never be able to ask him, will we?"

"What? You're fabricating a story just to wrap it up nicely. I know that your crew or gang or whoever was in my house. I stabbed one of them, him." I pointed to the door. "Before I escaped and Pinkman chased me."

Savage shook his head again, and this time there was a smile to go with the slime. "Sorry, you lost me, no idea what you're talking about."

I really didn't understand. He was denying being there; I mean, he was denying that he was responsible for killing Chris at all, saying Chris was already dead when they arrived. And then he changed his story, explaining that his crew had never been at my house, but he was perfectly happy to suggest that Pinkman, working alone, was responsible for Chris's death. Why?

And then it occurred to me why. Pinkman was chasing me – can't deny that. So it stood to reason he'd been in my house, where there happened to be a dead man lying in the lounge. What better way of giving the police a plausible story while keeping Savage and the rest of his crew out of the investigation. "But you're saying he was definitely dead when you arrived?"

He raked dirty fingernails through his greasy hair, and let his tongue molest his teeth again. "That's an end to our discussions about him." He looked at me, and I knew he could see that I didn't believe him, and with that, said, "I'm a man of my word. I am honourable."

I cocked an eyebrow.

"In this game you'd last about twenty fucking minutes if you had no honour. So I'm telling you now, just so you know, if you give me the list I will let you live, and I will not harm you."

The sobs came of their own accord. I couldn't see a way out of this; I couldn't make the idiot believe me! I was never part of that plan – all of that stuff went on behind my back. Chris said I didn't need to know about the transaction, and he never told me.

"Has your husband… I mean, *had* your husband told you about me?"

I shook my head.

"What, not a word?"

"No. Really."

He seemed to consider this, and then went on. "I met him last month. He promised me a list of names. In return I paid him a million upfront. Goodwill, call it what the fuck you want. When I got the list, I was going to give him another million. This is all in cash, mind." He leaned forward. "So you can see my predicament. I'm a million down and no fucking list."

"I swear—"

He held up a hand, shook his head. "I haven't finished yet."

"Sorry."

"I'm a million down, and no nearer to that list. He's dead so he ain't saying much. So that leaves you." He prodded his chest. "Now, I believe you, about the list, I really do. But what message does it send out to my business associates, eh, if word gets around that I've been fleeced and no one took a dive for it? What does it tell them? It tells them that I haven't got balls any more. It tells them all that I don't mind taking it up the arse and paying for the fucking privilege. Get my meaning?"

"I see your problem—"

"It ain't my problem, love. It's your problem."

He got up and walked around the desk towards me. I flinched as he blew smoke at the ceiling. I could see his neck, all the creases in it, the long hairs like spiders' legs. And when he smiled at me, his teeth were yellow, mostly; a couple of the lower ones missing so he looked like an apprentice meth-head.

"If I don't get the list or the million back, *you're* going to be the one who pays for it. See what I mean?" He peered at me as though wondering what I was. "I said, do you understand?"

I jumped, nodding quickly. "I see," I whispered.

"That's good!" He clapped me on the shoulder like we were old drinking buddies. "I don't want no more unpleasantness, see. But." His hand remained. "I will make it unpleasant if I have to." He moved away, sat on the corner of his desk again. "Because I like your tits." He winked. "I mean they're a bit on the saggy side, but still, you're what, forty-six, forty-seven? Anyway, I'm giving you a week, okay?"

"A week?"

"That's seven days, love."

"But I—"

"Let's not have any negativity. I'm going to get Streaky to drop you off, and we'll meet up again like old friends in a week, share pleasantries, and part like the honourable people we are. What do you say?"

My hand was on the door knob again, even though I knew it was locked. My chest felt tight and my head ached. "I wouldn't know where to begin—"

"You know what one of my favourite films is? It's an old one, mind, from the nineties. It had Rutger Hauer in it: *The Hitcher.* Brilliant film. In one scene, this woman wakes up, and her hands are bound together, and they're tied to the back of a truck. And her feet, they're bound up too, and they're tied to the back of another truck. Both trucks are revving their engines, ready to pull this bitch apart!" He stared into the distance. "I think it's fascinating. Shame they cut away before we got to see what happened.

"Well, in a week's time, if I don't have my money or my list, I'm going to find out what happens. But instead of tying your hands and feet to two trucks, I'll have one foot tied to each." He grinned, looked at the wall behind me as though it were a cinema screen. "I can picture it now, your sweaty arse parked on a stool, legs doing the splits." He laughed, and took a quick drag on his cigarette. "Streaky!" he shouted.

The door to my right opened, and the fat man walked in.

"This is Streaky," Savage said to me. "I'm not sure why they call him Streaky; either it's because of all the bacon he eats, or it's because he's skinny like a streak of piss." He laughed at his own joke. "Anyway, doesn't matter." He stared at the imaginary screen again. "Streaky is fucking you good and proper, them trucks are revving their engines, and I've got my hand in the air, clutching a Union flag. I'm very patriotic like that." He stood up from his desk and closed in on me, right into my face again, dark eyes inches from mine, nose almost touching mine. "As soon as he comes, I drop the flag and we see what kind of a mess falls off that stool." He took a step back, peering into me. "How's that sound, love?"

My hand was at my mouth. I was numb. All over. They say that when you become cold you start to shiver, but when you get really cold, life-threateningly cold – you stop shivering to conserve energy. Well, I wasn't trembling any more. I was beyond it.

"You can go now."

I didn't move. I stared at him, but not really seeing him. I was thinking of the trucks, of the flag, and of the fat man called Streaky. I was pretty sure my heart had stopped and I was only standing courtesy of the door I was leaning against.

"Oh, and one more thing." He reached into the drawer beneath the desk. "Don't try to leave the country." He waved a passport at me. "Could be embarrassing at the departure desk. You could do a runner, maybe try and hide in some remote place in the Highlands of Scotland, but I guarantee I'll find you within two days, three at a push. Guaranteed. And if that happens, I'll make sure everyone gets a go on you before I drop the flag. Okay?"

Chapter Fourteen

I felt the car come to a halt. I heard Streaky move in his seat, and he pulled off the stinking hood. I wondered how many other heads had been inside it, and immediately wished I hadn't. I blinked when the sunlight stung my eyes, and I found myself looking at him. I swallowed and looked away.

He said nothing to me, but I dared not just leave the car; I felt nervous sitting there, but I had to wait for permission. He was looking at me in a way that I found profoundly unsettling. His face might as well have been made of papier-mâché for all the emotion it showed, and his eyes were lifeless brown marbles – sharks' eyes.

Out of nowhere, he threw a punch into my face and my head hit the side window. Pain exploded from my nose and from the back of my head; for a second everything went white, and when my vision returned there were tiny white stars flitting around at the edges. I was too shocked to cry out, but my hand came away with blood all over it, and I could feel more dripping onto my jacket.

"That's for fucking stabbing me."

"I'm…" I stopped talking. I wasn't sorry, that's for sure, but I thought if I said anything further, he'd find an excuse to hit me again. My eyes watered, and I decided I didn't need his permission to leave after all. I opened the door.

"Seven days," he said. "Garforth Main Street. Same time. Don't dare to be late. And make sure you are completely alone."

I slammed the door, and the car sped off. It was a black Mercedes. That's all I can remember.

I never felt so much like just sitting down as I did there and then. My legs felt weak, and I was in some kind of shock, both from the punch and from my ordeal with Savage. I found some tissue in my handbag and dabbed it against my nose, sighing as it came away reddened. "Bastard."

I was in Swarcliffe, a north-eastern part of Leeds next to Crossgates, not more than a mile from Killingbeck Police Station; it's where Chris used to work before they transferred him to the new Elland Road Station. I decided to walk into Crossgates and find a Costa.

The barista could barely serve me; her eyes were all over my face, and I could swear she lost some colour from hers. I sat at a table in the corner and watched the steam rise from my Americano. Other people stared at me too. My eyes felt swollen, my lips certainly were, and my nose, though it had stopped bleeding, was still blood-encrusted, I could feel it there, cracking– a sharp riposte to the deeper, heavier ache in my face. And of course, Sienna's jacket was covered in it too.

"Nose bleed," I said, smiling, embarrassed. I shrugged as if to say, 'What can you do?' They looked away, unconvinced by my lie. I must have looked a right sight. I tried to stare back at them, but was quickly defeated. Instead I sipped my coffee, hissed at the sting.

The weight of dread pressed down on me, and I could almost feel the chair legs buckle beneath me. My whole body seemed in protest; my head ached, my belly ached, my back ached, and I came to realise that it wasn't just the physical punishment that made my body groan, it was the mental punishment, too. And by that, I mean Chris's death.

The grief had a weight all of its own, and it was crushing me; it was like a fog that I couldn't see through or even think through, enveloping me, filling my lungs and my mind like a toxin. Grief was a constant companion, and though sometimes I'd forget that Chris had died, the fog would always be there to remind me.

Aside from the injuries, I realised that I had one thing that I didn't have only a few hours ago. I had a million pounds. I had a million fucking quid! Chris would have been very pleased for me, that his plan had worked – to some extent. He would be cheering, in his own quiet way, perhaps nodding a glass of whisky at me.

What I did over the next few days would determine whether I got to keep it, whether I even got to live. But first I had to find it.

Wait though. If it was true, that Savage had kept to the deal so far and had given Chris one million pounds, why hadn't he told me? Wouldn't he at least give something away to me, a sign, a wink, anything? How could you keep news like that to yourself? How come I'd had to find out from Savage? Maybe Savage was lying – and why not? Despite his claims of being honourable, he wasn't exactly in an honourable profession, was he?

I began to convince myself that Savage *was* lying. About the money and about killing Chris.

And then something quite odd struck me. Why lie? He had no chance in hell of scamming me for a million! I had about three hundred in my account, so why not just ask for the list, why even mention the money if he hadn't paid it over?

"Because," I whispered to myself, "if I found the list and handed it over to Savage, I'd demand the money from him."

I thought about this as my coffee grew cold. The deal was, allegedly, for two million. One million before the transaction, and one after. If I handed over the list, I'd still be due the second million. If I had the balls to demand anything at all.

What I needed, if it ever came to arranging such a deal, was a lever. I needed something that would ensure Mr Savage stayed honourable. But all that was for the future. What I needed now, more than anything, was to find that list.

Chapter Fifteen

Coffee wasted, I headed out of Costa and into the ladies' toilets. I did my best to clean myself up; not because I'm vain, but because I got sick of people staring at me. They would actually stop talking with their companions, and stand to watch me as I walked by. And all this attention prevented me from thinking. So, I mopped the dried blood from my face, put on some lipstick to try and hide the busted lip, and eye shadow to conceal the bruise too. I threw Sienna's jacket in the bin and bought another from the nearest charity shop.

Now I could walk and think in obscurity.

I also needed a mobile phone shop. I took out the SIM card from the tiny hip pocket in my jeans, thankful that Streaky hadn't destroyed it, and thankful Sienna and I had been able to claw free of the smashed phone.

I aimed for the nearest, and began dissecting my meeting with Savage as I went. At first, I thought they stripped me out of my clothes to satisfy some perversion they had. But I remembered what Streaky said when he tossed my bag on Savage's desk. He'd said, 'Clear.' He'd been checking for bugs or whatever the term for listening devices or tracking devices was. It also explained why Savage wouldn't even speak to me, why he gave me his instructions from a screen. Savage was a very careful man, and I should have known that when he hooded me for the journey.

At last I had some indication as to what kind of game I was playing, and what kind of people my opponents were. It wasn't a game I even wanted to compete in, but now I was here, I decided I was going to win. Savage was not going to get the better of Becky Rose.

* * *

"It's me. Can I ask another favour, please?"

"Thank God you're alright! What happened? Where are you?" Sienna's voice was a mixture of relief, excitement, and frustration. "I've bitten my nails to the bone. What did he want?"

"I'm in the Arndale Centre."

"Gimme twenty minutes," she said, and hung up.

Twenty minutes was fine; it gave me a chance to think through the answers I was going to have to give her. Because if I knew Sienna half as well as I thought I did, she was going to ask and ask until I gave her something.

I sat on a bench in the car park, elbows on knees, and chin on fists. I remembered the book, *The Lord of the Rings,* and how those charged with seeing the ring of power destroyed actually sought it for themselves. Many failed the test when the opportunity arose to reject the ring. One character stood out: Aragorn turned his back on it. He was true to the cause and true to his friend.

I wondered if Sienna would be my Aragorn, and help me. I had no doubt she would. But when presented with a million pounds, what would she do? Part of me laughed at the problem, because it actually wasn't a problem at all. The stress of this morning had caused my reticence; she was a good friend and she'd make sure I got that money, and celebrate with me when I had. But there was a risk to all this; a risk that if she got one whiff of that cash she'd knock me out – or worse – and run like hell, filling her nose with coke along the way.

I don't know, it was somehow safer to distrust everyone and keep myself protected than to trust anyone and risk my life.

And did I deserve that million quid anyway? I think I did. Nothing would bring Chris back again, but if I was to be a widow with no job, no place to live… Hell, after losing Chris, after being stripped, after fighting for my life in my own fucking house, you bet I deserved that cash. And really, what better way to honour Chris than to reap the benefits he'd sown for us?

I know I'd played devil's advocate with Chris, that what he'd proposed was not only illegal but immoral too. But I'd decided, about the time Savage slapped me, that morals and questions of legality were out of the window for the foreseeable future.

Sienna's Corsa squealed to a halt right in front of me. I climbed in with a finger over my lips, and all I got back from her was a face full of incomprehension. I held up my new phone so she could see the screen. I'd typed: *Don't say anything, I think I'm bugged. But I want to be sure.*

She mouthed *Fuck*.

I erased my message and typed: *Please take me to Next at Colton Retail Park.*

She mouthed, *Why? There are shops here.* She hooked a thumb over her shoulder.

I erased, and then typed: *I need fitting rooms.*

She thought about it for a second and then nodded.

* * *

I've never been a classy lady. I mean that I didn't dress up once a month for an evening out. I didn't possess a pair of high heels, never owned any stockings. Never even owned a matching bra and pants set. I have always been a jeans and t-shirt girl, ever since my youth. And, as far as my mind knew, I was still in my youth.

I always nodded affectionately each time I saw an old man with a quiff, wearing brothel creepers and drainpipes. I never laughed at those old boys because to me it shouted that they still thought of themselves as young. And that was my aim. If I'd been born a male, I would have changed my name to Peter Pan, for I had no intention of ever growing up.

But a part of me had been forced to grow up over the last few days. Actually, ever since Chris had struck up that wild and compelling conversation in the lounge, I'd been forced to accept that there really was a serious side to life – like it or not.

I was in the fitting room at Next, the hooks laden with hangers of jeans, t-shirts, underwear, socks, and even a pair of trainers. I figured Streaky had my clothes for the better part of ten minutes, more than enough time to unpick a seam, slide one of those trackers or audio bugs in, and stitch it up again.

I'm a regular size 12, so all the clothes I'd chosen fitted well, and there was no messing about with grabbing different sizes: I pulled off Sienna's old clothes – they felt soiled to me now anyway – and slid on the new ones. Easy as that, three minutes tops. I dedicated another seven or eight minutes to running my thumbnail up and down the seams of each garment, and eventually my thumb stopped at the hem of the right leg of my jeans. Streaky's stitch work left a lot to be desired. Shoddy workmanship.

It was at this point that my heart-rate kicked up a gear. Despite the pain I still had, my memory of this morning's horrors had blunted slightly over the intervening hours, but this – this fucking bug – brought it back to me, and reminded me that I really was still a pawn in someone's game. And that game didn't concern money – not ultimately, not to me – ultimately it concerned whether I would live, or whether I'd join Chris.

I pulled at the stitching and the bug lay like a black disc, no larger than a coin battery, frighteningly small, in the palm of my hand. I took out my phone and photographed it front and rear. And then I surprised myself by being clever; I continued my search, even feeling along the seams inside my old bra. I couldn't feel any more new bumps, but I wanted to be safe, so I bundled the old clothes together; I'd dump them in a skip I'd seen just around the corner, along with the tracking device. I don't know anything about bugs or trackers, but I was pretty sure Savage's men would have a pleasant trip to the landfill site sooner or later.

I climbed back inside Sienna's car with a grin on my face.

"Never!"

I nodded. "Tiny little black thing the size of a thumbnail."

"The bastards!"

"Tell me about it."

"No," she said, "how about you tell me about it. From the top, Becky."

I hesitated. Should I tell her about the possibility of some cash, or keep it quiet? And should I tell her about the list? Chris had drummed it into me never to tell anyone anything. But he also said I had to work with what I had, and I took that to mean I should keep my allies onside. I needed Sienna, and since I'd known her for twenty-odd years, I figured I could trust her. I just didn't know how far. But when it came down to it, I didn't have much of a choice.

"Come on, come on, Becky. What did he want?" And then she shrank back from me. "What the fuck happened to your hair?"

"Savage happened to it."

"He cut your hair?"

"I think he was trying to prove a point: that he was in charge."

"What did he want? Why was he searching your house?"

Do not trust anyone.

"Becky?"

I looked at her and the smile at finding the bug had finally vanished, and she could tell I was debating whether or not I could trust her.

She sighed, and ran a finger over the steering wheel. "It's okay. I shouldn't pry; it's none of my business."

I almost said 'thank you,' and 'you're right, it's not.' But I didn't; I waited to see how angry she would get. But there was no anger; she turned to me and smiled. "Fish and chips? My treat. And then I'm going to see to that lip – it's breaking through your lipstick, girl."

And that wasn't the reaction I'd expected, not after all the excitement on the phone earlier. I expected anger, or a sulk. I got neither. And that upset me a little; I hadn't expected it.

* * *

That night, in Sienna's spare bed for the second time, I couldn't get to sleep again. I flitted between sobbing over Chris, and trying to work out what the hell to tell Sienna. Her tactics had worked well for her. She'd kept quiet, didn't ask anything further, never even hinted at wanting to know, and so it had driven me mad, so much so that I'd wanted to blurt out Savage's words just to get a reaction.

Perhaps she didn't need to ask because she already knew? It was something that I'd tossed around my mind for a while, but it was going nowhere. Just going around in pointless circles, the same as that other thought that kept bothering me: she never asked why Savage had killed Chris. Why didn't she? It would be first on my list.

Do not trust anyone.

They were the only words that stopped me. And only now in the middle of the night, listening to the traffic scooting by on Church Street, I had to decide what to tell her.

Chapter Sixteen

I could hear Chris's shaver up in the bathroom above my head. I heard it stop, and I heard the bathroom door close. I ignored the dishes in the kitchen sink before me, and sipped tea from my favourite Disney cup. I know, I'm forty-six, but come on, Disney never leaves a girl. Especially *Beauty and the Beast*.

As I sipped, I watched a pair of blue tits squabbling over seed on the bird table in the back garden. I use the term 'garden' loosely, for while I adore nature, I dislike tending it. Chris throws a mower at it when he has to, otherwise I like to call it 'as God intended,' and leave it at that.

The squabbling was a morning ritual for those blue tits. I couldn't understand them; there was more than enough seed for them and all the neighbourhood pigeons too. But still, it had become *my* morning ritual to watch them; they fascinated me.

I moved against the kitchen worktop to get a better view, and then I saw him. The neighbour's grandson, Bret. Fucking Bret.

What the hell was he doing?

He moved along the far side of the wall, edging his way to the dying conifers along the far side. Every now and then, I could see his head bob up as though assessing something. His belly must have been scraping the floor, and then I saw something in his hand as he stopped behind the conifers, and peered into my garden.

I had a bad feeling about this. Bret was trouble. Always was. And I had no doubt that today would be an exception.

He was assessing the blue tits, but now I couldn't see what was in his hands at all because of the conifers. "Get away from them, you bastard," I whispered. I put down my cup, leaned over the sink and banged on the window. "Shoo!"

Neither Bret nor the birds took the slightest notice. Bret crept closer, totally obscured now by the conifers. "Shoo, you bastard!" I screamed. Still no reaction. And before I could even think of turning and heading for the door, one bird took flight. The other fell to the floor, struggling to make its broken body work.

I shrieked and knocked my favourite cup onto the floor where it shattered, spraying hot tea everywhere. "Bastard!" I screamed at the mess, but my attention was drawn back to the scene outside.

I stood at the window with my hands over my mouth watching the poor thing flapping around in agony, suffering.

The other bird was nowhere to be seen.

"You evil fucker," I said.

"Who's an evil... Who's evil?"

Chris came in behind me, saw the smashed cup and tutted.

Just that one seemingly innocent tut spun inside my head like I was being judged and condemned as a stupid woman.

I folded my arms. I turned around to face him. "What did you say?"

He smiled at me, uncertainty skimming his mouth. "Sorry?"

"Did you just tut at me?"

"I tutted at your broken cup." He shrugged. "Why so uptight?"

I cocked my head. "Uptight? Do I look uptight?"

"Like you're ready to explode." He grabbed his sandwich bag and took a step back.

I felt my nostrils flare, and I pinched myself under the armpit to get rid of the tension. It didn't work. "He's killed a blue tit!"

"Who?"

"That little bastard—"

"Right." He shrugged. "I'll see you tonight."

"Don't you care?"

"Nope."

"You callous bastard, Chris Rose." I thundered towards the door, knocking him aside.

Once outside, I ran towards the conifers. I saw the bird as I passed; it merely twitched now. Its pathetic little chirps served only to heighten my fury. "You horrible little bastard," I snarled, leaping over the wall.

And there he was, Bret the Bastard, smug little murdering smile on his cod-like lips, greasy skin shining.

"Come here, now!"

Bret winked, gave me the finger, and ran off. I've never felt frustration like it. If I hadn't waited so long in the kitchen, I could've caught him; I could've wrung his worthless neck.

Panting through exertion and anger, I returned to the little bird that fluttered against the dust in the flower bed as it fought to get away.

I stared at it, and knelt down next to it. I felt so sorry for it; the toy of an evil creature, and now surely dying in a garden it thought was safe. Its tiny black bead of an eye twitched as it watched me, and when I brought the brick down and crushed it into the soil, I felt like I'd just killed a small child. I listened, and couldn't hear any birdsong from anywhere. They'd all watched me kill one of their own.

I cried.

I went into the house to get a ladle, something to dig a small grave for the poor thing, but as soon as I entered the kitchen, I saw Chris on his hands and knees, scooping up bits of broken cup.

I went rigid. "What are you doing?"

"Just lending a hand." He didn't look up.

"I can clean up my own mess, thank you very much."

He laughed. "I know," he said, "but many hands make light work, and all that."

"I don't need your fucking help or your ridiculous platitudes! Do you think I'm useless?"

He stood, trying and failing to smile at me, then he stepped away, palms outward.

"Go to work," I yelled.

I thought I would calm down when he did. But I didn't. I was hyper.

An hour later, I'd buried the bird near the conifers. And I waited there, ignoring my aching feet, and the thirst in my throat. When I saw Bret the Bastard walking back down the path towards me, I flexed my fingers, crouched, and held my breath.

I could hear his wheezing as he approached, and in a moment of released energy I leaped over the wall, grabbed him by his jacket and pushed him into my flower bed, not far from where his latest kill was still cooling.

The look on his face was a cross between shock and disbelief. I stood over him, my hands on my hips, as he rubbed the side of his leg that had grazed along the top of my wall.

"Not content to kill my birds," I said, "now you add trespassing to the list."

"What?"

I folded my arms; I'd caught him… but now what? I wanted to smash him up. I pictured myself bringing my heel down into his nose and feeling it break, I fantasised about standing on his throat until his own twitching stopped.

Instead I took out my phone.

"What are you doing?"

I smiled down at him, slid my thumbs across the screen as though dialling a number.

"I said, what are you doing?"

I ignored him, held the phone to my ear. "Oh yes, police please."

Bret tried to get to his feet, but I stood on his fingers until he squealed. It was ecstasy.

"What? Let me go, you fucking mad bitch."

I so wanted to kick him in the throat. "Ssshhh," I said, "I'm on the phone to the police."

"Why? What have I done?"

"Ah, yes," I spoke into the phone, "I'd like to report a trespasser and criminal damage, please."

"Please! Mrs Rose, get off me, I'll leave you alone!"

"One moment, please." I looked down at him, the snivelling piece of shit. "I beg your pardon, Bret."

"I'll leave you alone." His eyes were watering. "Really. Just—"

"How did you kill my bird?"

"What, I didn't—"

I pressed harder on his fingers, then twisted a little. His scream was a wonderful thing.

"Wait, wait, wait! I used a gun. An air pistol. Please!"

"Show me." I glared at him.

He yelled, "Grandma!"

I pressed harder, and I think I felt something snap under my foot. That's when he screamed so high that his voice broke and became inaudible. I eased off, but only slightly, and then he began sobbing, the cod-lip curled out, and a glimmer of snot showed itself. "If you ever want to use your stubby little fingers to give anyone the bird again, you'd better show me."

"Okay, okay," he pleaded, his left hand palmed at me the same way Chris had.

I took my foot away. His fingers had turned white, and red, and there might have been a shade of blue-ish purple in there too. I ignored his sobbing and his need to inspect his hand.

"You've bust my—"

"I'll bust your neck if you don't show me!"

He slid backwards a few feet, and then took a pistol from his inside pocket. He threw it on the ground.

"Pellets," I said.

A rattling tin landed next to it.

"Is it loaded?"

He nodded, his lip flapping, his eyes pleading.

I picked up the gun, surprised by its weight. "If I put this to your eye and pulled the trigger," I said, "would it blind you?"

He swallowed like a clucking hen, and then nodded vehemently. "Might kill me."

I slid the phone back into my pocket, and stared at Bret the Bastard as he stood. "Come near my garden again…" I raised my eyebrows. "Understand?"

He nodded, climbed back over the wall, holding his damaged fingers, and began running. When he was twenty yards away, the little bastard gave me the finger again, and shouted, "I'll fucking have you, you mad bitch!"

I laughed so hard that I peed myself.

Chapter Seventeen

I love my Chris. I was aware of sunlight coming into the room through the gently swaying curtains. I felt warm, secure, and loved here under my duvet. Chris breathed slowly beside me and I wormed an arm around him, pulling myself closer so we could spoon. My eyes were still closed as I nuzzled his neck, and sank ever deeper into love with him. I know how ridiculously sloppy that sounds, but it's the best way I can describe that feeling of bliss that melted me that morning.

He stirred and said, "Becky?"

I groaned, "*Buon giorno.*"

"Time to get up."

"Just another ten minutes."

"We have things to do."

I ignored him; whatever those things were, they could wait. It wasn't often we found ourselves this comfy, this close, and I wanted it to last until our time together ran out.

"Becky. Becky?"

And then he was shaking me on the shoulder to wake me.

"Becky, come on? I made you some tea."

But how could he shake me if he was lying in front of me? My eyes snapped open and I let go of the pillow I was snuggling into. I turned to face Sienna. The room was blue, the curtains pulled back already, and a grey sky leered at me.

"Come on."

"I'm…" Our time together had run out.

Three days ago. It came back to me in a wave of shuddering coldness, and it washed all the good feelings away with it. I felt cold, exposed, and… and lonely. I closed my eyes and tried to pull it back – the dream – the dream of me and Chris snuggled beneath a duvet, but all I got was prickled by goose down. He had gone. I had to begin my grieving again from the start. And it was harder the second time around.

I held my breath because I could feel the sadness crashing back to fill the void where Chris once lived, and it enveloped me wholly.

I can't begin to describe the pain of losing my Chris, but remembering him so vividly and sharing just a few minutes of lucidity with him was beyond beautiful. Having it kicked aside so abruptly was the antithesis of that beauty. It was cruel. I felt hollow. I had borrowed that memory, and now it was time to give it back, to let it go.

I felt dead.

* * *

"It's my dad's birthday," I whispered.

She held me tightly, and I sank into her arms. It was all getting too much for me. I loved my dad, and I always spent his birthdays looking back at photos of him and Mum, reliving the good times and sinking into a despair that I somehow found comfort inside, promising myself I'd come out of it the next day. I rarely did though; it took a week or more for me to come back around. But today, that despair was compounded by last night's dream of being back with Chris again; and the horror at learning he was dead hit me afresh this morning.

"They call it grief."

I stared into Sienna's eyes, aware that my chin was trembling and my fucking eyes were leaking again. "I can't come to terms with it. I'll never be able to live without him."

She held me tightly and for her kindness I soaked her T-shirt and dribbled snot all over it. She didn't complain, didn't try to pull away either. She just held me for the duration, rubbing my back, squeezing me.

"I want to die," I whispered. She said nothing for a long time. I closed my eyes and felt them stinging.

"I lost my boyfriend last year to—"

I pulled back, eyes now slits. "Boyfriend?"

She smiled. "Eric. Best thing to ever happen to me."

Eric was a six-foot-four arsehole, but just skin and bone. His eyes were sunken, swimming about inside the black pits of his cheek bones like sultanas in a burnt muffin. Chris and I used to joke about him, called him Eric the Viking. Not entirely suitable, I agree, but we couldn't think of another label for him.

He was a junkie – retired, he'd said. I suppose that alone was one of the reasons we didn't see much of them; we didn't approve. I feel shameful about that now, about judging him.

"I didn't even know you were still together."

She pulled away and sat down. "Didn't bother to find out, either, did you?"

I hung my head. The shame grew. "I'm sorry. Really."

She sighed. "Life is just death on hold."

I dragged an arm through the tears, and said, "You never told me. Sienna, you should—" She was away, somewhere, thinking of him, and now wasn't the right time to deflect my guilt by admonishing her. "What do you mean, you lost him?"

She gritted her teeth. "Heroin. Overdose."

My hand was at my mouth. "Oh, Sienna, I'm so—"

"He promised me he was clean. Said he had been for a year."

I knelt by Sienna's chair ."That explains why we didn't see you." There I was again, deflecting my guilt.

"It gets easier. That's what I'm saying to you. I know you can't possibly believe me, not right now. But it does, I promise."

"This is the kind of pain that nothing can cure."

"And you don't want to cure it. You want to live with it. You want to be able to remember it, have it visit you like an old friend from time to time." She shuffled off the chair and we knelt together, arms around each other, sharing shoulders. "Someone told me once that grief is actually a great gift. You have to let it lie for a while, let the sharp corners weather away. And once its ferocity has cooled, it shares all the best times with you, like looking through a window into your past. And when you're at your lowest, it comes to you and it brings you comfort." She pulled away from me, took me gently by the arms and said, "Don't fight it so hard. Live through it, Becky, one day at a time."

I thought about it for a while, and though I knew it was all bollocks, it was reassuring bollocks, and right now I needed some reassurance. "I'm sorry to hear about Eric." I moved away, back to the sofa, my tea, and a cushion. I'd come to a decision.

"We were going to marry," she said.

Luckily I didn't have tea in my mouth as it just fell open. I gawped at her. For the life of me I couldn't understand her shit choice in men. She was a good-looking woman, and I thought she could have her pick of a thousand shiny knights, but for some reason ended up with a scabby old Viking.

"And then he had a windfall." Her own tears ran, and I could feel mine beginning to surge in sympathy. "Only a few hundred quid, on the Lotto." She cleared her throat. "Well," she said, "if it's not meant to be."

"I never knew. Like the coke. That's two things about you I didn't know." I could imagine dying in a landslide or in avalanche, but dying of a windfall was a new one on me. What could I achieve with a million quid?

She smiled. "Life's boring if we give up our little secrets. Don't you think?"

What about the big secrets though?

"But you were going to marry him. And you kept it from me. Was I even going to get an invite?"

"Don't turn this into something it's not, Becky. I was thinking about it, that's all; we'd talked about it." She sniffled. "I always knew it would never happen anyway, it was just a silly dream." She smiled, almost embarrassed. "I never even began making plans with him. It was just talk. Silly talk to while away our time. And then before I knew it, there was no time left." Another shrug.

I looked away, crushed by her sadness. "And I wasn't there for you."

There was a pause, and then, "You really fucked up your hair, you know."

I marvelled at her grin, how she could shake despair away so easily. I patted the back of my head. "It's all the rage these days."

"It was all the rage in the seventies. Now it looks like shit. Let's tidy it up."

As she levelled it and layered it, I told her what had happened in Savage's crude little hut. If Chris had been in Sienna's lounge he would have put a finger to his lips and shushed me, and then he would have shouted at me to shut the hell up, and then he would have slapped me around the face. Well, maybe not that last bit, but he would have been pretty pissed at me for telling my secret to Sienna.

But I figured if I couldn't trust her, then who could I trust? And I really did need an ally; I really needed someone to help get me through this. I had no idea if there was a list of names at all. I'd never seen it, and he hadn't told me where to look for it. It was all rumour, really. And the million quid was just one gangster's word – worthless until it was in my hands.

When I mentioned the list, Sienna paused, brush hovering above my head. "I never knew things like that even existed," I said. But when I told her about the money, she dropped the brush, and I could see her jaw fall open. "Don't drool down my back, please."

"You are shitting me, right?"

"That's what he told me. I don't see he has a reason to lie about it."

"He put that bug in your jeans to find out where it was; the money, or the list. Or both."

"Maybe," I said, "but first we have to find them both. And quick."

Chapter Eighteen

"Do you think he's following us?"

"I'm not taking any chances." Sienna pulled into a space in the park-and-ride. "Be as quick as you can."

I walked the length of the car park, crossed the road and stood outside Elland Road police station. It was a grand white building, maybe two hundred yards long with glass running the entire upper storey length of its façade. To my right was a thirty-foot obelisk with the crest lit up in blue at the top, and beyond that, in the visitors' car park, was a flag pole with the West Yorkshire Police flag at half-mast. "For my Chris," I said and headed towards the rotating glass door.

I waited in the marble foyer for about fifteen minutes before the glass doors at the end opened up and Peter Ingram smiled out at me. As I approached, he held out his hand. "How are you?"

The doors closed after us and we dropped into a cooler, slightly darker, carpeted vestibule that stretched the length of the building. I remembered the comfy chairs and the water fountains from the last time I was here. "I'm okay," I lied. "Taking one day at a time."

We began walking. "It's a stupid question," he said, "but it's hit everyone in our office really hard, and each day we ask each other that question. As if anyone's going to say anything other than 'I'm fine.'" He stopped, and turned to me. "I'm so sorry. You must think I'm terribly insensitive. Of course our sadness could never—"

"It's okay, Peter, really. I'm coping with it. And he spent a great deal of time here, of course it'll affect you and your staff too. You're not being insensitive at all." I smiled my reassurance at him, and he eventually straightened. I followed him through two sets of double doors. "Did you know he used to hide my birthday presents here?" I was smiling at the memory.

"Did he? So you wouldn't go looking for them?" There was a film of sweat on his top lip.

I nodded, grinning, still holding my breath against a torrent of emotion that ached to be free.

He peered around the room. "Anyone in here?" he called. "It's the men's locker room," he said to me. "You get people walking around here in states of undress. I mean, because there's a gym," he added quickly, "people go there, and then shower, and—"

"I get it, Peter. Calm down."

He checked around again. "I want one hundred thousand."

"What?"

"Locker's down there," he said, all the friendliness gone. "I got a box ready for you if you need one. Go on." He placed a hand on my arm and pushed me along.

"Hundred thousand for what?"

"Are you serious?"

I stopped and looked at him. "Peter? What on earth—"

"For keeping quiet." He squinted at me. "Are you trying to pull a fast one on me?"

"About what, for Christ's sake? Emptying Chris's locker of his personal effects?"

We walked again, and stopped at the locker, Peter's jaw clenching repeatedly. He took a small key from his pocket, handed it over. "There," he said, "third one up. Sixty-one F. Chris's locker."

Through gritted teeth, I repeated, "One hundred grand for what exactly?"

"I'm his boss," he whispered. "I had to run a full audit on his workstation and report any anomalies." He closed right in to me. "I found it. The list."

He was trembling. I could tell his bluster was nothing but bravado, just a shop front, a grand façade like the one outside this very police station – a show of strength to guard against the realities of what might lurk within. "I haven't the faintest idea what you're talking about." I slid the key in the lock and turned.

"Twelve names. Each of them registered to Dougie Savage. Doesn't take a genius to work out what Chris was up to."

I thought fast. "Dougie who? Listen, I don't know what you're accusing my husband of, but—"

Peter pushed me back on to the locker by the throat. The door crashed and buckled, the echo danced around the room. He growled at me, "Don't fuck with me, Becky. We never compile those lists except for NCA, and only then with the express authority of a Chief Super or above. And no one from NCA has requested such a list."

"Let me go!"

He took his hand away and I took a step away from him, rubbing at my throat. It didn't stop him from snarling at me, "I've kept that audit quiet; it's on the farthest back-burner I can find. For now. Would take me fifteen minutes to flag it, a further half an hour to expose it to PSD. And then you couldn't begin to imagine the shit-storm that will descend on you if I do."

"Really? And what about your own shit-storm when I tell them of your demands?"

"Is that the best you've got?"

He was panting, but then so was I. I felt cornered, and I think he'd more or less called all my bluffs. But I wasn't ready to give up yet – this might be nothing more than an elaborate trap. Lull the little missus into thinking she was safe to do a deal – even though it was extortion. And then the cops would come out of hiding and slap on the cuffs. And they'd raise the flag again.

I croaked, then coughed. "Peter, if this is true, that he printed this list of names of… what do you think he was planning to do with it?"

He closed his eyes, nostrils flared, and I saw his hands clench into fists.

I swallowed.

"I respected Chris, you know. I did. And I respect you too, Becky. All I would ask in return is that you respect me, please. Do not treat me like some prick who's new to policing. He printed off that list for one purpose only: to escape. With you. So whatever Savage is paying you for it, I want one hundred thousand. I can buy you several weeks, maybe more." He looked right at me, eyes unblinking. "You can go on to tell me that he never confided in you if you like. And I'll politely nod my head and pick up the phone to PSD and you can spend a couple of days trying to convince *them* instead. How's that sound?"

I looked at the ground, I looked at the ceiling, and finally I looked back at Peter. To his credit, he wasn't smiling. I moved closer again. "I can't even find the list! I promise he didn't tell me where he was going to hide it."

Peter licked his lips, and I saw an inaudible sigh escape him as he relaxed a bit, having his hunch confirmed at last. But for a moment, I thought he was going to shout, 'She fell for it guys, come and get her!' "Then we'd better hope he left you a clue in there." He nodded at the locker.

I pulled the buckled door open. It was a two-foot cube of emptiness. Almost. There was a small cardboard box in the back. I reached in and dragged it forward, and then I sat on a nearby bench with it in my lap. My husband was the last person to hold this box and everything in it. Peter peered into the locker, ran his fingers across the topmost seam, and then came to stand over me.

Inside there was a West Yorkshire Police coaster. I looked up at Peter, puzzled.

"You can't get them any more. Hens' teeth."

I nodded, dropped it back in the box and pulled out a small clear plastic box with a West Yorkshire Police tie pin inside. I dropped it and picked up the only other item in there. "*The Barnbow Lasses*," I said, turning the book over in my hands. I opened it, flicked through the pages hoping that a folded-up sheet of paper might present itself. Nothing did. I shook it, flicked through the leaves again as I held the book upside down. "Where the hell is it?"

Peter slumped down beside me. "If you're trying to fool me," he whispered, "I swear I'll find the worst possible punishment for you."

"Really?" I threw the book back into the box and stood. I pointed a finger at him. "Savage has already promised he'll get his performing seal to fuck me, and then rip off both my legs with a pair of trucks. Do you think you can beat that, Peter? Do you?"

"I mean it. Do not mess with me."

"Or what exactly? You'll dob me in to the fucking PSD? Over having my legs torn off, I'll take them every time, you moron!"

He stood up sharply and nudged his sweaty forehead right into mine. Spittle hung from his lips as he growled, "Do not belittle me, woman."

I pushed him, and he pushed me back, harder. I lost my footing and went sprawling on the floor just as the door opened and an officer walked in. He stopped, said, "Is everything okay in here?"

Well, really, did it fucking look like everything was okay?

Peter was at my side, helping me to stand, smothering me with plastic kindness and empathy. "She fell." He walked to the officer. I heard him whisper something about being torn apart by grief, and hadn't he seen the flag at half-mast? He looked at me. "That's his wife."

The officer nodded slowly. "Sorry for your loss, madam," he said, turned around and left.

"Un-fucking-believable," I said as Peter came back to me.

"I'm sorry," he said. "I didn't mean to lose my temper with you."

I sat back on the bench, and said, "Look. Fine, you can have your hundred grand. But you have to understand two things first."

He folded his arms. "I'm listening."

"I genuinely do not know where the stupid list is. And I genuinely don't know where the money Chris was supposedly paid for it is either. Honestly!"

"Your problem."

I laughed. "My husband is killed, and two men in two days tell me his legacy is my problem. How the hell does it work? When does it become someone else's problem for a change?"

"It doesn't." He shrugged. "I'm clean. I don't know about the other man. But it stays your problem. Deal with it."

"Look, can't you just print off another list?"

It was Peter's turn to laugh. I was stunned. "I'm protecting an audit trail showing that Chris printed off a list of names. That's all the audit trail reveals. Twelve numbers are all I see on that trail. I see a collation, and then I see a print function. If I were to open up all those numbers and print them, what have I done? I've created an audit trail that leads to me. Not going to happen."

"But who's going to audit you? You're the boss."

"Look at me. It's not going to happen. I'm not planning on running away from it all like Chris obviously was. I still have to work here, alright?"

"But what if I can't find the list?"

"You'll find it."

"But what if I can't? Will you finally believe me when you see my murder in the news?"

"Figure it out, Becky."

"Might it be on a memory stick? Maybe I'm looking for a stick instead of a sheet of paper?"

"We don't have external drives. We don't have cards or card readers. We don't have disk drives because we don't remove information from computers. We're not allowed to, so we're not given the option to. He printed it. It's on paper."

He pulled me up off the bench, thrust the small cardboard box at me, and then led me to the carpeted vestibule. "You have two days' grace. And then I flag that report." He took a large breath, planted a sickly smile on his face, and ushered me towards the glass doors. "I hope you find comfort in that box, Mrs Rose. And please don't hesitate to call me if there's anything I can do to help you."

I walked along the marble floor feeling tiny and insignificant.

"Oh, Mrs Rose," he called after me.

I turned to him.

"Love the new hair."

Chapter Nineteen

I was still in some kind of flux as I approached her car. I have no clear idea what I was thinking about, but it involved surviving and not really knowing how.

It seemed to me that my mind was being rented out, like a time-share thing, and I was only in control of it for fifty percent of the time. I have no idea what happened to it the other fifty per cent, no idea who was in control of it. I only know that it didn't feel like me. I didn't know if it was strictly a time-share deal, or whether my capacity to determine what went on inside my own mind was dulled, as though I was on drugs or something. It was as though my ability to rationalise things had diminished until I couldn't see the dangers or the realities any more. I expect Sienna would have said this was 'grief.'

She was on the phone, and she dropped it into her lap when she saw me coming as though it was on fire. She smiled at me, clicked the door unlock button, and closed the phone off when I climbed into the passenger seat, and put the box on the floor.

"My mum." She smiled at me. She took another drag on her cigarette and launched it out of her own window.

I nodded, and despite biting my lip until it began bleeding again, I couldn't help crying again either. I covered my face with shaking hands and just wailed into them. Her arm was around me and she was trying to pull me closer to her, but I resisted. "Hey, hey," she soothed, "what's wrong, honey?"

I hate being called honey.

"He's demanding one hundred grand to keep his mouth shut."

"Who? This Peter fellow?"

I nodded, still seeking comfort in the darkness behind my hands.

"Bastard!"

"I'm scared, Sienna."

"I know, I know," she cooed.

Firstly, how the hell could she know? She was living through this second-hand, only living it through the words I gave her; she shared none of the emotion that went along with actually experiencing it. I know she was only being a supportive friend, but when you're hurting it feels like an empty platitude, and I hated… wait, wait, how many times had I said I hated something recently? Lots. What the hell was happening to me? I used to be so bubbly, but now, living in perpetual darkness and with perpetual stress, it had bent me somehow, and now everything was just annoying, everything was against me. Every *one* was against me. I couldn't trust anyone.

I took my hands away and looked at Sienna's concerned face. Could I really trust her? The part of my mind that still functioned insisted I could, but it also said that until Sienna proved herself untrustworthy I had no choice but to let her inside and allow her to travel with me. So, I closed off that particular discussion point and tried to move onto the next.

"I'm petrified."

"Don't be." She forced my hands away from my face and made me look at her. "Don't be. I'm here; I will come through it all with you. You have my word. I will help you."

I blinked, scrubbed at my wet face with bloodied hands and let her hold me. It felt good. It felt honest, and I believed her, wholly. She was working with me, and together we could get though it unscathed.

Besides, what choice did I have?

"I've got two days. And then he's declaring it. And if that happens—"

"You won't be able to get Savage's list in time, I know."

"What the hell do I do, Sienna?"

She was blank-faced, and I thought she'd fallen at the first hurdle, but then she looked at me, and winked. "We'll sort him out later." She started the car up. "But for now, let's find that money."

* * *

The book was a strange little thing. Small, the size of a pocket bible.

On the front cover, below the title, *The Barnbow Lasses*, was a photograph of some of the women who worked at one of the largest munitions factories in Europe, right here in Leeds. They were all young women, not much older than kids. It was well thumbed, but there were no folded corners, no bookmarks of any kind. And I checked each page much more slowly, much more thoroughly than I could while in Peter's company. I checked it for notes in the margins, signs and marks, and I found none. Part of me was pleased; I'm a librarian, and I hate to see books vandalised, though I would have been more than willing to overlook it this time. No such luck.

Christ, there was that word again: hate. Tut.

"So, what's it about?"

I turned the book over, skimmed the blurb. "It's an account of what happened in Room 42 of the Barnbow factory in December 1916. There was a massive explosion that killed thirty-five women."

"Oh, the poor buggers."

I nodded, wishing I could spend a little more time thinking about those who gave their lives so that we might swindle and defraud, and generally be so complacent about our existence that we freely abused it.

"Barnbow? Where's that?"

Chapter Twenty

Barnbow wasn't that far from where Streaky had dropped me off yesterday. Maybe two or three miles through Crossgates, along Austhorpe Road, and past the memorial in Manston Park eventually set up for the unfortunate Barnbow Lasses. Austhorpe Road became Manston Lane, and the scenery changed from large Victorian terraces to newly-built rabbit hutches.

As Sienna drove along, we passed a huge factory to our right; the Vickers tank factory seemed to go on forever. It was half a mile of decay. It was half a mile of British greatness sinking into the weeds. But worse, it was modernity forgetting the past.

The road grew narrower, more potholed, and pretty soon it became a country lane, with open fields to either side. "Slow down." I peered through the windscreen, sitting as far forward as the seat belt allowed. To our left were raised embankments, squares that were maybe ten yards across, covered in long grass that swayed in a breeze. "Those were the railway sidings," I whispered, "I remember now."

"What are you talking about?"

I jumped. I'd forgotten I had company. It came as a shock to realise it, but when I turned I expected to see Chris, and nearly screamed when it wasn't him at all. Cruel; it was cruel, my stupid brain playing fucking tricks on me again.

But I composed myself, smiled, and almost said, 'Hi, Sienna!' But I didn't. I said, "I've been here before."

"With Chris?"

I nodded. Who else would I come here with? My Chris.

"So, we're on the right tracks, then? He left the book as a clue."

"Maybe. Maybe he was just interested in its past."

We passed the sidings and parked on a small intersection with Nanny Goat Lane and Barnbow Lane; a pleasing triangle that afforded parking for those hunting history and for those hunting a future. At the very end of Manston Lane were some farm buildings – Shippen House Farm, the signpost read. But the place was deserted, and when I closed the car door and rested my hands on the roof, I couldn't see a single other person. No other vehicles, no signs of life. No noise except the very faint hiss of traffic to our south on the motorway maybe half a mile away. Bliss.

Sienna peered over the roof to me and asked, "Which way?"

I slung my bag over my shoulder and began hiking up the track called Barnbow Lane. I did little talking as we walked. Instead I did a lot of remembering. In fact, I couldn't believe how much forgetting I'd done in the time since we, me and Chris, were here last. It must have been two years ago, maybe three. It was autumn, and it had been beautiful.

This wonderful grave land, like a slice of history that tasted of cordite and TNT, left to disappear so that people wouldn't have to think about it – tucked away and left for nature to erase our horrors. The landscape was essentially flat with sunken land hiding behind thick bush land and thin woodland, spotted with marshes and bog in which reeds leaned as the wind grew in strength.

"I used to come here as a lad," Chris had said to me. "It was my own treasure, a pleasure to walk for miles and find no one else crowding into your space." I remember him looking at me, and I remember feeling privileged that he had granted me access to something so private to him. He was letting me in, allowing me into his space, and I squeezed his hand just a bit tighter.

He would tell tales of the buildings that used to be here, the canteens, the laundry, the places they stored shells. They were all just fields now, or marshland or woodland, the buildings dismantled shortly after the war, the foundations left to grow old alone, the memories seeping into the waterlogged earth.

Like poison leaching out of the air, my memories of that day and others began to come back to me. It was like a fog dispersing, and the wind grew ever stronger, bringing to life the bushes on both sides as though they were talking to each other, reminiscing. And soon the sky was coloured by a band of grey cloud that grew deeper with each minute, expanding so that it wasn't just a band across the distant horizon for long, but was now overhead, stealing our shadows and transforming the brightness of the lane to a dull brown ribbon stretching on until it was smeared by distance.

"You seem to know where we're going."

I stopped and turned to wait for her. I hadn't realised how rude it must seem to her. I was a good thirty or forty yards in front, marching to my own rhythm, keeping in beat with the past that came to me and spoke like it hadn't in months. I suppose I was walking alongside Chris, listening to his words again as though it was the first time I'd heard them. And I also suppose being pulled from those memories left me cold and impatient with her. I almost tapped my foot as I waited for her.

"Sorry." She panted. "I'm a bit out of shape."

"I was lost in thought," I said. "I didn't mean to leave you behind."

"It's okay." She smiled. "But do you?"

"Do I, what?"

"Know where we're going?"

I was still looking down the lane. "Room 42, of course." She caught up to me, but I didn't move over and continue walking at her side. I stood my ground, and she stopped before me, an embarrassed smile on her face. "Did you ever come here?" I asked.

"No," she said. "I didn't even know this place existed until an hour ago."

I searched her eyes and it seemed she was telling me the truth. I nodded, turned and began walking again.

"Why?" she asked. "What made you think I had?"

"I just wondered," I said without turning around. "Come on, keep up."

She trotted and then was in-step beside me as we crossed the Cock Beck shrouded in thick bracken, bushes reaching right over the water to join hands, hiding all but the sound of trickling from us.

"If you're so sure he hid it there, how come you didn't realise before? I mean, how come it took a book to remind you that it was a special place for him?"

I closed my eyes, never slowed my pace.

I didn't know the answer to that question. It's one I'd already posed, and I waited for an answer that never came. "We went to many places. How could I know which one he chose?" I have no idea if that was the truth; I mean, we did go to many places, but I couldn't be sure where.

We often travelled by train. We'd buy a ticket almost at random at Leeds Station if we couldn't make up our minds on a suitable destination, and just see what waited for us when the train stopped.

I'd always thought of photographing the places we visited, but back then I was more interested in the experiences themselves than recording them. I had no chance of remembering them all now. And I needed this to be right, I needed it to be *the* place without doubt. I didn't have the time to wait for inspiration. If the money wasn't here, I was in trouble.

But this was the only place we'd been to that he'd bought a book about. And it was the only book he'd left for me to find.

I remember how the mood had become more solemn, and once Chris and I got past the beck, he'd slowed until he stopped at a break in the hedge to our left. He'd looked at me, kind of a thin smile on his face – friendly, but inviting no words – and then he stepped through and disappeared from my view. I followed and stood alongside him, and all I could hear was our breathing. No birdsong, no wind stroking the bushes and bulrushes in the marsh.

"This whole area," he'd said, slowly turning in the muddy, sick-looking grass, "was a mass of buildings. If you stood here and looked around as we're doing now, buildings were all you'd see. No greenery. Just buildings and people. And there." He pointed to a stretch of land that looked no different from any other stretch. "Is where Room 42 was."

"It was a filling room," I told Sienna, "girls, teenagers most of them, filled six-inch shells with high explosives, then inserted fuses and used machines to screw the caps on." I looked at her, and it was as though she didn't recognise me; I was a stranger to her, and she to me. I was telling a stranger all this stuff that Chris had told me. "Tuesday 5th December 1916, 10.27 p.m."

"Thirty-five young lasses died," Chris had said to me. I felt incredibly sad then. I didn't know any of the girls – obviously – and I didn't know any of their relatives, but here I felt close to them, and I felt thankful for them, for their efforts.

"Becky?"

I snapped out of it, and there was Sienna looking concerned again. Of course she was fucking concerned. She was hunting a million quid.

"You okay?"

I nodded. But I wasn't. "If it's anywhere, it'll be here."

We stood together, turning slowly around, and it was then that it began raining. Heavy incessant rain that made my new hairstyle cling to my scalp in seconds, and caused the clothes on my back to become almost shrink-wrapped in position. It was heavenly.

Sienna squealed and looked around for shelter, but aside from the hedgerows and the scant bushes in this part of the field, there was nothing. She got wet right alongside me, but didn't seem to enjoy it as much as I did.

Mud splashed up our legs and pretty soon my new trainers were looking like contenders from a bog hopping competition. I smiled as rainwater trickled down my neck, and then I laughed as Sienna yelped and her T-shirt grew transparent. She pulled off her jacket and draped it over her head, whereas I revelled in the sensation.

"How big is Room 42?" she called over the rain.

I shrugged. "No idea." Chris never told me, and perhaps he didn't know the details, just appreciated the place for what it was: disappearing history. "Better start looking." I began walking towards the centre of the field, to where the landscape changed near Cock Beck. Down there, the lower bushes, the bracken and grass were prevalent, thick and inhospitable. It's where I'd look to hide something, away from casual observation.

"Are you sure he wouldn't have just hidden it in your basement?"

"Pretty sure," I said. "We haven't got a basement."

"Thought not. Anyway, how big is a million quid?" she shouted.

That stopped me. I didn't know. Could you squeeze a million inside a briefcase? Or would you need a wheelie bin? I took a guess. "Not sure, maybe a suitcase?"

"A fucking suitcase! He's not going to drag a suitcase out here, surely? A million must be heavy, too."

"Well I expect Chris wouldn't have accepted a cheque."

Sienna almost smiled. "Very good," she said flatly.

"Depends on denomination, I suppose. Anyway, look out for a large package."

"A large package," I heard her mumble as she splashed off in the opposite direction. "Well that helps," she shouted.

I squinted through the wind that raced around in gusts, whipping my jacket in all directions at once, hammering the rain against my face. I was growing nervous.

This was no egg-hunt; this was a life-saver – my life. If I gave it back to Savage he'd let me live, he told me so. And then I gasped as a fundamental thought struck me like a slap in the face. Peter wanted one hundred thousand, but paying him would get me raped and torn apart by two trucks. Or I could choose to pay Savage and go directly to jail where I'd get raped by some she-male called Trixie. Neither option appealed.

Everything rested on finding the money. *And* finding the list.

I turned, hoping Sienna was in earshot. She wasn't, but I wanted to know what her plans for Peter were. Did they involve killing him?

I couldn't do that. I just couldn't.

But we needed to put a stop to him.

I resumed my search of the field down by Cock Beck. I figured Chris would wrap the cash in something weatherproof, and it would have to be something quite substantial. I'd never tried to work out the dimensions or weight of a million pounds, but even if it was in fifties, it would be big and it would be heavy. How did Chris get it all the way up here? If indeed he did.

I looked at the twisted bracken, at the thorns and nettles, and wondered if I could have been more ill-prepared for something like this. "Only if I wore a bikini," I whispered. I tried to pick my footing carefully as I navigated my way, growing steadily colder, but there really was no 'carefully,' each step was as treacherous as any other. This was going to hurt. I tensed up and took a step into the bracken, wincing as the wet nettles stung.

"Becky!"

I stopped, and twisted around to see Sienna waving both arms above her head like she was guiding a landing jet liner. She was jumping up and down too.

Relief ousted my tension. I pulled my foot from the twisted thorns and ran through the mud towards her. By the time I got there my lungs were ready to pop, and I slipped onto my arse right at her feet. "You found it?"

She pointed to a section of reinforced concrete that the moss was slowly claiming. The concrete was like a finger, jutting out from the overgrowth, and its fingernail was a twisted brown length of rebar that pointed at us accusingly. Even over the rain, I could hear water trickling into some kind of gully that was lined with smashed chunks of sharp concrete and more fucking nettles!

I sighed. "I wish we did have a basement."

"The perfect place, don't you think?"

I admit that it had its merits. It couldn't be seen unless you were stupid enough to be standing where we were, certainly no casual passer-by would see it, and even youths wouldn't explore down there, the nettles saw to that.

We walked thirty or forty yards further away from the finger until the ground fell away more gently into the beginnings of that gully and the void beneath the collapsing concrete foundation. Sienna looked on as I slid into the first fronds of nettles that grew between slabs of fallen concrete. I could tell she didn't want to be left alone, but she needed to keep safe in case I got into trouble down there. Anyway, most of her reluctance was because she didn't fancy being stung to death or being trapped under the crumbling foundations as more of the subsoil washed away. She wasn't daft.

It was dangerous going. That first ten yards was treacherous. The rain didn't help, making every footfall perilously slippery, but the concrete too, ranging from fist-sized lumps to blocks the size of a single mattress, each coated with moss and stained red with rust from the reinforcement bars that were cast into them. I was surprised by how dark it suddenly seemed down here, and at how noisy it was. The rain lashed into the nettles and bracken, it slapped the concrete, pattered into the moss, and yet I could still hear it trickling down from the ground above as though creating rivulets through the cracks and fissures.

And then I saw it. The void beneath this foundation stretched out to my right like a giant black wedge, and for more than a moment I was afraid of what might be lurking in there. It was big enough to crawl inside now. I peered up, squinting through the rain and shouted to Sienna that I was going under. She shook her head and turned away.

I knew that if I hesitated now I'd back out and clambering up to her, forever wondering what was beneath our feet. So I chose not to think of the consequences; I ducked out of the rain and into the blackness.

I took out my phone and turned on the torch app. It wouldn't light up the Albert Hall, but down here, in my own private cave, it was more than sufficient. My thankfulness at being out of the wind and the rain was countered by a bravery-sucking claustrophobia that nipped at me as I thought of the tonnes of 100-year-old concrete hanging above my head. And that claustrophobia wasn't helped at all the by dozens of tiny waterfalls coming from the cracks in the porous ceiling. On my knees, I crawled a few feet inwards, and guessed I was right beneath Sienna about now.

The subsoil floor was crusted, with softer soil beneath. The moss grew sporadically across the floor and was thin, ill-looking stuff, but I've never seen so many bugs in one place. Spiders, things with long spindly legs and tiny spherical bodies, clung to the ceiling and spun untidy webs that were yards long, and millipedes meandered back and forth, surprised by the addition of light into their world.

There were slugs and snails aplenty, and I cringed each time I knelt on one or my hand crushed one. I shuddered at the sight of rats in the far corner, and the further into this horrible cave I crawled, the muddier I got, and the more apprehensive I grew. I paused for breath, looked to my left and discovered the huge bank of nettles and bracken that we'd seen from topside; so I must have been in the area of the concrete finger and the twist of rebar.

I didn't expect to duck beneath this concrete ceiling and find a stash of a million quid staring at me, but it felt like a possibility in the same way as a lottery ticket feels like a possibility. It could be me. The soil and the moss I crawled through looked undisturbed, and despair told me I had got it wrong. It said that Chris wasn't as easily deciphered or as predictable as I'd naïvely thought. It said that he'd been much cleverer than I'd thought. And still another part of me denied he'd even been paid by Savage at all, and all this was for nothing.

I started off again, heading towards the corner and the nest of rats, ducking through waterfalls and slipping in the clayey mud. Soon, the earth was close enough to the ceiling that I couldn't crawl on all-fours any more, so I found myself on my belly, hauling myself along and battling with an ever-increasing bulge of claustrophobia that seemed to gather in my throat like a lump of bile.

And then the torch went out.

Chapter Twenty-One

My instinct was to scream, but I surprised myself by staying calm, by breathing slow deep breaths. I became more aware of the sounds down here, of the insects and the rats moving about. I itched all over, and yearned for a shower.

I discovered that the torch had simply timed out. The phone was still good and so I turned on the torch again, glad that it pushed back the spectres of fear that had literally come out of the darkness to get me.

The rats' eyes lit up like glowing match heads and another shudder skittered down my wet back. To their right, near the back of the cave was a clump of nettles. They were dead. And I almost ignored them, almost started to circle around the rats and see what was beyond them. But instead, I looked at those nettles and wondered what the hell they were doing here. No light, no plants. Yet here they were, a large clump of them, all withered and dead.

It seemed as though I knew Chris quite well after all. He had hidden the cash here and covered it over. I crawled forward, clawing at the soil, knocking aside the snails and wafting a mud-caked hand through the cobwebs. I stared at the nettles with a grin on my face and a new anticipation in my heart. I pulled them aside and relief cascaded over me at the sight of a black luggage case.

The fear that had been building in my chest became excitement and I squealed – I couldn't help it. Right here, right in front of me was Savage's million pounds. And before I knew it, the squealing and the laughter had gone completely and the tears came back and ruined it all. What the hell was going on inside my head?

I'd like to think they were tears of joy, but they weren't. They were just tears, and I think they were tears for Chris. It was gratitude that had made me cry. Here it was, a case full of money that my husband had hidden for us. But now he'd hidden it for me, and he'd made sure I found it; he'd had a contingency plan in place should it have all gone wrong. And it had gone wrong, spectacularly so, in the worst possible way.

I reached forward, brushed aside the rest of the dead nettles, took hold of the handle and pulled. I edged slowly backwards, the phone torch in my left hand, and the luggage in my right, elbows and knees scraping along the floor, crushing slugs. The noises came back; the rain was still pounding down into the nettles and onto the concrete, the waterfalls were heavier the closer to the daylight I came and then I paused, turned off the torch and got to my knees, spun around and looked for my exit.

Despite the contrast with the cave, the sky appeared even darker somehow, as though night was close by. It wasn't of course, it was only about five o'clock, but it made me all the more wary.

I left the case, crawled out onto a large block of fallen concrete, and the rain soaked through my hair again, washing away the mud, and my face grew cold again as I peered over the foundation. The field beyond was empty. I wanted to shout to her, I wanted to tell her I'd found the money! But I stamped on the urge. Something wasn't right. She'd have been there, keeping an eye out, waiting for me. Where the fuck was she?

I shrank away from the edge of the foundation, and squatted in my semi-darkness again. This was the Aragorn moment where she would choose to help or choose to steal. And if she chose to steal, she chose to fight. I swallowed, looked around for a weapon and made do with a fist-sized lump of concrete with a sharp jagged edge.

"Becky!"

I peered over the top again, and from the bushes, she waved at me. "Where the hell were you?"

"Needed a pee. Sorry."

Her hands were empty. And she didn't appear nervous, like she surely would if she planned on fighting and stealing. I dropped the concrete and descended. You couldn't get much more remote than this, and she felt the need to find a bush to pee behind. I grabbed the luggage handle, and hauled it out into the open air. Rain pattered on its black surface and rolled away. I dragged it over the concrete and moss obstacle course until the foundations and the void became a long narrow wedge again, and when I looked up this time, expecting her to be reaching out to help me up the final hurdle and back onto the foundation, she wasn't there.

"Sienna?" I called. "Where the fuck are you?" I whispered through clenched teeth. I think the relief had bitten deep, and all I wanted was to get back to Sienna's as quickly as possible and make arrangements to see Savage.

I wanted this whole stupid mess cleared up. I know it's a million quid; it's a life-changer. But what's the point of having a life-changer if you've got no life to enjoy it with? Give it back, shake the dust off and carry on safe in the knowledge that Savage would leave me alone. As arranged.

I looked back into the mess of broken concrete down there, and wished I'd brought my weapon up with me.

I hauled the case onto the foundations, and arched my back. "Sienna?"

Now that I was on the foundations, I could see farther, into the undulations of this weird landscape. And in one of those undulations, only ten or fifteen yards away near the only clump of bushes around, lay Sienna. I rushed to her, skidding to a halt and slipping onto my knees. I could see her chest rising and falling, but there was blood in her hair. Rain beat onto her face, and mud splashed across her cheek and neck. I was on my knees, hand over my mouth, shocked at finding her like this. I was wondering if she'd slipped and banged her head when I heard a slapping noise of someone running at me from behind. I turned and recognised him immediately, but didn't associate his face with any actual danger until I saw the look of hatred on it.

And when I saw the wheel brace in his hand, I only had time to scream and raise my arm. Luck was on my side though; he was only a couple of yards from me when his feet slid from under him and he went down just as the wheel brace was arcing towards my head.

With the scream still on the air, I scrabbled backwards as he hit the ground; the wheel brace slammed into the mud, but his eyes never left mine throughout. They chilled me further, and there was no way on God's earth I wanted to go near him. I wanted to be away; I wanted to hop over that fence and run down the track as far away from him as I could.

But it wasn't as simple as that. Sienna was injured, possibly seriously, and there was Chris's million over there by the ledge; no way was I leaving that for this piece of shit to claim.

It was time to stand and fight.

I lunged forward as the surprise of the fall was still sinking in and before he could bring the wheel brace up again. I've always been afraid of physical conflict, and especially so against a man – even one not much bigger than myself. But now wasn't the time to compare bicep measurements or bravery points. Now was the time to act. I went in with my feet, and managed to kick Peter in the ribs. This had no effect on him at all; he just swung the wheel brace like an Olympic hammer thrower and thrashed in the mud, trying to stand. The wheel brace slipped from his hand and when he made a grab for it, I kicked him in the face. I know how bad that sounds for a librarian, but I had no option; it was him or me.

And it wasn't going to be me.

The kick knocked him off balance even more, and the half-stand he'd managed so far turned into a full fall across Sienna's legs, so I was winning! But he was back up on his feet in no time and I could feel the fear bite because that was it, that was my arsenal expended. I didn't have any other tricks up my sleeve.

He came at me, grabbed my shoulders and forced me backwards at speed through the mud and the long-flattened grass. My feet struggled to keep up, only just preventing me from falling backwards. I peered over my shoulder and knew we were heading for the edge of the cliff, for the end of the foundation and long drop onto the concrete boulders.

The rain stung my face, and the wind whipped my hair into my eyes.

I screamed at him. But he wasn't going to stop. There was a determination in his face that frightened the crap out of me. He meant to leave here today a damned sight richer than when he arrived; one hundred grand was peanuts compared to what Savage had paid, and he knew it because I'd readily agreed to his demand. He saw retirement, he saw a new life. The greed that had infected Chris and me was contagious.

I saw the edge coming up quickly. I dug my heels in, grabbed his arms and turned us both, momentum working with me. He didn't let go though, he *wouldn't* let go. His feet slipped as his legs tried to keep us both upright, but failed.

And all the time, he was looking at me. His eyes grew wide as we fell together. I watched him, aware that the ground was coming up quickly, and I saw his gaze leave mine, his eyes crept up to the tops of their sockets as he waited to hit the ground.

When it came, his whole face creased up, his eyes screwed shut, and his teeth clashed together. I felt the rush of his hot breath squeeze through them. His whole body stiffened, and as we came to rest, I felt a pain in my chest, a sharp, searing pain.

I rolled off him and he offered no resistance at all; he just lay there blinking against the rain with the rebar protruding from his chest. I looked up to see Sienna standing there, panting hard, hands on her knees, with a wheel brace held in one of them. Thinned blood was running down her forehead and dripping from the end of her nose. "Bastard!"

We both looked at Peter.

"I want..."

And that was all he said. Nothing else came out of him, except a glut of blood that stopped almost immediately. That blood washed down his shirt, and I had a flashback of how I'd found Chris: the blood had run down his shirt also. But Chris was different; there had been no rain to wash it away. Peter's wound was diluted to a pale pink within a few seconds.

"You're bleeding," Sienna said to me.

My chest was covered in blood. I thought it was Peter's blood, but it wasn't; it kept on bleeding. The rebar had gone right through Peter and had pierced my left breast.

* * *

We hobbled down the lane and over Cock Beck, making good progress towards Sienna's car. We were both panting hard, both exhausted, both injured. We had talked briefly about what to do with him. It seemed the best option was to pull him off the spike and roll him off the edge of the foundation and onto the same jagged blocks of broken concrete that he had intended for me. I didn't think it would take the rats long to realise their next meal was waiting for them. And just that thought alone made me shudder.

I didn't hear him land and I didn't go to look at him. My night's sleep would be thin and troubled as it was without adding to it.

Sienna launched the wheel brace into the thick nettles and bracken that I was about to wade into down by Cock Beck. And we didn't worry too much about leaving any of our blood behind or our footprints or the wheel marks from the luggage case, because as soon as we'd reached the lane, the rain had already obliterated them. This was a crime scene, but it would probably remain hidden for many years.

We should have thought about Peter's car, but we didn't, until we came across it parked behind our Corsa. By that time, it was too late. I certainly didn't volunteer to go down into that abyss and start searching his smashed body for the keys. Perhaps I should have, but I didn't.

Chapter Twenty-Two

During the drive away from Barnbow, with the rain beating down on the car as though we had a trio of percussionists strapped to the roof, we didn't whoop and high-five; it was the kind of adventure from which you felt lucky to have escaped. Our mood was sombre and composed. It was a time for reflection, not celebration.

We were lost in our own thoughts, with water, and in Sienna's case, blood too, still dripping from our hair, and the windscreen was fogging over, when I noticed a man with his dog walking into the woodland by the entrance to Nanny Goat Lane. Over his shoulder he carried a bagged rifle. It was just an air rifle, I guessed, but it reminded me of the airgun I had.

Bret's Beretta. I knew nothing about guns at all – except they killed people. He'd been kind enough to give me the tin of pellets too.

I'd spent a good half hour reading the instructions for this weapon on the Internet, and when I'd finished I was an instant markswoman. Certainly good enough to hit a teenager at twenty yards. And a few mornings later, as the bathroom door above me closed, an opportunity to test my skills had arisen.

With a plain white mug of tea in hand, I watched out of the window again. I saw a robin, and even a wren made a brief, flitting appearance at the bird table. But no blue tit. That made me feel sad.

"What the hell's that?"

I stiffened at the sound of his voice. Chris had been cold towards me for a few days, and communication had shrunk to the grunt level as though we'd regressed to being Neanderthals. And frankly, I thought his mood swing was an affront. He could see how upset I'd been and, rather than the leper treatment, I'd hoped for a little support. Looks like I was to be disappointed again.

"This is a Beretta Elite air pistol with a magazine capacity of eighteen pellets, and a muzzle velocity of over four-hundred feet per second. That's faster than any fucking kid."

"Are you serious, Becky?"

"I know, it's amazing, isn't it?"

"Becky."

I gritted my teeth. "He killed one of my birds. He killed one of many birds who felt safe in my garden. They felt safe in my garden, therefore I am partly responsible for their well-being." He didn't tut, or sigh. I knew the urge was there though, and I'd bet he was standing behind me at the very least shaking his holier-than-thou head at me.

"Honey, you can't go around shooting at a kid just because he killed a bird."

Inside I growled. "Don't call me 'honey'." I still didn't turn around, didn't feel the need. "And I can if he trespasses. And this is private property. So you can't stop me."

"You can't shoot someone for trespassing." His voice was whiny. "Look, it's just nature. You know what kids are like."

"It's nature if he eats the bird when he's killed it. To kill it for sport is just barbaric. But if it makes you feel any better, I won't shoot him in the head."

"You're sick." I'm sure those words just fell out of his mouth unbidden, and I also think he'd have retracted them if he could. But it was too late; they'd escaped into the open and they'd made it all the way into my mind and my memory. "I'm sorry. I didn't mean—"

I reached out and put down my horrible mug of tea. I picked up the pistol. I heard him backing away.

"Come on, Becky," he said.

I turned. "Move, Bret's here."

"What?"

"You have insulted me twice: you called me 'honey,' and you called me 'sick.' But you'll notice I kept my temper and didn't shoot you. However, that boy is back, so get out of the way!"

I made it into the back garden and had even raised the weapon before he got to me. He knocked my arm downwards and the pellet kicked up dust as it hit the grass. He took hold of my arm and tried to wrestle the gun from me.

The birds flew away. Bret stared at us; the widest smile his cod-lips could manage stretched his shiny face.

I can imagine that the scene looked like any one of a hundred cop shows where the officer is trying to get a weapon away from an assailant. Only in this case, it was a husband and wife who were performing like a pair of novice Morris dancers around a maiden. But our maiden was a Beretta. There was a lot of grunting, and on my part, a lot of swearing and shouting.

Eventually, Chris got the prize, and I stood there in a dishevelled state with my teeth bared and my finger pointing at him. "If another bird dies, it'll be all your fault."

Out of breath, he simply nodded at me. "I'm prepared to shoulder that burden."

"You bastard."

The neighbour's door opened and Gail Ferguson peeked around its edge. "Bret, come on, love, breakfast's ready." She saw me and Chris, and opened the door wider to get a better view.

Bret called back, "Coming, Grandma." He smiled at us and gave me the customary middle-finger salute when he thought he was a safe distance away.

Chris grabbed my arm. "Leave it."

I yanked free of him and marched over to Ferguson, Bret having already hightailed it inside. Her curiosity had kept the door open long enough for me to stick my foot in there before she could close it. "If that kid so much as looks in my garden again, I'll pull his fucking legs off!"

Chris was at my side again like an unwelcome smell, and he was pulling me backwards along the path. "I'm sorry," he said to her.

I think she caught sight of the gun in Chris's hand because that door shut so fast that the glass trembled.

* * *

"You're blowing this up out of all proportion," I said.

"I'm not. It's getting bad again."

"I care about those birds."

"Fuck the birds!"

I stared at him, shocked. Chris didn't swear – that was solely my domain. He was angry; I could see the veins in his forehead begin to throb.

"You can't go around shooting kids, and you can't march over to the elderly neighbours and scare the crap out of them, Becky."

"They asked for it, the nosey bastards!"

"There you go again. Flying off on one. Calm down." He looked hurt, but more than anything else he looked embarrassed. In our own lounge, just the two of us, he looked embarrassed. He seemed distant from me now, as though this was all getting too much for him.

I looked away, afraid I'd crossed the line this time, and those hateful tears came again. I wish I could have surgery and get the tear ducts pulled out. I smiled though, and I looked at him again, swallowed, and said, "You're right. I'm sorry; I got carried away." I shrugged, distraught that I'd made him feel wary of me, afraid even. Now *I* was embarrassed.

I touched his hand, and to his credit he didn't pull away, but neither did he respond. "It won't happen again. I've calmed down."

It didn't work; he still looked worried.

His solution to the problem was to pull up the bird table and destroy it.

My solution was Prozac.

I didn't see Bret walk by our house again, and Chris and I never mentioned it. He threw the gun out, too.

But I found it. And I buried it in the blue tit's grave.

Chapter Twenty-Three

I'd half expected to walk in here this morning and find the bloody thing gone, a note from Sienna in its place. But here it was still: the suitcase. It should have been a case full of new potential, but instead it was just a case full of problems.

I stood there with my arms folded, my attention divided between Sienna and the case. I needed to fix some new Steri-Stips across the wound on her head. It had begun bleeding again overnight, and she'd screamed first thing this morning when she woke to a bloody pillow, and a strip of hair like a red leather flap.

With bloody fingers, Sienna tried to part her blood-matted hair, but success was elusive. I managed to get the strips in place but there was no guarantee they'd stay put. We had slept together last night because we both deemed her spare bed just too uncomfortable for me after the day we'd had. I say 'slept' in the loosest of terms; it was a fraught night, one filled with aches and pains of the physical kind for both of us, and of the mental variety for me. And probably for her too, actually. I shuddered as I imagined the blow to her head. It could so easily have ended in her death.

We'd walked from her room like a couple of old women. My arms were bruised where the bastard had grabbed me and pushed me along. And, of course, my chest was a dull ache where the bar had punctured it. My new bra was ruined. My t-shirt was crusted with diluted blood, fit only for the bin. But it was the desolate feeling he'd left us with that lingered; the expected triumph had never really materialised, and we were left feeling cold, dismal, and lucky to be alive.

The case was where we'd dumped it after we got home from the chemist. Its bottom corner was ragged where the rats had

had a go at it. At least the rain had washed away all of the mud. We'd checked inside and seen that Chris had packed the cash into a stout vacuum-sealed bag that was still intact. I don't know how he'd taken delivery of it from Savage, but he'd repacked it. I recognised that vacuum bag – it had my wedding dress in it last week. A previous life. And knowing Savage, the original delivery would have had a tracker inside somewhere so he could 'reclaim' it, so it's no wonder Chris didn't take the chance.

Sienna stood up straight, and I saw she'd been crying.

"Hurts like a bitch," she said.

"Well, let's see if we can cheer ourselves up with a million quid."

She looked at me sideways on. "You're giving it back, aren't you?"

"I wasn't planning on it. Depends if we find the list or not."

"Savage didn't find it. The police didn't find it, as far as we know. Play it safe and take the money back. Then we can all get back to normal." She shuffled away into the kitchen. I heard the kettle clanking under the tap and then I heard a knock at the door. "Get that, would you?"

All I wanted to do was take a long hot bath. I closed my eyes on the way to the door, thinking that maybe she had a point. But I also thought it was a little strange that she didn't even want to hunt for the list. We still had a few days left before Savage's deadline. And we'd successfully found the cash when we thought we had no chance.

I turned the key and swung the door open. I'm sure my chin clicked as it hit the floor.

"Hello, Becky. Can we come in?"

It was the man with a long single eyebrow and the woman with no tits whatsoever. My face must have given the game away – I'm not good with names.

"DI Steve Hughes and DS Alison Merchant?"

It was stated in question form, as though I was stupid. I gritted my teeth, propped a smile onto my cheeks and stood aside. "Of course," I said. "Forgive me." I closed the door behind them and laid my hot forehead on the cool glass, wondering when it would all end and leave me the hell alone. "Would you like a cup of tea?" I followed them through into the lounge and the first thing my sore eyes fell on was the case. The case of money; hot money, money so hot that it was liable to self-combust at any moment. Fuck. I headed towards the kitchen as quickly as I could. The last thing this situation needed was a woman dabbing blood from her head walking in as though she'd been mugged.

"Coffee for me, please," said Hughes. "No milk. One sugar."

"Same for me please, thank you," Alison said.

The kettle made a noise that I thought would have been loud enough to mask the coppers coming in, so I touched Sienna on the shoulder and when she looked, held a finger to my lips. I whispered, "The police are here. Best if you stay in here till they're gone." She rolled her eyes to the ceiling and mouthed 'bollocks.' I thought it an appropriate response and nodded my agreement.

I took their drinks through and sat in the chair opposite, holding a cushion to my chest.

"Going somewhere?" This from Hughes, who nodded at the case.

My heart kicked. "What? No, no, it's my friend's. It's full of books. She's going to take them to the charity shop."

"Oh," Alison said. "I love reading. What are they?"

You're fucking kidding! "Erm, I don't really know. Romance, I think."

"Just my thing."

Well it would be, wouldn't it?

"Everyone says I'm strange because I don't like crime thrillers, but it'd be like a busman's holiday, wouldn't it? I work at it all day, why would I want to read it too?" She laughed, and it was a tinny, shrill laugh that no doubt set dogs barking somewhere.

She was strange anyway – had nothing to do with books. I smiled, pulled the cushion in tighter. "What can I do for you?"

"How have you been these last few days, Becky?" said Steve. "I see you changed your hair style. It looks good on you."

I smiled again. "I'm okay," I lied. "Just waiting for the grief to abate. It's still very painful." This was one of those times where having puffy eyes from crying so much came in handy. It masked the swelling from the beating at Savage's. At least I hoped it did, or there would be more awkward questions coming my way.

"Of course, of course," he said, not giving a shit. "Anyway, we bring news that the criminal investigation into Chris's death is concluded. We and the CPS are satisfied that Pinkman was responsible, that he." He paused. "That he..."

"Murdered Chris in the course of a burglary." Alison finished for him. I saw the stabbing glance he gave her and knew that she'd be in for a lecture when they got back to the station.

"Anyway," he continued, "the file has now been passed to the coroner for him to proceed as required."

"You'll be notified when the hearing is due to take place," Alison said.

"But you're under no obligation to attend," Steve blurted out, compensating for his colleague's sudden attack of subtlety-death.

I nodded to him, a gentle blink of my eyes to indicate that it was okay, and she wasn't upsetting me. Well, that's what I wanted it to say; it probably came across that I was tired, because she said, "We can call back if you'd rather go and lie down for a few hours?"

I gazed at her. Passive-aggressive bitch; she'd seemed so nice before. "I'm fine," I said. "Thank you for your concern. Do carry on." My mouth smiled brightly.

"You'll be issued with a death certificate as soon as the paperwork gets through the channels. You're free to make funeral arrangements." She stared at me like I'd put salt in her coffee. Wish I'd spat in it.

I nodded, trying to keep speech for when it was necessary. I was choking up; I couldn't help it. All this talk of Chris...

"Anyway," Steve almost shouted, and reached into his pocket, "you'll be happy to hear that we've brought Chris's house keys back."

"Your car's still in the compound though."

I felt like stabbing her. It was about then that I wondered if little Miss No-Tits there was on Savage's payroll. He told me he had someone on the inside. Was she his mole? But surely if it was her, she'd do her best to keep that hidden, wouldn't she? She wouldn't change her demeanour and arouse suspicion.

"I'm afraid you'll need to sign for them," he said, waving them at me, "for the keys. And I'm not sure what condition it'll be in, the house, I mean. We do try to be considerate in our scene examinations, but sometimes..." His voice trailed off and he ended his sentence with a gentle shrug.

She passed over a form, and then thrust a pen at me. I tried to read the form but she shoved her finger to the bottom and said, "There. Just sign there."

I pulled the form away from under her finger and stared at her until she backed off. I didn't know what the hell was going on. This woman couldn't do enough for me the last time we met; she was very considerate and gentle, and now she was all bitch. "Have I done something to annoy you, Alison?"

She smiled, backed away from me, and turned to Steve. "We're almost done. I'll wait in the car."

He nodded, and she left without looking back.

"Is it because I made instant coffee?"

"The coffee—"

"Or because I wouldn't let her look at the romance books?"

"No, I don't think—"

"Because they're not mine," I said, "how would she like it if someone rooted through her stuff when she wasn't there?" I was shouting, and he'd shrunk back into the chair slightly. I felt the tears pricking, the nose blocking.

"I'm sorry," he said, reaching out but making no contact. "She's a bit upset."

I rubbed the cushion across my face, blinked at him. "*She's* upset?"

He stood, straightened his jacket. "I'd better leave."

"Why is she upset?"

"It's no concern—"

"Oh, I think it is." I stood and he started walking to the door. "Stop," I said. "I want to know why she's upset, and why she thinks it gives her the right to be rude to me. Did I let myself into her house and murder her cat? No. Did I let myself into her house and put rotting fish down the back of the radiators? No, I didn't. So what exactly did I do to piss her off so much?"

Steve cleared his throat, looked at the doorway to make sure Alison wasn't in earshot. "Peter Ingram." He watched me, but I gave away nothing.

"What about him?"

"You came to see him at Elland Road yesterday."

"I wanted personal effects from Chris's locker."

He nodded. "I know. But was there anything else, anything out of the ordinary?"

I looked up, took a big breath, and let it out around the words. "Nothing strange happened. I mean, I wasn't paying full attention to my surroundings. I was a bit distracted, you see."

He was nodding again. Pretty soon his head would fall off.

"But no, nothing strange. He was fine with me, very polite. Though I could tell that he was distressed by the whole thing. Why do you ask?"

It was his turn to take a breath. "Peter hasn't been seen since your meeting with him."

I did well. My eyebrows nearly slid off the top of my head. "But. How do you mean?"

"Just that. After you left, Peter went back to his office, picked up his car keys, logged off the system, and left."

I didn't know what to say, so I said nothing.

"We know that you were distressed in the locker room, that Peter told an officer you were upset, but after that – nothing. Nothing at all."

I looked to the floor, noticed his brown shoes, how his feet twitched as if to some unheard tune. "I'm sorry to hear that." I looked up. "But I don't understand why Alison was so rude to me."

"I don't think she means to be. She's Peter's girlfriend," he said. "He didn't come home last night."

I found that my hand was at my mouth; it was a true shock. Seeing a dead person is all well and good, but when you encounter a relative of theirs it puts a whole new perspective on things – it's like looking at remnants of that dead person. And in this case, remnants that *I'd* left behind. *I'd* caused her anguish, and it was likely to be anguish that would last years because there was no way his body would be found, not for a very long time, if at all.

Now I felt bad.

But I remembered Sienna in the kitchen, how close she came to dying because of him and his stupid greed, and a flash of my anger hit Steve right between the eyes.

"Then I suggest you do some investigation into why two members of your intelligence staff have recently died." I saw his eyes widen, and I've never wished so much for the ability to turn back the clock.

"How do you know he's dead?"

Fuck. "I don't," I whispered. "I mean, I'm just trying to express that it's more than a coincidence that my Chris is killed and now another member of his team is missing. Don't you think it's strange?"

"Do you seriously think that hadn't crossed our minds? Do you seriously think we drive around all day looking for coffee stops, or... or looking for Lord Lucan?"

I said nothing for a while, just looked away, grinding my teeth, wishing I hadn't been so stupid. The trouble was, I was about to get even stupider.

"I apologise for my insensitivity."

"I wasn't going to mention it to you. Alison wanted to, and I'd refused her permission. That's why she's in such a mood; she was hoping Peter might have said something to you to indicate what his intentions were."

I shook my head. "Nothing. I'm sorry."

His feet stopped tapping. "I'll leave you in peace." He turned to go.

"You need to find the common denominator." I didn't need to say it, that's the stupid thing! He could have left none the wiser, but I had to state the obvious, didn't I? I had to get the last word in. A person with no involvement in Peter's disappearance would *think* exactly that. But more than likely, they wouldn't have *said* anything at all, because it was the obvious conclusion. The person who actually *had* some involvement with Peter's disappearance *would* have said that as a bluff.

He picked up on it too. He closed up to me, and I swallowed, on guard now, starting to get a little scared. "Your chest," he said. "It's bleeding."

I looked down and sure enough there was blood leaking through Sienna's t-shirt in a J shape. My mouth dried instantly. I licked my lips with an equally dry tongue. "Scissors," I said. "I'm clumsy, I fumbled, and I managed to stab myself."

He looked into my eyes, and without expression said, "You're the common denominator."

When I closed and locked the door after him and came back into the lounge, Sienna was standing there like some ghoul.

She said, "He knows."

Chapter Twenty-Four

I stared at her for a long time, and I knew she was right. He'd come in too close, too cocky; a man who was just as bad as I was at keeping his cards close to his chest. The only straw that I could clutch at was that he was pissing in the wind. It was a hunch he had, that's all. I hoped.

Sienna looked shocking and my heart went out to her then. She looked so sorry for herself. "Want some painkillers?"

She nodded, looked at the case. "What are you going to do with that?"

I was happy to hear 'you' instead of 'we.' There was one million pounds right there within easy reach. One million pounds! I'd dreamt of having a million quid all my adult life – who hadn't? But right now it was poison, so I turned out the disco lights at the party that my brain was having. "It's out of bounds. It's not mine. It goes back to Savage, and then I move back home until I can find another place, and you concentrate on healing that hole in your head."

Sienna went into the kitchen, slid open the medicine drawer and downed a couple of paracetamol. Then she turned on the kettle. I'd followed her in because I knew this conversation wasn't over – it was just beginning. It smelled of cigarette smoke and toast in here. We were doing the dance, each testing the other's reactions; my presence here showed her that I was willing to play tag, and she wasted no time in coming at me.

"I've been thinking. You can't hand it back. If you step foot on Savage's land with that cash, he'll take it and he'll kill you. And if he ever figures out a connection between the two of us, he'll kill me for knowing you."

I half-laughed. "Why would he do that? He made me a deal; freedom for the cash or the list."

"You think he's honourable? You really think that's how men like him operate?"

I shrugged. "I had hoped so, yes."

"Think again. And this time don't be so naïve about it. If you walk out of his place intact, what kind of risk are you to him? You could march straight into the nearest nick and spill the beans. He's not going to let that happen. While you draw breath you're a threat to him."

She poured the drinks, and I watched some men in waterproofs down in the courtyard to the back of her flat strimming grass and clipping hedges. Rain tapped against the window, a rhythmic accompaniment that added tension to an already stressful time. It was miserable. And so was I. "Why does it rain all the bastard time?"

"Look what he did to your Chris."

That snapped me back from the damp gardeners like a slap round the head. I blinked and took the tea she held out to me. "So, what do you have in mind?" I followed her back into the lounge, and both of us fixed on the case again.

"It's not my place to tell you what to do with your money. I just don't think you can go to him; it'll leave us both exposed."

"Look," I said, easing the path to frank discussion, "don't worry about money." I nodded at the case. "If it ever becomes mine, I'll see you right, you know that. You're my best friend."

"And your fucking chauffeur." She smiled. "Thank you, Becky."

"Yeah, and my chauffeur. Call it petrol money."

"Call it danger money!"

We both laughed at that, two women beaten half to death, groaning at our bruised bodies.

"Okay, if I have a say in its future, and *our* future, I say we do one. Wales. South Wales; get up in the hills…"

I was already shaking my head. "I'm not running. He made it perfectly clear to me that he'd find me. And I believe him."

"Like you believed he'd cut you a deal?"

"I'm not running, Sienna. I don't want to spend the rest of my life looking over my shoulder. I want to be free of all this shit once and for all. If we can't run, and we can't hand it back, we only have one hope of getting out of this thing alive. So far as I can see, we have to give him the list."

She snorted like I'd told a bad joke. "How?"

I didn't know. I sat down with a thump and hissed as tea spilled over the rim and caught my hand.

"The cops and Savage have been through your house like a horde of termites. So it's not there. Where else would he hide a sheet of paper?"

I stared at her, lost for an answer. Except for the termites bit: it's a colony or a swarm. Not a horde. Once a librarian, always a librarian. Sadly.

"There must be a thousand places you could hide a sheet of paper. Ten thousand. It's a non-starter."

"We thought finding the money would be a non-starter, remember?"

"Look at the size of the fucking case, Becky! There's not many places you could hide that thing. Christ, you could shove a single sheet of paper up your arse – and he might have done that for all we know. And who's to say he actually printed a list off? Who's to say there actually *is* one?"

"Peter. Everything the Intelligence Unit does is recorded, it's auditable, and Peter found the trail to show he printed a list. The list is real."

"Right. But it's paper. It could be mush in the bottom of some toilet somewhere. We have *no* option but to run. And the sooner we do run the better." Sienna sat down next to me. "I have a shit life, always have, always will, but at least it's a life. It's the only one I'm likely to get and so I'd like to keep a hold of it."

I pulled a cushion over me again, and it reminded me of the visit from CID, and that reminded me of the blood leaking out of my boob. I pushed the cushion away, and listened to some more of her pleading. I was beginning to think that she just didn't want to find the list. And I could understand that: she didn't want to have to deal with Savage, she wanted to run. But better deal with him now than when he's got a shotgun to your head.

"If you say you'll see me okay with money, then it means I have a stake in what we do. I have a share of what's in there, and I'd rather take my chances in South Wales."

"That list is in my house. Still." I stood and left the room. "I'm taking a shower," I called back.

* * *

The shower left me in equal parts drained and invigorated – I can't explain it better than that. When I walked into the bedroom, Sienna had left me some of her clothes out.

The second time I entered the lounge, the money had gone. There was no note.

My heart skipped a beat and I semi-screamed, ready to begin a short journey into a rage, when I heard her crossing the lounge behind me.

"I'll have a quick shower too," she said without looking at me. "Case is in the kitchen."

It was standing on newspaper, the remaining mud and water collecting around its wheels, and I wondered if I should open it again just to check the cash was still in good order. But did I really want to do that? It would only cause Sienna to flare up on the 'running' argument again, I knew it would. She'd see it, and her imagination would carry her to South Wales and a fucking cottage with flowers around the door and a bag of dope on the porch. I left it shut.

When she'd showered and dried her hair as much as she could, I fixed some more strips over the wound. It was looking better.

For an hour we avoided each other as much as being in a two-bedroom flat would allow. I was lost inside my head, weighing up Savage's words, and trying to balance it with what Sienna thought we should do. I had no doubt that Savage wouldn't enjoy losing a million quid. I had no doubt he'd try to find us, and probably succeed. Find *me,* anyway. But I also thought that she was right, that Savage would want us, *me,* out of the way.

"I'll make a deal with you," I said.

She stood by the kitchen window, arms folded, hair tied up over the wound, a cigarette in the ashtray on the counter next to her.

"I'm not staying here," she said. "I don't care whether you give me any money or not. I'm leaving first thing tomorrow." She turned to me. "If you don't want to live at your house, you can stay here as long as you want, the landlord won't mind. So long as he gets his money, he won't ask questions."

"Don't you want to hear my deal?"

She puffed on the cigarette, then stabbed it out with rather more force than was necessary. She looked at me, a frown on her face.

"We go to my house and spend the rest of the day looking. If we don't find it, we leave with the money first thing tomorrow, well ahead of his deadline." It was a shit plan. But it was all I could come up with.

Chris didn't go out to the pubs, he didn't partake in any outside activity regularly; he was a homely man, preferring to spend his time in front of the television, or reading, or grudgingly throwing a mower at the weeds. So, wherever that list was, it was at home. It was the golden ticket, and it was the only thing that would keep me alive and relatively prosperous.

She swallowed and turned away from me again.

"What have you got to lose?"

She lit another cigarette, and as she stared out of the window, I saw her fingers tapping on the counter top matching the rain tapping the pane. "Okay."

Chapter Twenty-Five

D espite the agreement from her, I sensed – knew – there was something wrong. She had no enthusiasm for it, and was just a bag of sighs all the way from getting our shoes on to driving the mile to my house.

It was a standard three-bedroom, semi-detached house on a quiet road in the middle of a housing estate full of other standard three-bedroom, semi-detached houses. When you looked at it like that, it just said 'boring.' But today was, for me at least, anything but boring. I was returning to the place my husband died. I was also returning to the place that the police had examined, so Christ knew what state it would be in.

I was also returning to the place that I'd shared with that man for the last sixteen years. I tried to bolster myself against any outpouring of emotion, but knew the bolster would give out at some point and I'd have an episode or two.

We cruised around the corner and down the slight incline and there it was up on the right, looking exactly the same as it had the last time I'd been there. The road was almost deserted, one parked car outside the Ferguson's, and right on cue I saw their net curtains twitch. I suspect if it hadn't been raining they'd have had a fucking picnic in the front garden just to see what was going on.

Sienna parked out front, and I steeled myself against the embarrassment that had somehow tagged along for the ride. The Fergusons had created that feeling in me but I was unable to shake it until I closed the back door. It was covered in some kind of white powder. Messy bastard police. And there was more across the hallway floor.

It smelled chemically in here, and it was cold too. And even though the furniture would still be in all the rooms, the rooms we'd turned into our cosy nest where we could relax and be ourselves, it felt alien. It felt like the kind of place that would echo as you walked through it. The soul had died too. I shivered, sank my head into my shoulders.

"So," she said, "where do you want me to start?"

I threw the keys on the kitchen worktop and reached around to take hold of my shoulder bag just as I'd always done, but there *was* no shoulder bag. I closed my eyes, great start. "I've left my sodding bag back at yours."

She looked at me. "So? You don't need it, do you?"

"I feel naked without it."

"Then feel naked for a while. Where should I start?"

This was going to be a fucking long day. "I know you don't want to do this, but come on, humour me. Think of what I'm going through just by being in here!"

I found myself in the lounge staring at the same patch of floor I'd found Chris lying on.

She curled her hands around my arms and rested her head on my shoulder. "I'm sorry," she whispered. "I didn't think. It was insensitive of me."

Damn right it was! "It's okay." I pulled away from her and turned to face her. "I'm glad you're with me. I'm not sure I could do this..." I swept a hand across the room. "By myself. And there's no one else I'd rather have here." We smiled at each other, but it wasn't right; it wasn't the same as it had been.

There was an atmosphere, the kind you'd expect to find between two people newly introduced to each other, where their guards were still up and they were probing each other to see if they could get along. Arse-sniffing dogs springs to mind.

Chris and I had moments like this. Especially during the last few months or so, when things hadn't been running especially smoothly; that was about the time he'd begun thinking about his super master plan that would end all our worries. Fucking did a good job there, Chris!

These were the kind of moods we'd experience in the aftermath of an argument when we were slowly coming down and sensing the other person's demeanour, and whether we dare approach them. Typically, I didn't approach him; I suppose that might sound aloof, but he always took a longer time to come down than me, he was prickly for a lot longer and so he always came to me.

"Want me to go back and get it?"

"Get what?"

"Your bag? You feel naked, remember?"

I smiled, I was being silly. "No, forget it."

She went to the bookcase. "I'll make a start here."

"No." I was at her side in seconds, my hand on hers. "Want to start upstairs?"

"Okay," she said. "My favourite bit."

I watched her go and wondered what she was thinking. I felt unsettled but put it down to the spectre of Chris. I didn't believe in any of that shit – once you were dead, you were gone. No lingering, no haunting. But still, I had a feeling that didn't sit well. You'd think that if my man was here, I'd feel a warm, loving presence. I didn't. I felt cold, unwelcome.

I sat down and listened to the noises she made as she moved around in my bedroom. I knew which part of the room she was in by the creaks the floorboards made. I sat down so I could think; Savage's search would have been hasty, cursory, only semi-thorough, especially with three or four men rushing through the house like a thunderstorm.

They'd go straight for the bedside cabinets; they'd rip the spare room to shreds in seconds, hoping for a home file or a small desk with drawers. When they exhausted that option, they'd go back to the bedroom and pull all the drawers out, upping the thoroughness, being more careful, searching the drawers for an envelope taped to the underside. They'd check under the bed, under the mattress. They'd do all this because it was doing something, it was doing something that didn't take any thought. Blind action. Better than nothing, but only slightly.

Chris was far more intelligent than that. Plus, he'd had the time to think where to hide a single sheet of paper, and he knew the house. He could have hidden it under the carpet in the spare room because it had come away from the tread plate and would be easy to access. But he wouldn't hide it there because although it was easy to access, the gripper plate with the evil little nails poking out might snag him, or it might snag the paper.

So next they'd go deeper and rip off the bath panel. Like he'd ever consider hiding it there! They'd check inside the toilet cistern in case he'd hidden it inside a plastic bag in there. Nope, it would be messy and noisy.

I heard Sienna moving onto the spare room. She wouldn't have a lot to look at in there because everything would be turned out, upside down. All she had to do in there was observe.

I looked around the lounge, pulling my eyes from the red stain in the carpet, remembering the knife over there by the doorframe, feeling the terror all over again as men thundered through my house upstairs. And then I thought I heard the gate squeal, and my eyes pinged wide and my heart kicked. I was gripping the arms of the chair, but eventually the fear inside me abated and I came back down again, and began to look around the lounge, trying to see it through the eyes of someone wanting to hide something.

The fifth stair cracked and again my eyes widened, and I was gripped by a panic that chewed at my already frayed nerves, sucking every last ounce of juice from them. I was holding my breath when Sienna walked in.

"I've got it," she said.

"The list? You've found the list?" I was out of my chair.

"What? No, no, not the list. Jesus."

I felt deflated. "Then what the hell have you got?"

"Where he's hidden it, of course."

I took a long breath and watched my fingertips tremble. "Go on."

"He took out a PO box."

"He what?"

"A Post Office box. You can hire them. They keep things for you."

"No. He needs instant access. Even over a weekend. He'd want to keep it close by." I had no idea, of course, what kind of a bargain the two men had come to, or when Savage would want the list. But I figured that Savage would give him next to no notice for fear of Chris having the chance to set a trap.

"Hmm." She turned around and I heard the fifth step crack again. "Get searching, stop sitting," she shouted.

I sat back down. Thinking would get us there much quicker than blind searching; that was Savage's way and he'd come up with a fat blank. And then there was the police search too. I'm pretty sure they didn't find it because none of their questions led to it. They were still in the dark about Chris's duplicity. If they knew about it they'd have frozen our bank account, searched through transactions, studied other criminals who'd been too lucky for too long, and even looked at who got double-tapped recently. They hadn't done any of that, so they hadn't suspected anything.

And if they hadn't suspected anything, they hadn't been looking for a single sheet of paper. All they'd be concerned about was gathering forensic evidence and having a laugh at any sex toys they came across. They'd come up short on the sex toys. Game over.

I found myself staring at the carpet again as my subconscious watched Sienna tramp from the spare room into the bathroom, probably unzipping the laptop bag on her way.

I suddenly stood up. He wanted quick access, he wanted to be sure no one tripped over it by accident, and I was looking at the very thing. Our bookcase spanned the wall either side of the chimney breast, and among the delights living there were two or three books about Formula One. They were big books, the size of a kid's comic book annual. The perfect place to hide a sheet of paper – or a ticket.

Actually, there were four books about Formula One and I chose to look in none of them. I had an almost ritualistic method of cleaning and sorting my books; I knew them all individually as other people might know their friends, or their DVD collections or whatever. But today, I sidestepped the big books – my usual starting place – and went straight for the others.

It took me three-quarters of an hour to flick through the hundreds of other books on those shelves, and at the end I stood and arched my aching back and massaged my throbbing knees. I stared at the unstable piles of books surrounding me on the floor, and at the near-empty shelves, and began crying again. I have no idea why; perhaps it was the upheaval my life was in, it was a metaphor for me. And it was horrible to see it all laid bare, exposed, and rummaged through.

"You okay?" Sienna called down.

"Yep." No, not really. Actually, not at all.

And then she was on her way down the stairs, and I sighed. As I stretched my back I looked out of the lounge window. There was a car parked over the street. Maybe sixty yards away. It was difficult to see through the rain and wet window, but from here it looked as though someone was sitting in it.

"Cuppa? Although I need a pee first."

"Come and look at this," I said.

Sienna stood beside me. "Who is it?"

"I don't know." I was whispering. And then I noticed my hands were trembling again. I'd never experienced a nervous breakdown before, but I heard how devastating they could be and how suddenly they could occur. I wondered if it was my turn. I always thought I was much too strong-minded to have a breakdown. Okay, I was on fluoxetine, otherwise known as Prozac, and had been for twelve months. I'd told the doctor I needed them because I was going through a bad patch at work – high pressure, bad atmosphere. You always get those in a library, I was tempted to add.

I'd intended getting more from the doctor because the police had my house locked down and I couldn't access those by my bed, but I had forgotten. In fact, I hadn't taken them for a week or so.

And so, I countered the impending breakdown thought with one concerning the effects of withdrawal. I left it at that, ready to revisit the debate if, or when, things got any worse.

They were about to.

"Someone's getting out." She clutched my arm and my whole body prickled. I felt slightly sick, and inside my mind I ran around in circles panicking, screaming, looking for the exit, and looking for a kitchen knife all in one quick loop that played over and over. "It's a woman."

I squinted. "It's that copper." I turned to Sienna. I felt all the heat drip from my body as though I'd been relocated to the freezer department. "What the hell does *she* want?"

"Where were we last night?"

"What?"

The gate squealed.

"Last night, when Peter died? Where were we?"

"Shit. I don't know. What was on telly?"

"What? I don't watch fucking telly!"

There was a knock at the back door. The one I hadn't locked. Again.

"We were just talking, alright. And drinking." I hurried out of the lounge. "Talking and drinking," I hissed, making sure my hair was respectable – why the hell did I do that? And that made my silly mind drift to wondering where my ponytail had gone, and suddenly memories of being in Savage's little hut came back just as she knocked on the door again.

I stood before it, calming myself down, breathing slowly and practising a smile that I didn't need. In the end I just opened the damned thing.

Chapter Twenty-Six

"Hi, Becky." "Alison." I wiped my sweaty hands down the sides of my jeans. "What can I do for you?"

She looked out into the street again. Over her shoulder I could see the Fergusons' curtains twitching. Bastards. Then she looked back at me. She seemed agitated. "Can I come in? I won't stay long."

"Yes, of course." I stood back and she slid past me like a fog as I lost myself in thought again. I blinked, saw Gail Ferguson staring at me, and slammed the door. I could hear talking from the lounge, and rushed through.

Alison turned to me. "I was just telling Sienna how lucky you are to have someone at a time like this."

"Still no sign of Peter?" I said, clasping my hands before me.

She shook her head. "I wanted to apologise for my behaviour this morning. It was very unprofessional."

I hated that – there's that word again, but it's true. She was apologising for how unprofessional she was. How about apologising for how fucking rude she was! "If anyone understands how you must feel, it's me."

"*I* don't know where my man is though."

Simple words that cut right through me. As though I didn't have a right to grieve just because I already knew my Chris was dead. I think people call this a pissing contest. I was still winning. "No, I appreciate that, and of course I accept your apology. But I can't shed any light on his whereabouts, I'm afraid."

"Did he say anything to you yesterday? I mean anything out of the ordinary?"

You mean like, 'Gimme some money, I know what your husband was up to?'

"No, nothing. He was very kind; showed me into the locker room and allowed me to empty Chris's locker. He expressed his sorrow, and said his whole team was suffering."

She nodded, looked at the floor, eyes pulled to the blood as mine had been.

"We didn't speak much more," I offered. "I collected Chris's things, and he showed me back out."

She thought for a moment, and then said, "An officer came into the locker room, and he described the scene as frantic."

"Frantic?" I half-laughed. "I was..." I shrugged. "Beside myself with grief. I don't know how, but I ended up on the floor in tears. Peter tried to help me stand, and that's when the officer came in." I stared her in the eye, never flinching. "I expect it did look frantic to anyone who only caught a brief glimpse of what had happened."

She nodded, licked her lips quickly like a lizard, and then her face lit up with a false smile. "I've taken up too much of your time, forgive me." She held out her hand and we shook.

"No, no problem at all. I'm sure he'll be home soon." I bit my lower lip as I followed her to the door. I felt horrible, yet vindicated. Perhaps I'd saved her from a life of despair at Peter's hands; hell, she should be grateful.

At the door, she stopped so I could squeeze past and open it. "Might I ask where you went after you visited the police station yesterday?"

I took a deep breath, aware that her plastic friendliness towards me was fracturing, and through it I glimpsed something violent struggling to break out. "I went back to Sienna's flat, where you came this morning."

"Did you go out again last night?" More fracturing.

How much did she know? Had they found Peter's car at Barnbow? Were they already looking for his body? Had they found it? Think!

"We stayed in." Sienna appeared out of nowhere, standing behind Alison, sandwiching her between us both. "We drank plenty, and we talked more bollocks than you could shake a shitty stick at. And we have a bastard's hangover to show for it." Sienna folded her arms, stared. No smile. She was only a couple or three degrees away from being overtly aggressive.

But Alison seemed oblivious. She turned her attention back to me. Her raised eyebrows said she was posing the question to me.

I stuttered. "Stayed in and drank myself silly." I smiled, I couldn't help myself. "Just like she said."

"That trolley-case in Sienna's flat. It was covered in mud at the bottom edge." She nudged a little closer to me, and I felt sweat growing on my top lip. It itched but for some reason I daren't scratch it.

"It's been to the charity shop more times than you could shake another shitty stick at it," Sienna said. "It's a muddy track behind my flat, and that's the route I take to the main road. It's a battered old thing, so it doesn't bother me how muddy it gets."

All the time that Sienna was speaking, Alison's eyes were closed as though she was summoning all her powers to stop from screaming 'who the fuck asked you?' Although more cracks appeared and the beast was clawing at me through them, she remained almost calm on the outside.

As her eyes flickered open, she smiled at me, and I returned it, teeth and all. "Will that be all?"

"I find it very strange that your husband is killed by a rogue gang member, and then my partner goes missing the same day you visit our station. Both men work in the same intelligence department. Becky, do you find that strange?"

Condescending cow!

"Well—"

"Shut up, Sienna," Alison said without taking her eyes off me. "Do you?"

The beast touched me, and I went cold. "I've already had this conversation with your inspector. Perhaps you'd like to ask him what my response was."

"You are the common denominator."

"I'm not sure I like your tone. Are you here as Alison or as a detective sergeant?"

"I'm here as a woman, wondering if anyone knows what might have happened to her partner."

"Then I believe I've answered your question as fully as I can. I bid you a good day." On some other level, I felt my heart stop; if it'd had nails it would have been chewing them by now.

The beast broke free, and Alison pushed me into the wall by the door. "Fucking tell me what's going on, Becky." Her hand was at my throat and her arm was across the wound on my chest – it hurt like a bitch but my mind took little notice of it. "I know there's more you're not telling me, and if I find out you withheld information that could help me locate Peter, I swear—"

Suddenly her hand was not at my throat, it was frantically reaching up behind her head. Sienna pulled her back along the hallway by the hair, and I saw Alison grimace, teeth bared, and then she ducked and spun around all in one movement, but Sienna didn't let go. They ended up in an untidy scrum by the lounge door.

"Stop!"

They didn't, so I screamed again. "I'm ringing the police right now, Alison. Think how good that'll sound when they play it back to Inspector Hughes!"

They stopped as if suddenly frozen in place. Gradually, hands slackened, and almost gracefully they parted. They were panting and, once out of arms reach, straightened up their clothing. Alison walked out without looking at me, and I was about to swing the door closed when she said, "You're involved in something so fucking warped that it'll send you down for decades, Becky."

I wanted to come back with a really good put-down, but as usual my mind shrugged its shoulders and left me to fend for myself. "I will never see you again," I said to her. Best I could come up with.

But her eyes were smiling at me. Her face was red through exertion, and you could tell she was rattled, but her eyes shone with joy. "Oh yes you will. I'll be the one throwing away the fucking key."

I slammed the door, and I locked the bastard.

Sienna and I stared at each other for some time, wondering what the hell all that was about. It was as though we were searching for the correct emotion to assign to what had just happened. I thought I was going to the floor on my knees where I'd bawl into the powdery mess that the forensics team had left, but that didn't happen.

We laughed about it. We laughed hard enough to have us coughing, hard enough to make our ribs hurt, and when Sienna quoted me, "I bid you good day," we burst out laughing again, and then Sienna said, "I don't need a pee any more." We laughed again so loudly that I expected Alison could hear us even if she was half way back to the police station.

It faded though, minutes later, and we found ourselves sitting on the hall floor going over what had just happened between gasps and little giggles that soon perished. "Thanks for hauling her off me. Well, thanks for just being there, actually. She was an animal." I looked past Sienna into the wall mirror and I could see myself; I could even see the red marks around my neck. "That fucking hurt." I rubbed at my throat. "I should kill her for that."

Sienna sat upright, and she glared at me.

I winked at her in the hopes it would degrade the effect those words had on her, but the wink was confetti in a storm. "I wasn't serious," I said. "Jesus."

"Who killed Chris?"

Whoa! No warning, no preamble, just wham. You can't ask a question like that without prepping someone first! Unblinking, unfeeling, and with a strange honesty, I said, "I'm looking at her." My voice was cold, croaky, but my eyes were fixed, my breathing halted, everything on high alert.

"How dare you say that? If you really think that then move aside and let me the fuck out of here. You're on your own, do what you like with the money, just get it out of my house." She stood and walked towards me with a purpose that only physical contact or wise words could stop.

"Relax," I said. "Of course I don't think it was you! It was Pinkman."

She stood over me, one battle ended but another on the way, prepared and ready to fight her corner. Sienna almost growled, "Say it again."

"Pinkman killed Chris. Who else would it have been?"

"Then why say—"

"I was joking! Fuck me, Sienna; I'm stressed out, I'm at my wits' end, and my head is all over the bloody place. I thought it was funny, and it turned out not to be."

"Funny?"

"I didn't know what I was saying, cut me some slack, would you?" I did know what I was saying. Of course I did, I wasn't drunk or high or anything. The trouble is that sometimes what you say is what you're wondering. Sometimes it's what you know to be true deep down on a level where sunlight cannot reach. It's on a level where lies don't exist.

"How could you think that was funny? Really, think about it, how the hell could you think that was funny?"

"I don't think I should have stopped my Prozac so suddenly." I offered my hand, and reluctantly she gripped it and hauled me to my feet. I didn't speak, I just embraced her, and there I cried with my head buried in her neck. "I'm sorry," I croaked. "I am, I just said it, it just came out." I pulled away, looked into her eyes,."And no, it wasn't a Freudian slip – it was just…" I sighed. "I don't know what it was; it was just hot air." I pulled her tightly into me. "Of course I don't think you killed Chris. My God! I was just upset by that silly bitch invading my house and assaulting me."

"You were putting out feelers, Becky. You were checking my reaction because you already said that he was cooling when you found him, and Savage denied killing him."

"Of course Savage killed him! Pinkman killed him; and they'd done it hours before I came home. They'd been searching for hours."

She pulled away, looked at me with softened eyes, and she stroked the hair out of my eyes. "You sure?"

"I was frazzled. I'm sure. Come on," I said, "let's find that list."

I closed all the drawers in the kitchen, filled and plugged in the kettle, and we both settled down to a hot drink in the lounge with Chris's blood for company. I couldn't take my eyes from it.

"You coming to stay with me again tonight?"

I thought about it. It was either Sienna's or a hotel room. And although the deep friendship we enjoyed was now dented, it remained strong enough that I could share a bed with her without feeling like she was going to stab me in the middle of the night. I nodded. "If you'll have me."

She laughed. "Of course, I wouldn't fight with a copper for anyone else."

A lull drifted over us like the shadow of a cloud, and we sat there sipping our drinks, lost in our own thoughts. I knew what she was thinking though, and it turned out I was right. It's all in the eyes.

"We're not going to find that list, Becky. Let's just get going, get a good head start over Savage."

"We haven't finished yet."

"Come on, we have to call it a day. I've finished upstairs, and you've done down here."

"I've only done the lounge."

"So what's left? The kitchen? The hall? The cupboard under the stairs?"

"Savage searched under the stairs pretty thoroughly, there are only wellies in there. And shopping bags. And he wouldn't use one of those in case I actually remembered to take them shopping with me."

She sighed a big one. "So that leaves the kitchen. All the drawers were out, the cupboards opened. They searched thoroughly in there too."

And that got me thinking. Chris would need instant access to the list. And it didn't matter where he was, he'd need to be able to lay his hands on it immediately as soon as Savage called. And Savage might call while he was at work as well as when he was home. He didn't go anywhere else. Work. Home.

"Spit it out."

"What goes to work with him that he brings home too?"

Her mouth turned down at the edges, and she shrugged again. "Briefcase?"

"Doesn't own one."

"Come on then, the suspense is killing me."

Chapter Twenty-Seven

It was on top of the fridge freezer, lying on its side, top flap unzipped and open. Chris would never leave it like that. Chris always made sure he closed it and placed it squarely away into the corner of the walls.

"Sandwich box? You're kidding me?"

I reached up and dragged it into my hands. It was a soft black cooler-type sandwich bag with a zip around three edges. The top flap opened and you had ready access to your insulated food. It was an old thing, and it was showing signs of wear: the handle was frayed, the paint on the zipper was worn away, and the white wipe-clean plastic lining was torn across the top seam. It was the perfect place to slip a folded piece of paper. It was the perfect medium for innocent transport to and from work. No one would bat an eyelid. And no one would think of giving the thing more than a cursory glance if they were searching for a piece of paper worth a million pounds.

I held the flap back and Sienna and I peered inside. I pulled the torn lining back and it stared at me – a folded piece of white paper. Sienna stepped away, resting awkwardly against the counter top. She had gone quite pale, and appeared to be hyperventilating.

"You okay?"

She nodded, turned away.

I pulled the list out, tossed the sandwich box back on top of the fridge. I opened it up, and there was the West Yorkshire Police crest at the top, Intelligence Department below in bold, and below that a disclaimer, headed *CONFIDENTIAL*. Below that it said, *Data Protection Act 1998. This document is confidential. Unauthorised use of disclosure is unlawful. Any disclosure, copying, distribution, of the information contained herein is strictly prohibited.* This was the real deal.

"Sienna." I smiled at her. "We found it. We found the list!" She didn't react. "Don't you know what that means? It means we own the money! It means we can go to Wales in safety if that's what you want." I had no intention of going to Wales. I had my eyes set much further afield. But I still needed her on side.

My heart felt full. I had the damned list; therefore, I now had that money. I'd dreamed of having that money. I felt like screaming, running around the house in a joyful frenzy. I eyed her. She remained indifferent. I wondered what was wrong, because something sure as hell was. And I didn't like it. She rubbed her eyes and her hands were shaking.

I went to her, held her arms. "My God, love, you're trembling. What's wrong?"

Still with her eyes covered, she said, "Read the list."

My full heart exploded. I stepped back away from her, almost afraid to look at the names on that sheet of paper. But I did. I propped myself against the fridge and sure enough, the sixth name on the list of twelve was one Sienna Middleton. Alongside was her address, and then her known associates. There were further blank columns for aliases and such. There was some code at the end that I didn't understand, but my entire focus was those two words: Sienna Middleton.

"Have they got this wrong?"

She shook her head, her hands slid down her face revealing damp eyes that were hurting and sorry all at once.

My eyes flicked to the knife block in the corner by the kettle, and I wondered for a moment how safe I was. Her name on this list made her desperate. "You knew?"

"Yes."

"That explains your reluctance to try and find it. In fact, you hoped we *wouldn't* find it." I shook it in front of her, angry that she… hold on, a more fundamental question flipped to the top of the pile. It was waving its arms at me, and though I couldn't hear it, it was screaming at me. But I ignored it for a minute. "How did you know? How did you know there *was* a list? How *could* you know there was a list?"

Her face creased up. At first, I wasn't sure if she was getting ready to cry, or if she was getting ready to grab a knife. "You told me, remember? When you said there was a list of informants against Savage, I knew I was on it. Had to be."

The fundamental question waved at me furiously now. I cleared my throat. "Chris must have known you were on this list. He read it, he printed the entire list, and he couldn't edit it out." She was looking at me, waiting for that fundamental question. "Didn't he contact you to warn you?"

"No, the first I heard of the list was from you three or four days ago. Honestly! Becky, you have to believe me."

No, I didn't have to believe her, and I definitely did *not* believe her. I knew Chris; I knew he would warn her – she was a family friend. The deal with Savage was under way already, or her inclusion on that list didn't mean more to him than a million quid; either way, he would have told her. Make no mistake about that – he would have warned her.

"He would have told you, Sienna. He wouldn't want Savage getting hold of you."

"No, he didn't!"

I thought back to the hallway, where I asked her if she'd killed Chris, and her vehement denial. "Surely if he told you, you would want to dissuade him from giving that list to Savage, wouldn't you?"

"He didn't fucking tell me!"

"He'd feed you to the wolves? Is that what you're saying?"

"Yes!"

"He wouldn't." I shook my head. "Not my Chris. So you came here and you tried to talk him out of giving it to Savage." I looked at the ceiling, I could picture it. They were standing in the lounge. Chris had let her in because it was an old friend of ours, Sienna. And he'd contacted her, told her she needed to get out of town. Perhaps he didn't tell her why, because it would implicate him; it would give away his plan, and she might run to the police and spoil it all. "Did you threaten him with reporting it to the police?"

"You're drawing conclusions that are irrelevant, Becky." She moved closer to me, away from the knives, tried and failed to smile at me.

I folded the list up, slid it into my back pocket, and crossed my arms, resolute that she wasn't going to get her hands on it.

"It never got that far, I swear. He told me to leave, yes."

"So he did warn you!"

"Yes, alright, he warned me."

"You lied to me!"

"I'm trying to protect my life here; of course I lied to you."

"What else have you lied about?"

"Nothing. Look, he told me I was on a list, and he said there was a high chance that information would find its way to Savage. And that to stay safe I should leave while I could. Honestly, Becky, that's it; that's as far as it went."

"You told me that you didn't kill him," I whispered it because my mind was working, humming away at the possibilities this revelation proffered. "I believed you. I apologised for even suggesting such a thing." Mind working underground, processing the truth against the lies she'd told me, and against the lies that I'd made myself live by. "Now I know why you were so close by when I was in that phone box. You were hovering, waiting till they'd gone so that you could come and find the list yourself because Chris wouldn't tell you where it was."

"Hovering? I fucking live—"

"You were here that morning." I paused; the lie grew wings and flew, growing larger and larger, more menacing as it approached me.

"No."

"You pleaded with him to give you the list, and he refused."

"No, Becky that's not—"

"And you killed him. You really *did* kill him!"

She slapped me and burst my fucking lip open again. Now I was angry. "It wasn't Pinkman at all, you lying bitch—"

She slapped me again, and I lost my balance and went down like a sack of shit. "I *didn't* kill—"

I kicked her legs and she joined me on the floor, hitting her head against the corner of the dishwasher. She rolled from side to side holding her head, and the wound must have opened up because blood trickled out into the creases of her knuckles, flowed under the rings she wore and dripped onto her arm and then the floor. I got to my feet first.

"Get up."

She continued to roll around, hands clasped over the open wound.

"Get the fuck up, Sienna!"

"Why won't you believe me?" The words slurred out through a mouth that was too busy grimacing at the pain to form them properly.

"I said get up."

She stopped rolling, took her hands away, grimaced at the blood on them, and then slowly stood, keeping as much distance from me as she could. "I promise that I didn't kill him. I wasn't here that morning, Becky. You have to believe me."

I clicked my fingers as another suspicious image crossed my mind. "When I came back to your car, after the meeting with Peter, you were on the phone."

She stared at me.

"When you saw me, you shut it off and dropped in your lap."

"I'd finished the call."

"Who to?"

"My mum, I already told you that."

I smiled, chalked up another lie. "It was Savage, wasn't it?"

"What was Savage?"

"You were talking with Savage. Telling him what we were doing next. You've been in cahoots with him all this time!"

Her face was a picture of confusion. "You've no idea what you're talking about."

"Really?"

"I was telling Mum that I wasn't able to visit this week, that's all."

I smiled at her. "Bollocks." I took the chance to lunge, and I caught a good one across her face. I could see her hair sweep across her face like a shampoo advert; it was kind of graceful if a little gruesome. And then she looked at me and hit back. My eyes closed reflexively as the punch connected. I went down again, but only for a few seconds, and when I opened my eyes, I was alone. I heard her rushing along the hall and then she was outside. The gate squealed.

My jaw throbbed. I couldn't help but smile.

Next to the kitchen bin, almost out of view, half hidden under the side of the cupboard, something caught my eye. I slid my way across and picked it up. It was a piece of pottery. I studied it closer; it was part of my shattered *Beauty and the Beast* cup. This piece that I turned in my fingers showed the head of the beast.

Chapter Twenty-Eight

I almost tripped over the damaged bath panel that lay across the bathroom floor like a pale giant's tongue. I peered into the mirror, and Sienna's blood was smeared across my left cheek where she'd punched me with her blood-soaked fist. My own blood had leaked out of the bust lip and leached across the fold between my bottom lip and chin. It looked like I had two mouths. I washed, dabbed the bottom lip and re-evaluated myself. I was okay, physically, though I was starting to wonder if that lip would ever heal.

Mentally I was not okay. I was wading through a pool of lies and semi-truths, and I was having a hard time keeping the sediment – the *horrific* lies that I'd laid into dormancy – settled at the bottom where I needed it to lie.

I smiled at myself in the mirror and the other me, the one with the red cheek, smiled back at me with blood between her lower teeth. There was no sparkle in her eyes any more; now they looked predatory, a little too evil for my tastes, but I guess that's what happens when you live in a pool with that sediment pluming around you.

I vowed that I would correct it all one day. I vowed that I'd make the horrific lies float where I could deal with them, maybe never really accepting them, but reconciling them, learning to live with them until they became just another part of me. Like the grief was becoming a part of me, and shaping who I was becoming.

I changed into clothes that belonged to me, and I felt a little more comfort at last. But I needed a jacket, something lightweight that had an internal pocket. I rummaged through the wardrobe and found the very thing.

* * *

I pulled the back door closed and locked it. I slid the key into my jeans pocket, checked the list was still there – it was – and walked past the Fergusons' giving them the finger as I did so. I got great satisfaction from seeing the shock on their faces – nosey bastards. My walk turned into a jog.

At the top of the street, I turned right, and within fifteen minutes I slowed to a walk and finally came to a stop behind Sienna's blue Corsa. I rested there for a full minute, thinking of my next move. If I'm being honest, I couldn't believe she was still there. I thought she'd have shoved the case in the boot and been on her way to the airport by now. If the roles had been reversed, that's what I would have done.

I walked to her door, took a deep breath, flexed my fists and took hold of the handle. I didn't even need to push it down as the door swung open by itself. On the mat was a length of wood from the doorframe. The door lock itself was still in the locked position. I peered in and saw no one. But I heard someone. I stepped inside and pushed the door closed behind me, and the sounds of Garforth quietened to a hum, and I could smell fresh cigarette smoke.

Sienna was lying on the sofa, face buried in a cushion, and I could see her back in spasm. "Sienna?"

She paused, but then her crying resumed with renewed vigour.

"Sienna? Are you alright?" A stupid question to ask, especially after we'd just been fighting like a couple of drunken men, but really, what else could I say? Except, "What's happened?"

She lifted her head and a string of snot snapped and joined a pool of it on the sofa. Her eyes were swollen – partly because I'd slapped her, but mostly because she was crying like a woman about to be split in two by a pair of trucks. It took a while for me to process what she said because she was talking like a two-year-old. "The money."

I rushed into the kitchen, and there on the floor was a sheet of muddy newspaper. "Fuck."

Back in the lounge, Sienna had turned over and sat up, and she looked pitiful as I walked back in.

"Where is my money?"

"I don't know." She nodded to the door. "I've been burgled."

I began to speak several times but couldn't get the words out. Eventually, I managed, "Are you shitting me?"

She said nothing, only hitching her breath like she had hiccups, unable to speak because she was sobbing so hard.

"Someone broke in while we were away and stole a muddy suitcase? They took nothing else? Nothing else was disturbed?"

She shook her head.

"Savage."

"Must be," she managed.

"Back in a minute," I said, and rushed outside. I searched her car, just to be sure it wasn't some kind of bluff; it was empty. How I kept my abject fury under control is beyond me; I do not know how I didn't kill her – even though she wasn't responsible, but I just wanted to take it out on someone, and who better than one Sienna fucking Middleton?

"I don't know how he found out where I lived. And how the hell did he know I had the money here?"

I snatched her handbag from the floor and ripped a cigarette out of the packet. I puffed that thing until I felt like throwing up. I felt the drug spinning through my body and my mind, and it was wonderfully disgusting.

It was a good question. "I wonder if he put a tracker in the bundle when he gave it to Chris?" I answered my own question before Sienna could even begin to think about it. Maybe he had; but it's probably one of the reasons he re-packaged it. It was in one of my vacuum bags, so I knew he hadn't trusted Savage either. No, it hadn't been tracked. Besides, Savage would have found it at Barnbow, wouldn't he?

Sienna reached for her handbag too and the cigarettes inside.

And that's when it hit me. My handbag! "The slimy bastard!" I got my shoulder bag from the side of the sofa where I'd left it today, and tipped it out across the floor. And then I did the same thing I did when I'd bought the new clothes in Next. I ran my thumbnail along all the seams. But I found nothing.

There was a tear in the lining at the bottom though. I pulled the lining up and out of the bag, ripping it free. And the tracker fell out.

It was nothing like the small black disc that I'd found in my old jeans. This was bigger, a small box something the size of a matchbox. The disc had been a distraction, a simple decoy, and stupid me had fallen for it – and I thought I'd been so clever! I looked at the mess Sienna was in and I felt deflated; I felt like rolling into a ball and just crying myself to death. When would this ever end? When would I be free of that man's grasp?

I dropped it onto the floor, and brought my foot down on it. Another three attempts and the tracker was in small pieces. I kicked them across the room, and then I kicked my fucking handbag there too. I wouldn't need it any more, not after tonight.

And then there was a knock at the door. "Hello? Sienna?"

Sienna climbed from the sofa, dragged a sleeve across the snot on her face, and walked to the smashed front door. I saw a streak of red in her tangled hair. "Anything?" she asked.

She came back in with a small, skinny woman with tattoos up both arms, and big black rings inside her ear lobes. She looked at me. "This is Patti from next door," she said. "She has CCTV over her door."

She nodded at me, a 'hello, pleased to meet you' look on her pointed face. "It reaches across to Sienna's door." She smiled. "I think I got him."

* * *

We stood, a strange threesome, in front of Patti's laptop as she scrolled back through footage from the camera over her front door. "Here we go," she squealed, excited by the possibility of catching a burglar. Though this was no ordinary burglar, and I waited to see one of Savage's gorillas come into view. "At 14.29 p.m. Here we go, wait for it. You can see him, there. There he is!"

A large man wearing a sports jacket came into view. He didn't look around, he didn't look shifty. He looked as though he had every right to be there. We watched as he approached Sienna's door and practically walked right through the bloody thing!

He didn't pause, just lowered the handle and shouldered the door, and he was inside within half a dozen seconds. I was standing there in Patti's lounge with my hand over my mouth, staggered by the ease with which he'd gained entry. "Bastard," I whispered.

"Wait, wait, wait. He comes out again in, three, two, one."

And sure enough, the big man in the sports jacket came into view as he silently swung Sienna's front door open and casually wheeled away a million pounds. It was Streaky. "The big fat bastard!" I screamed and hurried out of Patti's house, ignoring the hurt look on her face.

Chapter Twenty-Nine

"I need a drink." Sienna skulked into the lounge just after I'd lit another one of her cigarettes, and walked straight past me and into the kitchen.

I followed her. "Tell me why you were on that list."

She paused at the kitchen counter, bottle of vodka in her hand. Slowly she turned and said, "Because I give information about him to the police."

"Precisely."

She looked at me as though I was singing the Danish national anthem, and began unscrewing the top of the vodka bottle.

"You know things about him, right? Savage? You know where he operates from."

The bottle chinked against a glass, and it reminded me of Chris pouring a whisky at home. How that now felt like a hundred years ago. "Why do you want to know?"

"Take a wild guess."

"You're not thinking of getting the money back!"

"I have the list. The deal's still on."

She drained the glass and reached for the bottle again. I slapped her hand away and she recoiled. "I can't believe you'd sell me out. How long have we been friends?"

"Who said anything about selling you out?" I threw the cigarette in the sink, closed my eyes for a moment and tried my best to mellow out a bit, to calm down. But really, after having a million pounds snatched from under our noses, it was a very difficult ask indeed. I tried a smile, and it felt okay, not too strenuous. "You're my best friend, Sienna. You've been the one I turned to for twenty years. And when my Chris was killed, you took me in; you came on a wild adventure with me. And you'll never know how grateful I am. Never. So why would you think I'd sell you out for a million quid? Why would I?"

"An hour ago, you accused me of killing Chris!"

Good point. "Of course I did. I wanted to see your reaction; I was fishing, Sienna, for Christ's sake. And can you blame me after all the lies you've told me?"

She looked away, her face ever so slightly flushed with, I hoped, embarrassment rather than anger. And then she said, "But the list. You just said the deal's still on."

"It is. In theory. Just tell me what you know about the man."

She sighed, and I did nothing this time when she topped up her glass. "I know where he works from, yeah. But you won't get within a hundred yards."

"What else do you know about him?"

"Huh?"

"Come on! The police pay you for information against him. So, what do you know? I need to find a weakness."

"He doesn't have one."

I lost my smile and my mellow dropped down dead. "Sienna."

She shrank away again, and whispered, "What do you want to know?"

"Let's grab some tea," I said, looking at the vodka bottle, "and go sit down. Let's see if we can figure something out."

Had I been Sienna right then, I would have picked up a knife and stabbed me in the back. I would have *known* that Savage would find out I'd snitched on him – one way or another; irrespective of any proposed plan, I would have known that. And the only way of Savage not caring one way or the other if I'd snitched on him, would be if he were dead. And I, Sienna, would doubt that Becky would commit murder to protect me.

That's what I was thinking as I strode from the kitchen; I was kind of wincing, expecting a blade between the shoulders any second. It didn't come, and I breathed a little easier as we entered the lounge.

It was a missed opportunity, I thought. One she'd end up regretting. Shouldn't have had that last vodka, love.

We sat down, and Sienna tossed an ashtray across to me, and opened a fresh packet of cigarettes. We each lit one, sighed out a cloud of blue smoke and sat back in our chairs, me staring at her, she staring at the carpet. "Tell me about his business."

Initially, she seemed to struggle with some inner turmoil. Maybe she was fighting the urge to tell me because of some misplaced loyalty towards him, or towards the police, I don't know, but she hesitated for so long that it became a refusal. "Sienna?"

"He deals in drugs. High-end stuff as well as street level."

"High-end?"

"Posh folks. And we can get through this quicker if you don't stop and ask questions at every point I make."

"Of course I want to ask questions! It's how…" I found myself sitting forward, pointing a pair of smoking fingers at her. And I stopped it; I calmed down, rested my back into the chair, and took a long slow drag. "I want to see where each point could lead to. There might be an opening, something we could negotiate with. I don't know, some way we could strengthen our position."

"We should have run while we had the chance." Her voice was filled with something approaching hate and despair, but her eyes showed remorse, a missed chance, an implied acceptance of her fate, and it was obvious she thought this exercise was a waste of time.

"Maybe," I said. "But we're here now. And don't think of running, Sienna, because if he doesn't catch you, I will. I want some answers; I want something I can work with."

She shook her head, folded her arms.

"What else? High- and low-end drug dealer. What else?"

She sighed again. I was getting fed up of this reticence. But then she said, "I can't prove it, but I think he's a stop on some people-trafficking route from Europe. The trucks stop there, and I've seen vans coming to pick up people who weren't there before the trucks came in."

"What a bag of shit." It was all awful news; and I expected more of the same, but so far there was nothing substantial I could use against him. "What's next?"

She thought for a moment, smiled and said, "I know he has a wife and three kids who live in Monk Fryston. He doesn't go home much because he hates them all. Not exactly a family man. I've heard him say he'd have them taken out if it wasn't for some hard nut of a brother of hers in Newcastle – who wouldn't hesitate to come down and return the favour."

My eyes lit up. But the light in them extinguished pretty quickly. It wasn't anything I could use; since they both probably hated each other, they probably had a mutual respect, or at least had come to some sort of stand-off that neither seemed eager to break. It was a dead end. "Go on."

She shrugged. "He has a frozen food network, a small fleet of vans that he uses as a front for his other businesses. Oh, and I know he's killed at least three people."

That was the wrong time to take a sip of tea. I blew it across the floor. "Fuck's sake, Sienna! You *know* he's killed people?"

She nodded, matter-of-factly.

"And they still haven't arrested him?"

"No bodies. No witnesses. I'm pretty sure they did some covert stuff on him, but it either turned up nothing or they're holding it back until they hit the jackpot."

"And what's the jackpot?"

She laughed. "They're hardly likely to tell me, are they?"

"No, suppose not." I mopped tea from my chin, and stared at her, "Just how the hell do you know all this?"

She said nothing to me, but eyed me as she reached for yet another cigarette. "I could really use another drink."

"You haven't finished your tea. Try that."

"I feel very uncomfortable—"

"Please tell me you're not shagging him."

Her eyes fell away as she flicked ash.

"Jesus, Sienna! How the hell could you? Have you seen—"

"Don't you dare judge me, Becky Rose!" Had she been closer she'd have clawed my eyes out. "You've no fucking idea what I've been through since Eric died, and I don't need no prim-and-proper fucking librarian preaching shit at me as you look down your *fucking nose at me!*" The rage dripped from her mouth like the blood had dripped from the bust lip she gave me earlier. Her eyes were fierce, lips drawn back in a snarl, and it's the closest to being utterly petrified I've ever come in her company. Taught me a lesson. I didn't know what she'd been through, except Eric's death last year – which I only found out about recently.

I bowed my head in shame. "He's not exactly Richard Gere though, is he?" I tried to smirk, hoping it would relax the situation, but the tension was clearly still there, and the snarl stayed on her face until I swallowed, and said, "I'm sorry. It was wrong of me to judge." But I still couldn't get the image of him out of my mind. I shuddered. "Does he come here?"

"Don't worry," she snapped, "you haven't slept in the same bed he has."

I sighed gratitude inside, but stared at her still.

"Eric owed him money." She shrugged. "So, I… He sends a car. I meet it on Main Street. I don't want him knowing where I live."

"I thought for a second you were going to tell me he was your landlord."

"No, he's not. But you can imagine why I don't want him getting a hold of that list. If you think two trucks ripping you apart is bad…" She didn't finish her sentence, but she didn't need to. I shuddered again. How low could humanity reach?

I had often wondered how she managed to live like she did, and though it wasn't exactly opulent, I nonetheless wondered how she could afford the cigarettes and the booze and a decent amount of rent each month when she didn't work. Now I knew. And, of course, she was getting money from the police to supplement whatever he paid to her. This was all very Mata Hari, and I sensed in myself a streak of envy and even of pride in her. I wasn't sure where that streak had come from – I sure as hell wouldn't do what she did if I had the choice. But maybe she didn't have any choice, maybe that's what her whole point was.

"So, you think I'm prim?" I lit a tiny smile, not trying to eradicate the seriousness of what we were discussing, but just trying my best to bring the tension down a notch or two. It didn't work, the flame died.

"I'm not in a good place, right now," she said. "And I don't mean to be rude, but don't try and funny your way through this because I'm not enjoying it at all."

Ouch.

I sank into thought as Sienna went into the kitchen – probably to get another shot of vodka, I thought, but instead I heard her fill the kettle again. So far, everything she'd given me was background, and it was mind-blowing, but I'd heard nothing I could use against him. I wanted to exchange the list for the cash without getting my hand chewed off in the process. And so far, I had come up blank.

Except… there was a kernel of a plan forming, but it was right at the bottom of the pool of lies below my feet, stirring up the sediment of its own accord. I was sure I wouldn't like it, but I was even more sure I would use it, whatever it was.

I took the list out of my back pocket just as Sienna walked in with fresh drinks.

"If you're going to give him that list, then I'm leaving after this farewell drink."

I was surprised she was still here. If getting that money back meant giving him the list, then that's what would happen, with or without her blessing. "Don't worry, it's the last thing on my mind," I lied.

"You have a plan?"

"Getting there." I read the list properly for the first time, studying it as she watched me over the rim of her coffee cup. "Do you know anyone on this list?"

She held out her hand, and I raised my eyebrows. Like I was that stupid! I'd rather shove wasps up my arse. "I'll read them to you."

She pulled her hand away, singed, and I saw the small shake of her head. Because of that, and that alone, I knew tonight would not end well.

I read through eight of the twelve names, even mentioning those in the alias/original column, and for each one, she shook her head. I missed out her own name, but the next one, number ten, caused her eyes to widen slightly, and her body jerked. She put her fingers to her temple. "He's a drug supplier, I'm almost sure of it."

"Why would he be a police informant?"

"They must have offered immunity, I suppose."

Name number eleven meant nothing to her. I looked back at the list. The last name was, "Paul Richmond?"

She shook her head.

The column next to Richmond's name was headed alias/original, and I said, "How about Paul Bacon?"

She looked to the ceiling, thinking, and her mouth turned down at the edges again. "Don't think so, no."

I wondered if Paul Bacon – if that was his original name, probably changed by deed poll – was a certain fat bastard in a sports jacket called Streaky. He probably thought if he used his legal name, the police wouldn't check to see if he was originally known by any other. Bacon. Streaky. It made sense, and if the police had caught him in some kind of trap, or had evidence against him for some crime or another, I wondered if they'd recruit him on a deal of immunity from prosecution too.

Imagine if that were true. Imagine what Savage would do to his most trusted right-hand man. Skin-peeling came to mind. I began to wonder if I might be able to use Streaky to get my money back. Maybe he'd prove to be a lucky streak after all.

"So, Savage doesn't know you live here?"

"No. Why?"

"Because this is where he found his million quid. If your name is linked to mine, then—"

"That's why I was so careful he wasn't following us, remember?"

I did, and I hadn't known the full gravity behind it back then; I thought she was being paranoid, and only now, because I knew of her connection to Savage and what he'd do to her if he found out we knew each other, did I fully appreciate her willingness to chauffeur me around at all. She was a true friend. Had things been different, I would have valued that friendship.

Sienna cleared her throat, and I looked up. "So, am I leaving?"

That plan, the one stirring the sediment, bobbed to the surface and I grabbed it eagerly with both hands. It was amazing. I looked at Sienna. "No need," I said.

"What's your plan?"

"Have you got his mobile number?"

Chapter Thirty

This was the hardest thing I'd ever done in my entire life. Really, my entire life. I punched his number into my phone with difficulty; I was shaking so much that the phone was a blur. My mouth was dry and my heart hammered somewhere low down in my stomach. I stared at Sienna, and she could see I was well outside my comfort zone, and for a moment then, as she held her hands up to her mouth, I considered hanging up. There must be another way, there must be.

But then he answered. "Yes."

"Savage, it's Becky Rose."

"Ah. I wondered if I would hear from you."

"You stole my money. I want it back." I marvelled at how direct and forceful I sounded, but inside I was just a scared and pathetic little kid.

"How did you get my number?"

"I want my money back." I stared at Sienna, her fists screwed up at her face, too afraid to peer at me. I could relate to it.

"I consider this to be a new transaction. The one I had with your husband is… how shall I say it? Dead."

"Bring my money to me this evening. I have the list."

There was a significant pause, and that was sufficient for me. I had him, he had the bait, and I had his full attention.

"Prove it."

I was confused. "How the hell can I prove—"

"Read a name from the list."

"What?"

"Have you gone deaf, Mrs Rose? It's not difficult, read me a fucking name."

I wasn't expecting that, and it took me by surprise. I wedged the phone between my shoulder and my cheek, took the list from my back pocket, and shook it out. I kept my eye on Sienna all the time; she knew what was happening, and I saw her holding her breath, wondering whose name I would choose. I saw her stance change too, she became offensive, ready to strike me maybe, ready to run. Or just ready to grab the list.

Of course, I wouldn't give him Sienna's name, but I was so tempted to give out Streaky's. The trouble with doing that was it would deflect attention from me and my money. I didn't want to ignite any internal retribution this evening; I wanted his attention solely on me. And another thing, I might need to play that pawn later. I selected the first name. "Craig Gomersall. Alias is 'Gummy'."

I heard clunking, as though he was moving the phone away from his face, a hand over the mouthpiece. There was muffled shouting. I couldn't make out anything he said specifically, just the word, 'now,' and then he was back on the line. "You have a deal. But let me just make one thing crystal clear for you. I have two trucks here, and I'd like you to picture yourself between them. You remember our conversation?"

I remembered alright. I could hear him moving his tongue around his mouth, and it sent a shiver crawling through me. But one thing struck me then: just how important this list was to him. I hadn't given it too much thought before; I'd assumed he would be able to eradicate his competition, turf out some non-loyal people in his line-up perhaps. But I got his sense of urgency, and I began to understand that this would be a turning point for Savage.

I began to understand just what power I held in my shaking right hand. "Leave your trucks out of this; I already proved I have the list." And I've no idea why I said it, but I blurted out, "And I'm amending the deal. I want two million."

"What?"

"That was your original deal with my husband. I want you to honour it."

The line went dead.

I looked at the phone, confused.

"What the fuck did you say that for!" Sienna screamed at me. "Jesus, this isn't about your fucking money any more! This is about keeping alive, Becky. Oh Jesus, no." She buried her face in her hands, collapsed to her chair and wailed.

My heart thudded, and for a moment I thought I was going to faint. I too sat with a bump, let the list fall to the floor, and dropped the phone. I reached for the cigarettes, and decided it would be healthier if we both booked into a hotel for the night, maybe set off from there at first light, running away with our tails between our legs. It wouldn't take him long to muster men to go and break down my door, and then they'd be back here too, even if they didn't understand the connection I had with this address.

I picked up the list, put it back in my pocket, and spoke around the cigarette dangling from my trembling lips. "Fill a carrier with stuff you'll need overnight. We're leaving. Now. And grab your passport."

Without looking at me, she got up and headed for her bedroom. "You've fucking ruined it!" She screamed at me.

I had nothing to pack. All I had was the phone and the list and my shoulder bag I retrieved from the corner of the room .Travelling light. I waited for her by the broken front door, peeking out every few seconds to make sure Savage didn't suddenly appear, chugging on that cigarette like it would be my last.

She came out of the bedroom like a steam train heading straight for me. I took a step back.

"Call him. Call him back. Tell him you've reconsidered. You'll take one million."

"I'd rather go empty-handed. If I back down now, we get nothing."

"Nothing is fine, Becky. Nothing is good. At least we'll still be alive."

I retracted my retreat and took a further step forward. "He'll give us the money. The money means nothing to him. It's chicken feed. The list means everything to him. It's a list of those who are disloyal, it's a way of purging his team. He can grow stronger from it. That's what he wants. Once he has it, he'll forget all about us, and the two million."

"Call him!"

"Car keys," I said. "Come on."

"I said call him." The knife came out of nowhere. I felt the tip at my throat, but it was her eyes that frightened me more. Her pupils were wide, and the whites were yellow, and the snarl was back, lips tight. "Give me the list."

I wondered if she'd had a quick snort while she was in the bedroom. "We can still get away with this, Sienna."

The knife went in, I don't know how far, but the pain was excruciating, like billowing heat inside my chest. I wanted to cry out, and my eyes started watering. I tried to pull back but she had her left hand around the back of my neck. This was the new moment of greatest fear in my life. Forget speaking with Savage, this was king of the castle now. "How much further would you like me to push?"

I reached into my back pocket, and then someone said, "Want me to fix the door?"

I gasped but Sienna held the position, just stared over my shoulder and across to Patti who stood on her own front door step, the encroaching darkness turning her into a vague shadow among other shadows. I could just see her out of the corner of my eye.

"I see you've had no joy with getting a joiner. I could fix it temporarily for you. You know, till you can get hold of someone."

"Go away, Patti," she said.

"It's no bother. At least you can sleep soundly."

"Go away!"

My attention came back to Sienna, but I heard Patti's door slam, and then her eyes came back to me. "The list."

* * *

My fingers touched the paper in my back pocket just as the phone in my front pocket rang.

A ripple of sparks burst through me, and Sienna and I stared at each other.

"We can go where he'll never find us," I whispered. "We can *do* this, Sienna."

She blinked.

"A million each. Think about it." I pulled the phone up and out of my pocket, gently, slowly. I watched as her eyes narrowed, her snarling lips covering those teeth again. The knife came away and she stepped back. She said nothing, just nodded.

Another missed chance, I thought.

I felt blood trickle down my chest, and the hatred I felt for her then solidified as the wound began to sting. I hit the green button. "Yes."

"We have an accord."

I closed my eyes and nearly fell forward onto the floor with relief, but I checked myself quickly, gritted my teeth and said, "I have two conditions."

"There are no conditions."

"I want the money in one large case, wheeled. I will check the money and the case for trackers, bugs, and tracers, and if I find any, you will not get the list."

"I don't have time to dick about."

"Is that agreed, Mr Savage?"

"Yes, yes! Agreed. Go on."

"And I will weigh the money, so no short-changing me."

"Is that it?"

"No, that's not it, Savage." I dabbed at the wound in my throat, and my fingertips came away bloodied. Sienna swallowed and looked away. Bitch. "Don't forget my passport."

"Right," he said. "This is where we're going to do the exchange."

"Wrong. You will ring me back in an hour, and *I'll* let you know where we're doing it."

"I will not—"

I ended the call. My hands were still shaking.

"It's just a game to you, isn't it?"

I stared at Sienna; she looked like a kicked puppy. "If you ever put a knife to my throat again, you'd better push it all the way home."

She dropped it. "I'm sorry," she said, her bottom lip curling out. The tears came next, and she reached out to me but I knocked her hand away. "Please, don't give me up to him."

I felt like killing her. And really, would it matter? "Go and get me a sweater."

She looked at me as though I'd grown a second head.

"To cover the neck wound you just gave me."

She hurried away to the bedroom again, and I looked down at the knife.

When she came back, she tossed the sweater to me.

"I want an envelope for this." I waved the list at her. "And get your car keys. Do it now." I checked my watch. It was eight-forty-five. It would give us plenty of time to get where we were going. Then we'd sit tight, watch, and wait.

Crunch time.

Chapter Thirty-One

The whisky tasted luscious. I held the glass under my nose just to get that stinging sensation in my eyes again. I smiled across at Chris and the reflection of the TV in his spectacles. "Okay?"

"*Ti amo più di qualsiasi cosa.*" I nodded. Everything was okay. The airgun incident was a week old and I like to think we'd got past it fairly well. We hadn't mentioned it again since, which to me, was a sign that it was water under the bridge. We'd both learned a lesson from each other and I think we had become stronger because of it.

"What?"

"It means I love you," I said. "More than anything."

He smiled back, turned off the TV. "More whisky?"

I drained my glass and held it out for him.

He was back with a healthy shot in two minutes, and despite already feeling its effects, I relished the thought of more. No work for either of us in the morning so we could stay up chewing the fat as late as we liked. He turned out the big light so there were just a couple of lamps casting their gentle glow over the lounge and it lent a cosy, intimate atmosphere to our receding inhibitions.

He sighed into the sofa alongside me, and we got comfy, me with my head against his chest, him with his arm around me. I loved my Chris.

The fat I chose to chew this evening concerned one Dougie Savage and his millions. "How are your plans going?"

"Plans?"

I laughed. "How can you forget The Plans," I said. "The life-changing plans?"

"Ah," he said, "those plans."

"Those plans."

"I don't think it's such a great idea any more. I've binned the idea."

I pulled myself free and sat up. "Why? You were raving about them."

"I thought about what you'd said, about being able to sleep at night."

He was smiling at me, trying to disarm me, but I knew he was talking bollocks – the way he'd mouthed off about lack of money and being sick to the back teeth of Savage living the highlife as a criminal. I tilted my head, waiting for the punchline.

"What?"

"Come on. You're not serious?"

"I am. It was a big risk, and even though we're always broke, we can hold our heads up high in our honesty. I want you to forget all about it."

Was this a pre-prepared speech? "What about the new life, the new beginning in some foreign land away from the bad winters and bad taxman?"

He cleared his throat, sat up straight, and adjusted his spectacles. "Leave it, Becky. I've had time to think it through and it's a bad plan; it's full of holes and it's too dangerous."

"How so?"

"Come on! This guy is a killer."

"You knew that when you planned it. You said the risks were manageable, that he'd stick to his part of the deal. And he's getting a good deal, you said so."

"I said a lot of things, but really, this is just too dangerous. From both aspects – the police and Savage. And not to mention the people on that list."

"What about them?"

"Well they're not on that list because they do good in the community; they're bad people too, Becky."

"Don't patronise me. You had all bases covered. You knew the police risk but said it was easily achievable, you knew about Savage, and you'd even met him, sussed him out. And we'd be a long way from here before anyone on that list knew who'd spilled the beans. So, come on, what's the real reason you're bailing out of it?"

"That's the real reason. It's too dangerous."

"Bollocks."

"Don't turn this into something it's not. There's nothing else. It's just too dangerous, that's all."

"What about living life on the edge for a change? What about ditching the idea of us painting the town beige, and go paint the fucker red for a change."

He took a long sigh, tapping his glass with his fingertips as it sat in his lap.

"Think of it this way," I said. "It's a new start for us, as a couple. A chance to get back our youth and do the things we should have been doing all these years but couldn't afford to."

"It was a pipe dream, Becky."

"It was not! Chris don't you dare pull the fucking plug now."

"Stop swearing."

I breathed deeply, remembered my routine, how I'd let the anger slowly drain from me as I breathed it away. I thought about a place down by the river in a summer meadow, trees swaying in a sweet-smelling breeze, a bottle of red in the wicker basket. "Okay, I'm sorry."

"That's alright."

I growled inside. The fucking river bank and meadow didn't work this time. "Do you love me?"

"What? Of course I do."

"Say it."

"Come on, Becky—"

"Say it!"

He sipped whisky. "I love you."

He was good. He stared me right in the eye, didn't blink, and it came out naturally, not forced, not plastic. If it hadn't been for the pause I would have believed him. I put the glass to my nose and got the vapour in my eyes. The sting came but the tears this time were real. "Okay. Consider this then. If you loved me—"

"Come on, we agreed never to play that game."

I nodded. "You're right. I didn't mean it like that, sorry. What I meant was that if you cared for me, perhaps you could consider my well-being, that's all. I'm suffering here." I was about to say like a blue tit tormented by a cat, but I knew that would bring back bad memories, so I left that simile alone. "I hate the library job. I know you hate working for the police, and the money is getting to us both. A new start would reinvigorate me. Really, it would. A new start with enough behind us to make plans for the future, to begin living properly instead of merely existing, would change my outlook on life, Chris. I know it would. The pressure would be gone." I clicked my fingers. "Like that."

He disappeared inside, thinking. I left him alone for a moment.

"I'd be back to my old self," I said. "Remember the old me?"

He snapped a look at me then, and I met his eyes with a warm smile, inviting. "More whisky?"

"No," I said. And in unison, we said, "Lots more," and then we laughed like we used to.

* * *

Afterwards, I pulled the duvet up to my chest and stared at the ceiling, a certain reinvigoration already achieved. I smiled to myself.

"What are you grinning at?"

"Us," I said. "I love the idea of us, don't you? I think there are certain people in life who are really meant to be together. And we're one of those pairs."

He looked away. "We're lucky."

"We are. And think how much more relaxed we'd be without the stress and pressure."

"You're not talking about the Savage thing again, are you?"

"We could do it, Chris."

"No."

It was my turn to look away, I was losing the argument, and I could see that idyllic future slipping back into the sludge we lived in right now. "What's the biggest regret you could imagine?"

"Being shot to death."

"Mine's reaching my death bed and wishing I'd taken more chances."

"Hmm."

"I always wanted to go on a zip wire. Never had the courage. But how many people are killed on a fucking zip wire?"

He shrugged.

"So, I really should give it a go. It's a bucket list kind of thing." I rolled over and faced him as he stared into nothing. "I don't want to arrive at my death bed wondering what would have happened if we'd taken the chance."

"And I don't want to arrive at my death bed next week. Longevity and poverty over a week of riches gets my vote."

"You're a boring old fart. The possibilities are endless. You just need some imagination," I said, "and yes, a bit of luck too. But you could do it if you wanted. You have the power to change our lives. You really do have the power. How many people get that chance?" I reached behind me and turned off my bedside light. "Or have I already spoiled things between us?"

"How do you mean?"

"My… illness. The depression, the aggression, the swearing?"

He turned his light out too, and we settled into a silence in the darkness.

As I was drifting off to sleep, he said, "I'll think about it."

I smiled and draped my arm around him. But, looking back on it, I was fairly sure he'd already made his decision, the damage was already done – and I was the one who'd damaged it. He was going to do the job, but only one of us would be starting a new life in the sun, and though he'd tried to get my mind off it, he'd failed to deflect my interest.

He wasn't going to take me with him.

Chapter Thirty-Two

The journey across Leeds to the train station was horrendous. The car was full of fear. You could feel it; hell, you could touch it. My hands were sweating, and each time I wiped them across my jeans, they became instantly wet again. I had the shakes too. We both smoked almost constantly and pretty soon there was a fog roiling around that joined the fear, and it made our eyes sting.

Sienna said nothing, just drove, clunking gears, forgetting to brake, forgetting to indicate. It was a miracle that we didn't get pulled over by the police, and it was a miracle we didn't rear-end someone.

"It's going to be fine." I think I was trying to reassure myself more than her. She didn't reply, and I didn't blame her. It wasn't going to be fine. I'd read enough books and seen enough films to realise this was always the most dangerous part of any clandestine deal: the exchange. Perhaps I'd have been better fixing the exchange remotely, like a drop-off. But I knew he'd stitch me up, and I'd end up between those two trucks just to fulfil his need for sick amusement.

I wondered what he'd think of the list. Seeing his most trusted man on there and his mistress too. I could imagine the fury, and it played on my mind. How would he react if I was still within striking distance? He'd think I was doing it to spite him, giving him some bad news. But on the upside, I'd hoped he'd be too preoccupied with finding some so-called business partners on there too. That would light his eyes up. Bastard.

"Where'm I going?"

"Aire Street car park."

Leeds City train station was a huge triangle. Wellington Street was along the top slope, New Station Street along the bottom slope, and along the left side was a car park; this was Aire Street.

Inside the triangle was a large concourse that ran from the Wellington Street entrance all the way to the bottom tip of the triangle where the two-dozen or so platforms and the British Transport Police office was, a distance of over two hundred yards.

It was full-on dark when Sienna reversed the car into a space just outside the Aire Street entrance. The floodlights did their job well, but there were still dark shadows around the periphery, like a vignette, that the normal streetlights just didn't seem to penetrate.

She lit another cigarette, her third of the journey, and offered the packet to me. I shook my head. If I'd taken another I would have thrown up. "You coming?"

She shook her head in turn. "I'll stay here in case I need a quick getaway."

"I could use your help," I said. "I need to recce the place."

She looked at me, squinting, "Recce? Have you heard yourself? You're enjoying this."

"I'm as nervous as you are. More probably! I have to meet him; I have to worry about him grabbing me. What the hell do I do if he grabs me and you're not there?"

She stared. "Scream."

I got out of the car and slammed the door, heard her lock it after me. And that was the first minor hurdle cleared; I didn't want her with me. I didn't need the aggro, I didn't need the whining, because I had urgent things to do. If Savage turned up early I was screwed, so I needed to move quickly and lay the foundations for what would happen afterwards.

The first thing I did was head straight for the Left Luggage place. It was at the top of the triangle right next to the round foyer of the Wellington Street entrance. It was empty of furniture and of people. There was a couple standing just outside smoking, but in here it was deserted. And the best thing, there was only one

CCTV camera, just inside the concourse, so most of this foyer would be a blind spot.

I entered the shop, and there was one man in there in a tired brown uniform reading a book. It looked like a place someone had tried and failed to modernise. A laminated counter top and a lick of yellow paint around the doorframes had sadly failed to overwrite the creaking floor and array of tarnished brass lamps hanging from the high ceiling. It looked like a seventy-year-old woman with false boobs and stilettos.

The shop was covered by two cameras.

He marked his place by folding the corner of the page over, and stood. I cringed, and almost chastised him for defacing the book, but I had more important things to get done right now. I smiled. "How's your day?"

"Fine," he said, tapping his fingers on the desk.

I could tell he was in the running for the annual customer service award. I put the envelope on the counter. "Can I deposit this, please?"

"Fine." He slid a form over to me; I had to declare it wasn't a hazardous substance or an incendiary device, but the whole process took no longer than thirty seconds.

"I'll collect it in about half an hour."

"Fine. So long as you have this." The printer threw a ticket at him, and he handed it to me. I didn't read the fine print, but stuffed it in my back pocket where the list had been. "Can you store large items in here?" I asked. "You know, those large wheeled suitcases?" I knew the answer before he opened his mouth.

"Fine."

I was right. "Great," I said, "I'll be depositing one with you soon."

"Fine."

"Bye." I left Mr Customer-Service and headed back out into the main concourse, looking for a cash machine. The concourse was sprinkled with cameras. You wouldn't be able to spit in here without hitting one. It was the size of a small aircraft hangar;

high domed ceiling, shops and fast food places down each side. I spotted a bank of cash machines just as my phone rang.

I felt out of breath already, palms still wet, and I was breaking out in a sweat. I was so high on tension that I was getting light-headed. I leaned against one of the billboards in the centre of the concourse, and answered. "Yes."

"Stop dicking me about, and let's get this thing done."

"Leeds train station." I closed my eyes, remembering the instructions I'd pre-recorded in my memory. "Park on Wellington Street, outside the Queen's Hotel. Enter the train station at the City Square entrance on Wellington Street. If you're not here in forty minutes, I won't be either."

My eyes snapped open as I heard him laughing. "You haven't done this kind of thing very often, love, have you?"

"I want this transaction to go smoothly. So I've put things in place to make sure they do."

"Ooohoo, good for you, lass," he said, mocking me.

"There are British Transport Police officers patrolling too, so don't try anything."

The line went dead. I always thought it was very rude of people to put the phone down without saying goodbye first. It irked me, but I got over it quickly and continued to the cash machines, keeping my eye open for those officers I'd mentioned. Not one in fucking sight. Great.

I was counting on what I'd told Sienna back at her flat to be correct; that he was interested only in the list, that we and the cash were insignificant. And certainly, that's the sense I'd picked up again from our conversation. Still, that reassurance didn't stop me trembling.

I pulled out our last £300 and wasted no time heading outside to the Wellington Street taxi rank. I went to the last one in the line, and typical of taxi drivers in a queue, he was outside the car, cigarette in hand, coffee cup on the roof of his cab, reading a newspaper. "Excuse me," I said.

He didn't look up. "Go to the front, love."

"I don't want the front one," I said.

He tutted, looked at me over his reading glasses. I had five twenty-pound notes in my hand, and that little fan of money got his attention. "I'm booking you for an hour's wait."

"I'll still be here in an hour, anyway, love," he said. "Slow tonight."

"I realise that, but I'm *booking* you. I'm guaranteeing your service. I want you here for an hour. I don't want you accepting any other fares or nipping off to place a bet." I waved the cash in front of him. "One hundred."

He craned his neck in suspicion, the way a pigeon does when it walks. And then he looked up towards the front of the rank, and without glancing at me, casually took it, folded it, and thrust it into his pocket. "One hour," he said.

"Don't leave, stay with your car."

"Okay, keep your hair on."

Was I being threatening? I'd intended to offer an air of assertiveness, that's all. But anyway, he could take it or leave it; it was my show and I could be who I wanted to be, I could speak how I wanted to speak.

There wasn't a taxi rank on the New Station Street side of the triangle, but there was one in Aire Street, where Sienna had parked. I hurried through the concourse again but stopped at the ticket machine. I paid for a first-class ticket to Manchester Airport. I figured it would be a good idea to go for first class. Firstly, you can't beat relaxing on the first leg of your journey in a little opulence; secondly, it would grant me access to the first-class lounge where I could seek temporary refuge should I need it; and lastly – I deserved it!

Throughout this whole charade – and that's exactly what this was, a charade – I'd wrestled to the death with a madman on an old ammunition site, been stabbed in the boob, been beaten up and almost strangled by a copper, been slapped, and stabbed in the neck by my only true best friend. How much more challenging could life get? I hoped not to add 'split in two' to that list, and that prickle of dread crept through me for the hundredth time today. So yes, I deserved it.

I checked my watch. Twenty-five minutes until Savage was due to show, and that meant he'd be here in fifteen – it's what I'd do.

So now, I had to rush. I walked down the concourse again, hurrying, but trying not to look as though I was hurrying. I walked past groups of people milling around waiting for their trains, or like me, waiting to meet a member of their party. I'd seen this place rammed with people, but now it was relatively quiet, just huddles of people gathered in seemingly random places throughout the concourse, others sipping drinks, even someone playing *Sweet Child Of Mine* on an acoustic guitar outside one of the fast food places.

I exited into the Aire Street car park, back into the chill of the evening. I saw Sienna's car to my right, but managed to skulk into the shadows and skirt to my left, going roughly around the outside of the car park to reach the taxi rank.

Taxi drivers are clichés in their own right, and the guy at the tail end of the rank could have been the first driver's twin. He, too, was outside his cab, smoking. There was no coffee or newspaper around, but otherwise I couldn't tell them apart.

I booked him and his services in the same way as I had his twin, but I added something more specific. He wasn't offended by my tone as the first one had been, all his wide eyes saw was the cash, and it kind of made me wonder where he'd drive me if offered him a grand. He was the kind of man who'd betray his wife of twenty years for just one glimpse of a pair of tits. They were all the fucking same!

I skirted back the way I'd come, and tapped on Sienna's window. I was pretty sure she left a head-sized dent in the roof. She wound down the window, stared at me with eyes that were one blink away from falling out of her face. "Scared the shit—"

"Are you okay?" I said.

"I *was*!"

"Sorry, just checking up on you. Not checking *up* on you, just checking *on* you." I tried to smile but it was agony, there was nothing to smile about right now. I had less than ten minutes, and I'd either be waltzing away with a shitload of cash or I'd be dead in some scrapyard somewhere. No happy medium.

"Has he rung?"

"He'll be here in ten minutes."

"Oh, shit, shit, shit." She closed her eyes and I thought she would never open them again.

"Want me to get you some more cigarettes?"

"I have more. I'm okay."

"Okay—"

"Why must I be here? I'm too close to all this, Becky. I should be away from here, I should wait for you in a hotel somewhere."

I crouched down so we were eye to eye. "I'll tell you why. Because I don't fancy loading a bag with two million quid in it into the back of a fucking taxi! I'm taking as much of a risk here as you are. More in fact. The least you can do is wait for me, wait for your share!"

"Sorry," she muttered.

"One more thing. Where does Savage operate from?"

"What?"

"Come on, I don't have the time to say everything fucking twice! Where does he work from, where's his base?"

"Scholes. Remember that old Ford garage at the top of Main Street off Leeds Road? It's on some land just behind there."

"That's a petrol station now, isn't it?"

She nodded and resumed puffing on a cigarette. I left her as she wound up the window.

She would get her share alright. I'd see to that.

Chapter Thirty-Three

I entered the concourse again, dazzled by the comparative brightness in here, and the smells of fast food shops hit me hard enough to send my stomach into hunger cramps. I hadn't felt the slightest bit hungry until now, but food was a luxury that would have to wait.

The sounds of heels on marble, and of the buskers, and the train announcements bombarded me too, and for a second or two I was paralysed; didn't know what to do next. I stood next to the billboard where I'd taken Savage's call, and ran through the checklist inside my head. And it came to me: I had nothing else to do but wait. I headed for the entrance on Wellington Street where the two people had been outside smoking. I stood there amid a crowd of smokers and looked out.

Waiting was the worst part. I had nothing to occupy my mind other than what he'd like to do with me. It was a nightmare that I saw again and again on some kind of loop tape in my head. I couldn't let go of it. And he grew in stature until I pictured myself looking at a man barely able to get inside the concourse. He was everything now; nothing else existed, and I became that pathetic child I'd imagined myself to be while speaking with him on the phone earlier. I was a bug about to be crushed by his shoe.

Who was I kidding? Me, a librarian. A librarian with anger issues and a mind that had a mind of its own, was in the ring against a man for whom they didn't make boxing gloves big enough. I was growing cold again, and I was getting nervous almost to the point where I was ready to back my way inside the foyer, turn around, and run back to Sienna's car.

It was one thing acting cool on the phone, but seeing him again in person, knowing he'd slashed off my hair with a knife and punched me in the stomach without even being especially cross, made me quiver.

Someone was kind enough to offer me a cigarette and I took it, but then I became rude – not intentionally – as they continued speaking with me, and I just disappeared inside my head, nodding occasionally and hoping I got it about right. I apparently didn't, as they stubbed out their smoke and headed off without so much as a goodbye.

I'd like to say that it was quiet, a calm rippling backwater, inside my head, but that wouldn't be the truth. It was as noisy as hell and as busy inside there as it had been in the concourse. Not with music and tannoys, but with voices, and with memories. Of times when Chris and I had been here, the places we'd travelled to, the walks we'd enjoyed.

And before I knew it, I was in tears again. How come I could get stabbed in the throat and control the pain, could control the scream that wanted to come out, yet I couldn't stop the tears coming whenever I thought of him? I missed him so very much, I really did. And I'd give anything to be back one month ago with him telling me about this criminal he was investigating, this criminal called Savage for whom he held so much envy. How I wish I could have been more forceful when I'd told him that at least we could sleep at night.

I was seriously beginning to think that even if this transaction went according to plan, I would never be able to sleep again.

I saw a black Range Rover pull up on the kerb outside The Queen's Hotel, and wondered why it didn't surprise me. All these gangsters watched too much television. I tossed the cigarette aside and concealed myself behind the group of smokers still there until he began walking towards me. Another man got out and headed off to the New Station Street entrance.

I could have flicked the sweat off my palms now. I waited in the round foyer off to the right, hands under my armpits, squeezing the skin there, trying and failing to calm the hell down. The last thing I wanted was him getting a whiff of my nerves and trying to exploit them.

He came in with Streaky, who pulled a wheeled bag twice the size of Chris's, and my blood stopped dead in my veins. I almost ran around them and out through the exit. But I didn't. It was this or nothing, for ever and ever, amen.

"Savage," I said. He turned and I pointed to the single CCTV camera that caught this part of the foyer. "Look at that." He followed my pointing, and shaking, finger and got himself recorded on the camera. He walked to me, long greasy hair draped around the collar of a black cotton jacket, flakes of dandruff dropping like ash from a bonfire all over the fucking place.

"List." He held out a hand.

"Money," I countered, trying not to breathe in his odour of weeks-old sweat.

Streaky hauled the baggage closer, stood it up next to me.

"Unzip it." I stared at Streaky, daring him to defy me. Streaky looked at his boss, and Savage nodded.

"There's nothing in there but money," he said.

"Forgive me for not trusting you."

He brought his stench close to me and said, "I'll have you one day." And Streaky stood up again.

I desperately wanted to come back with some smart response, something that would have him quaking in his boots every bit as much as his comment had got me quaking. I searched my brain, but it just shrugged and mouthed 'give me notice next time!'

"In the meantime," I said, "my passport?" I held out my hand and he dropped a black leather passport wallet into my palm.

"Come on, woman, I'm losing my patience," he growled.

Flustered, I opened it and checked my passport, but he grabbed my arm.

"Get me the list. Now."

I zipped the wallet back up again. A group of people walked past us and didn't give us a second glance. Smoke drifted in from

Andrew Barrett

outside and I craved a hit of nicotine. Looks like I was addicted again.

I slid it into my jacket pocket, and out of sight of the CCTV camera, I laid the baggage down, pulled open the flap, and stared at the money inside. I looked up at Savage and Streaky, but their faces were straight, no hint of a smile, no 'gotcha' moment imminent.

"Get a move on, woman."

I recognised the vacuum bag – the one that had my wedding dress inside once upon a time, and a second bag, heavy clear plastic. I pulled open its end and peered inside, ruffled one of the stacks to make sure it wasn't just strips of blank paper.

"I'm going to beat the shit out of you in a minute."

"And I'll scream the place down." How I kept my composure is beyond me. I zipped up the case, stood it upright and walked towards Left Luggage. "You," I said to Savage, "come with me." Streaky began to walk with him, but Savage held up a hand, and followed me inside alone.

Mr Customer-Service sighed and folded over the page again. He didn't even bother to smile as he stood. "Come for your envelope?"

"I'd like to deposit this, please." I stood the case upright.

He peered over the counter, and I heard another sigh escape him. Work, huh? Who needs it? "I'll have to scan it," he said, coming around the counter. He took hold of the side handles and strained to lift it onto something like an airport x-ray machine.

I said to him, "Erm, can you tell if there's anything electrical in there?"

He eyed me suspiciously. I acted dumb and embarrassed. "I've lost my mobile phone. I don't fancy unpacking that lot to see if I've left it in there."

He nodded. "Fine." And pushed a button. The case disappeared through the flap doors.

Savage stood to my right shoulder, he watched Mr Customer-Service, and whispered, "You'll never live long enough to spend it all."

I turned to him. "Oh, shut up, you stupid man." I turned front again, feeling quite proud of myself, but thinking that maybe I was the stupid one; why antagonise the idiot? He might have forgotten about me, content to kill those people on the list, but now I'd insulted him. "I'm very frugal," I said, "so I should hope not."

"Nothing electrical in there, love," said Mr Customer-Service. "Sorry."

"It's fine, thank you."

"Looks like a lot of paper." It wasn't a question as such, more a statement, but it lingered long enough to become one just the same.

"It's a manuscript," I said. "The original *Lord of the Rings*."

"Joking?" He slid the form across to me and handed me a pen, thoughts of his own book in the far distance now.

"Nope."

"Must be worth a fortune!"

"About two million." I raised my eyebrows.

Savage coughed. "My list," he said.

"That'll be six quid, please, love."

I looked from him to Savage, raised my eyebrows.

"You taking the piss?"

I nodded to the CCTV camera above the counter. "Pay the man." I signed the form.

Savage dug in his pocket, came out with a twenty, and hurled it at Mr Customer-Service.

"Keep the change," I said as he handed over my ticket.

My heart was still rattling and sweat dripped from my fingertips, and in all honesty, I wasn't sure how much more of this tension I could cope with. I wasn't sure how I'd managed to hold out so long in the first place.

I'd have to deal with a lot more before tonight was out. Once Savage had that list, he wouldn't just going to walk out of here, he'd open it in front of me to check its authenticity, and of course he'd read it. And he'd see Streaky on there as well as a host of other surprises. God knew what would happen then. I wanted to stay and watch the fireworks, but from a safe distance. Of course, I wouldn't.

Once we were outside of the Left Luggage place I wanted to be gone, not waiting around for the goodbyes and the courteous handshakes.

When the luggage was safely inside a locker, I dug out the ticket for the list and handed it over, feeling sorry for working the poor man half to death.

"You want this out?"

That was the general fucking idea, Sherlock. "If you don't mind."

I turned to Savage. "Get on the phone to your man at the New Station Street entrance, and recall him."

He stared at me aghast.

"Do it, or the list stays here and I rip up that ticket."

Mr Customer-Service came back with the envelope and took the ticket from me. I held onto the envelope tightly and peered through the door into the circular foyer where Streaky was leaning against a wall, arms crossed, unblinking eyes on me. His companion joined him within a minute. Savage ripped the envelope from me, and I followed him back into the foyer as he pulled the list out and inspected it.

"Mick, Streaky. In the car."

Streaky hesitated, eyes flitting between me and Savage. "Go on," he said again.

When Streaky had left, he turned to me. "Thought you'd have been on your toes by now, love."

"I have one more thing I need from you first." I felt for the knife tucked beneath my belt and covered by Sienna's sweater.

His forehead creased up. "What's that then?"

"The list. There's a Paul Richmond on there."

He cocked his head. "Never heard of him."

"That's his alias. His real name is Paul Bacon."

His eyes widened then, but still he said nothing.

"Streaky?"

He brought a hand to his mouth, but it was false, like a satirical gesture. I was confused. I'd wanted to skewer him with more bad news, I'd wanted to see him squirm as the list proved his empire was a sham, full of treachery and backstabbers and... but he was smiling at me. And then he was laughing at me.

"What?" I said. "What's so funny?"

"Streaky's on that list because I put him there. He feeds the coppers shit information."

It was my turn to be shocked.

"It's all a big game. And you're not as good at playing it as you'd like to believe." He turned and started to walk off, shoving the list into the inside pocket of his jacket. "I'll be seeing you," he called.

Maybe he was right, but I was learning fast. I waited until he was in the CCTV blind spot and then I pulled out the knife. As a group of people passed us on their way into the station I lunged, and in one swift movement I grabbed Savage's long greasy hair and I cut that fucker right off. He spun around, his hand going to his new skin-head-cut up the back of his scalp, and snarled at me, taking a step forward. I held the knife up, tossed his hair into his face. "Now fuck off," I whispered. "We're even."

"We were," he said, and turned around and walked out of the station.

I instantly regretted doing that, but I've never felt so satisfied with anything since I kicked a lad who had been bullying me in school when I was twelve years old. He never bothered me again, and I hoped the same might be true of Savage. But I got the creeping dark feeling that I hadn't just overstepped some invisible mark, but done an Olympic-level long jump over it and landed on my arse in the shit pit. I hoped I wouldn't regret it.

For now, on the surface at least, I felt wonderful – except for my left hand, the one that had clutched Savage's disgusting hair. I longed for some alcohol gel, but for now I'd have to settle for wiping it vigorously down my jeans.

I rushed back into the Left Luggage place. Mr Customer-Service saw me enter and slammed his book down in frustration.

* * *

I walked through the concourse again and out into the floodlit night of Aire Street car park. I saw Sienna's car, and the gently rising plume of smoke from the driver's window. Holding onto the case handle, I took out my phone. Tonight wasn't over, not by a long way, but I had just one more call to make.

Chapter Thirty-Four

I approached her car from the rear, along the driver's side. Her window was cracked an inch or so, and even more cigarette smoke billowed out. I tapped, but she'd seen me approaching in her door mirror. She wound the window right down, and peered up at me. I had a massive smile on my face. I pointed to the case. "Sienna, may I introduce you to two million quid."

She squealed and was ready to open the door, but instead I reached in and took the keys from the ignition. She stopped laughing pretty abruptly. Now she thought I was playing some kind of game with her. She looked at me, still a sly smile clinging on.

"Becky?"

"I need these for the boot," I said. "Gonna stash it there, *honey*."

The smile came back and she tried to open the door, but I wouldn't let her, I wedged the heavy case up against it.

"What's up?"

"What's up?" I said. "I'll tell you what's up."

"Where's Savage?"

"He's driving, don't worry about him."

She twitched her head. "So, what's all this about?"

"It's about being a librarian."

"Uh? Look, shouldn't we be making tracks? We can talk about your job another time."

"We should," I said, "but I'd rather get this out of the way once and for all." I had my hand on the roof of the car, case keeping the door tightly closed, keys in my right hand so she couldn't just drive away. I peered at her through the open window. "I love being a librarian; one of the best bits is that I get to work flexihours. I can come and go as often as I please. I can start at seven in the morning and be home by nine if I want. Great."

She looked at me, swallowed. I think she had an inkling about what was coming.

"I want you to look me right in the eye and tell me about you and Chris."

She almost puked. She started to say something but her tongue got wrapped up in the syllables, and it made no sense at all.

"Try again, didn't get any of that."

"There's nothing to tell, Becky." She shrugged. "We were just friends."

"Good friends?"

Another shrug. "Yeah, suppose."

"Lovers?"

No instant denial, no shouting, proclaiming her innocence. Just a pathetic, "No. No, we weren't. Honest."

Really, she could use some lessons in lying. I'm quite good at lying now; been doing it to myself and to everyone I met for the better part of two months. I'd had an excellent teacher. Chris was a master of lying. "You need to try a little harder to convince me of that, Sienna. I mean, you could try being a bit more forceful, show more conviction. And you could try looking me in the eye; that always goes a long way towards having people believe you."

Her left hand searched the passenger seat for her cigarettes. When she couldn't find them, she looked up at me, and a pair of perfect tears trickled down her perfect cheeks. I felt like grabbing the knife and sticking it through each of those perfect eyes. I pictured myself doing it and screaming victory into the night.

But I didn't. It was cold out here, the sweat under my pits was cooling, and I had begun to shiver. Shivering – or shaking– because I had the bitch who'd been shagging my husband in something of a corner, waiting for her to admit to me that she had ruined my life, had taken everything that I held dear. For I held nothing more dear than my Chris. He was my hero in every way, and I'd die for him. But I wouldn't live a lie for him. I'd only do that for myself.

"You want me to lie?"

Here I was, in some shitty train station car park exchanging pleasantries with a woman who would see me alone and homeless, and oh how I wanted to kill her there and then. Nothing would have pleased me more.

"Tell me," I said, "and maybe we can learn to live with it and get the hell out of here." See what I mean about being an accomplished liar? I have certificates.

She was boxed in; literally and metaphorically. She had nowhere to run, she only had me left, but she had to tell me they'd been sleeping together. I was never going to believe that they hadn't. So, she was in a tight spot: admit it and we could be on our way, or deny it, and stay here until something bad happened. I could see it in her eyes: those were the options. She knew it, and rather than stay here protesting her innocence, she said, "Okay. It's true."

"See." I oozed calmness, even maintaining a smile. "Wasn't so bad, was it? Tell me how it started."

She swallowed, rushing the words out. "He got in touch with me, to tell me to get out of town, that he had information that Savage was about to be privy to."

"So I was right?"

She nodded. "He wouldn't tell me more. So I went round to see him. You were at work. He let me in." She stopped, looked at me, probably to make sure I didn't have an AK47 pointing at her. Unfortunately, I hadn't. She continued, her eyes flitting all over the place, looking for the words, searching for the best way to tell me. "I made a move on him, and—"

"You 'made a move' on him?"

She screwed her face up as though all this was becoming too much for her to compute, like she wanted to back-pedal. Too late for that, love.

"You learned that there was money at the end of the fucking rainbow, Sienna. You found it out from him as you lay in our bed.

My bed! You learned all of this as you fucked my husband's brains out in my fucking house!"

People had begun to notice us, but I made no effort to keep my voice down.

"We didn't—"

I was going to struggle. "Liar!"

"It was only once."

Lying bitch wasn't doing herself any favours.

"It just happened; it wasn't premeditated. We couldn't help it."

I gritted my teeth. "You can when it's someone else's fucking husband. It's called a moral compass; it's called having some fucking willpower!" More people looked.

"If that's what you suspected, why didn't you say anything before now? Why leave it till now, Becky!"

"Why would I say anything?" Right on cue a black Range Rover crawled slowly into the car park. She saw me nod at it. "I'll let him do the talking. I was going to take care of you myself, or pay someone to." I patted the case. "But since I found out you were on that list, I figured I'd be silly to waste my time and my money on you, when he'd do it for free."

She tracked the Range Rover as it grew ever closer, her mouth opening and growing steadily wider until she realised who was inside. "You bitch, you fucking bitch! You promised me." She shouldered the door, but I held it closed, revelling in her panic, enjoying every moment of her fear, like I'd suffered every moment since I'd discovered the wet patch in my bed, since I'd discovered Savage and his men tearing my beautiful house to pieces.

Savage's men got out of the car, and I watched them. I saw something else too.

Chapter Thirty-Five

I saw a plain blue Peugeot come to a stop where the taxi rank was, some hundred yards or more away, and from it climbed a woman with absolutely no bust whatsoever. Alison looked right at me, and then she smiled.

Sienna realised that Savage's men were close and she switched from trying to get out, to trying to stay inside. She locked the door and started winding up the window. I stepped away, and she looked at me with loathing in her eyes, and I knew right then that I'd killed her. Standing here, I watched her lose any hope of life.

"We were going to run away with that money," she screamed, trying to hurt me with empty words. Her eyes went to slits, and she spat venom at me. "We were going to start a family. He said he couldn't stand living with a psycho bitch any more!"

I smiled at her, edging away all the time. "I know," I said. "That's why I killed him."

Her mouth turned into a perfect O. "You? You killed him? You even accused *me* of killing him!"

"I'm a wonderful liar." And then it hit me. *I had actually killed him!* Me! I stared into nothing, perhaps looking through a fog into the past; and then that fog cleared and I saw it, the whole thing, how I—

She was screaming at me, and I found myself with hot tears stinging my eyes. I blinked and they fell. The reality of the situation slapped me awake. I looked around at what was happening.

I turned and walked quickly to the train station entrance. Behind me I heard a scream, and I took a glance back to see Streaky punching through the ascending window, then they were dragging her out, a writhing mass of arms and legs, hair catching the light from the floods.

I allowed myself one glance towards Alison, not surprised to see Steve – the single eyebrow man – at her side. I saw the dilemma on their faces, the indecisiveness as they looked between Sienna and me. I hoped they went to Sienna.

"Move!"

Four British Transport Police officers almost mowed me down as they thundered from the entrance. I didn't pause any longer, though I was desperate to see whether Savage made it out with Sienna, I daren't stop and stare with the other groups of gawpers. I had to run. Literally.

How the hell had Alison worked it out? Maybe they'd gone through the audits again, perhaps they'd found Peter's car at Barnbow, and maybe his wheel brace up in the Cock Beck. It was all speculation, but I didn't have the time for it now.

Chapter Thirty-Six

I did run, right up the centre of the concourse. People paid me no attention; someone running in a train station, pulling a luggage trolley wasn't anything out of the ordinary. I ran up the ramp that took me into the ticket area and the turnstiles. I headed for one with an attendant, flashed my ticket and asked, "Which platform for Manchester, please?"

He pointed across the tracks. "There, love. Platform sixteen."

"Thank you," I said, glad that I had to go up and over the bridge. It would hide me from the coppers who would definitely end up chasing once they sorted themselves out in the car park. I knew that once Alison got the Sienna thing sorted, she'd chase me too – she had a personal investment in meeting with me again.

I hauled the suitcase along, chose the escalator, and then climbed that too. Once on the bridge, I took a look over my shoulder, happy that I could see no signs of anyone giving chase. I didn't slow though; I knuckled down and ran across that bridge even though my legs were on fire, my lungs were ready to explode, and the case was wrenching my arm out of its socket. I guessed that money must've weighed a hundred pounds or more. By the end of the bridge, I had sweat dropping from the tip of my nose. My heart hammered against my ribs and demanded I sit down and rest. There would be no rest, not yet.

The case thudded down the steps, but instead of hopping onto the platform and heading for number sixteen, I headed down another flight of stairs, scattering people who'd turned to look at the noise and the heavy breathing, wondering what the hell this crazy woman was running from.

After what seemed an hour, I plunged out into the cold night air on Dark Neville Street, and there was my taxi, fifty yards away. I smiled as I ran, waving at him.

As I approached, the driver climbed out and popped the boot. For one horrible moment, I expected to see Streaky grinning at me, or maybe Steve, despite seeing them both in the Aire Street car park only ten minutes ago. My mind was fragmented, and I couldn't think straight. "You waited," I tried to say, ragged breath tearing the words to shreds.

"Of course. Let me help you with that." He threw the case into the boot, slammed the door, and said, "Where to?"

"Horsforth Town Street."

As we cruised past the station on Wellington Street, I peered behind me but could see nothing. I desperately wanted an update on the Sienna situation, not to mention the Alison situation. I'd hoped to throw any pursuers off the scent by sending them to platform sixteen – shit, I even went to the trouble of buying a first-class ticket! I hope it had worked.

I thought I could still hear Sienna's screams. It was my mind playing tricks on me, the way it had done throughout this awful episode, the way I'd allowed it to. Seeing her being dragged away like that, left to a death that, despite everything she'd done, still made me shiver with revulsion. I felt cold with shame when I'd expected to feel hot with the victory of retribution.

I sat back in the seat, letting the hum of the engine and the intermittent glow from the streetlamps as they swept over me calm me down. I allowed those subversive stimuli to take away the past eight hours and slipped into to a time where my mind could think about everything I'd done.

It had gone like clockwork. Everything I'd planned right from the moment Chris's heart stopped beating had worked wonderfully, and I should have been proud of my achievements. I'd managed to push aside – really push aside – all thoughts of my killing him. I'd managed to become a grieving widow with all the inherent frailty that status afforded, especially when becoming a widow under such vile circumstances. I'd managed to float on the top layer of thought and keep the dreadful stuff at the bottom, in the sediment, and that action allowed me to convince the police, and Sienna, that I was innocent.

I had won.

And now I had to really think about that victory. Winning was my motivation. I had stabbed and killed the man who'd betrayed me. I'd sent his mistress to her death, and I was two million pounds in the black. And I was alone. The two people I cared about most in my life were gone.

While we travelled, I couldn't help but recall the way it had all started. How my life had changed because of nothing more than a cruel flip of a coin. Or so it seemed to me; it was just one of life's tricks that had turned my Chris into a stranger and me into a killer.

I had lost.

Chapter Thirty-Seven

The night before had been awful. The sleep in between had been disturbed, fretful. And this morning showed no sign of becoming any happier. If my mood had been a weather forecast, it would have gone from unsettled to wintry outbursts with hail storms and six feet of snow. Not good for late August.

The Prozac didn't seem to have any effect at all, but did I really expect it to? It was like giving the Titanic's captain a thimble and telling him to get on with it. But it wasn't just a mood, it was a lack of order in my head, it was a constant jumble of colliding thoughts and emotions; it was like a fireworks display in an electric storm.

I stared at him, as he rubbed his electric shaver up and down his face, pulling his jowls taut. I felt something akin to hatred towards him. My Chris. Not the saint I'd always believed him to be. He was the cause of the hail storm; he was the reason the Titanic's captain was crying in frustration. And yet, there he was as though nothing had changed. I was sure that if he could whistle, he'd be on some catchy fucking Abba tune right now.

"When do we go?" I asked. I tried to create cheeriness in my voice, hoping to provoke cheeriness back, hoping to lull him into a false sense of my loyalty. Who's a good wifey, then? I might be able to lie to him, but I found it difficult to convince myself. I'd asked that question every morning for the past week, but he always shrugged, said he didn't know, but suspected it might be around the 27th.

"I can't hear you," he mumbled, switched off the shaver, and stared at me in the bathroom mirror.

"Aren't you excited?"

"Not long now, dear." He smiled and winked at me.

Yesterday was the 23rd of August. And yesterday I'd decided to rearrange my bookcase after work. I hadn't anything else planned. Tea was in the slow cooker, the house was tidy, and the bookcase had slowly become more and more disordered as the weeks since its last sorting had passed. I knew we wouldn't be in this house for much longer, but it might be another week. Even for such a short time, I couldn't stand it, knowing those books were in a dishevelled state. It wouldn't do at all.

I began, as I usually did, with the largest books on the bottom shelf. That meant Chris's books on Formula One and those tomes on astronomy by Hawking and Cox. But I'd been clumsy and they'd fallen out of the case before I could get a hand to them. Normally I would have shrieked at the prospect of damaging any book – even those I had no interest in at all. But that time, I didn't shriek, I looked at what had spun out of one of the books as they'd hit the floor.

It was a paper wallet. A Ryanair paper wallet.

My heart had skipped. These were the tickets. *The* tickets! This was our passage to a new life in Milan, the one we'd talked about for weeks; the one my mind had prepared itself for. I bent to pick them up and to file them away back in Chris's little hiding place, but I wanted to look them over first. It was one of those times where one takes an opportunity to create a memory for the future, and this was a memory I wanted to hang on to. Of finding our future inside a boring book about Formula One.

But it wasn't what I'd expected.

It would be one of those memories I'd come to wish I could forget like I'd 'forgotten' so much over those weeks. This was a gift ticket. It was dated for the 25th of August, two days before we'd provisionally agreed. At first, I was confused, and I thought I'd made an error, but I hadn't. He'd definitely told me he thought the deal would happen on the 27th of August – my late father's birthday, that's how I'd lodged the date in my mind. The ticket holder was Miss Sienna Middleton. The booking date was

Andrew Barrett

yesterday. That meant he'd done the deal with Savage, and gone straight to the travel agent and booked the tickets.

The strength in my legs left abruptly, and I found myself on the floor among the books. All this time he'd been telling me of his plans for our future when in fact he was telling me plans for their future! I didn't figure in his plans at all. He was going to leave me. And he was going to leave me in a house that I couldn't afford to keep, all alone with nothing but memories of a failed marriage and a wasted life.

And that single thought represented Chris to me now, just the most callous of men.

And then another thought had struck me. When he didn't show up for work and all of this came out in the wash through the audits he'd told me about, who would be left to answer their fucking questions? Me. And so who would take the fall for withholding information – if there is such a thing? Me. It would all come down to me, and I'd bet my bottom dollar I'd do time for it, too. I'd finally get to meet that woman called Trixie and all for no gain. Lots of pain, no gain.

Bastard!

I really have no idea how I kept myself together when he finally came home, kissed me on the cheek, smiled, and asked how my day had been. I should have got a medal. But I'd remembered what he taught me. About lying. How to be good at it. And so I'd practised for the rest of that evening. I'd blocked out the plane ticket completely. I shoved it into a small box and kicked it to the very back of my mind, and I concentrated on making that lamb casserole the very best lamb casserole I'd ever made, and when he slapped me on the bottom, I'd giggled as though I'd enjoyed it.

I drank with him that evening, watching him, knowing he was going to abandon me tomorrow, and there was not one single iota of foreboding in him, not a regret, not a qualm. He didn't even look at me, didn't study my face and wonder what condition I'd be in this time tomorrow.

There was nothing.

I had lost him. But, I'd grown competent enough to hide those things away in that small box and carry on with the here and now. I'd done such a good job that in only a few days' time I'd be able to fool the police completely.

For I'd learned something else too – if Savage didn't get that list on the hour that he'd requested it, he'd come looking for it.

This morning, the 24th, the day I had the fireworks display in my head, the day before he and his lover were due to fly out and begin enjoying my new life, I left him in the lounge slurping the coffee I'd lovingly made for him. He was seated in his usual chair by the window, but he couldn't keep still; crossing and uncrossing his legs, fidgeting with his phone, flexing his fingers. Weird.

I'd also made a plan for him; it'd certainly leave a much stronger taste in his mouth than my decaf had.

"What are you doing today then?" I'd asked.

"Uh, nothing unusual."

I stared at his sandwich bag as it sat on top of the fridge. It didn't occur to me then, but it was an odd sight. It was a work day; it should have had his sandwiches in it. But it was empty. It was further confirmation of a done deal. Either way, he had taken a risk that I wouldn't notice it was empty and begin asking questions.

"Do you ever wonder when the last day of your life might be?"

I heard him gasp, or choke or something. He coughed and said, "You morbid sod."

I laughed. "Do you though? I'm just curious."

"Think like that, Becky, and you'd petrify yourself for whatever time you had left."

"So you wouldn't want to know then? Even if you could?"

"No I wouldn't! I'll just take my ticket when the time comes."

I almost laughed my tits off. What a choice of phrase! Well, I selected a blue-handled knife from the drawer; it was an oddment, we didn't have any others like it. I marched into the lounge, and as he turned to face me, I stabbed him in the chest as hard as I fucking could. The look in his eyes was a picture – it truly was one of those memories I'll never forget. "Your time has come," I whispered.

He hit the floor sideways on, and I nudged him with my foot so he was lying on his back as he squirmed and bucked. "That, my love, is what happens when you fuck my friend behind my back." His eyes, wide already, widened further, and his hands tried to dig into the carpet as though holding onto life. "And planning to take *her* away instead of me, leaving me here to pick up your pieces and do your prison time, is not conducive to my being a good and happy wifey." I knelt at his side. "Do I make myself clear?"

He tried to reach up to me, gargled one word that could have been 'Becky' but sounded like 'geck.'

"Sorry," I said. "No time to chat, I'm going to be late for work." I dropped the knife by the lounge doorframe and left, leaving the back door unlocked. I might have been wrong, but I thought I'd heard his phone ring. I paid it no attention, just washed my hands under the tap in the back garden, and skipped over the low wall as I always had.

Today was my last day at work – I'd booked a week off; I thought that would have been enough time to make preparations, and to get the hell out of the country with my Chris, without having to field any awkward phone calls. So much for making plans.

I felt no grief at all. That had all been part of the mental conditioning process I'd been through. There was a time and a place for expressing that emotion, and the anger that had grown in me, and this was not it. So, I concentrated on my day, one second at a time, the same way I'd concentrated on the lamb.

I must admit, though, like feeling cold at Sienna's demise, I'd anticipated feeling almost high on endorphins after I'd dealt with Chris's 'situation,' but instead I found myself feeling more depressed than ever; more fireworks exploded. Was revenge the way forward? Who knows, but self-respect and pride wouldn't allow me to remain inactive, a bystander, a passive victim of the deceit they had cooked up together.

Betrayal on that scale deserved the ultimate punishment.

Chapter Thirty-Eight

I cleared my throat and leaned forward in my seat. "Excuse me," I said

"What's up, love?"

"Can you stop for a moment, please?"

He indicated and brought the car to a halt at the side of the road. I felt it sway each time a car passed, like a rocking motion. I sat back in my seat and ignored the driver staring at me in his rear-view mirror.

"You okay, love?"

No, I wasn't okay. I was a very long way from okay.

"Not going to be sick, are you?" He turned in his seat, fearful of finding puke all over the back of his car. When he saw I was crying, he nodded, turned front and pulled the mirror to one side.

I was sick. In the head. Nothing I could really do about that, I decided. And I guess I'd made my sickness worse by killing Chris. Then again, maybe I'd made it better – there was nothing more invigorating than clearing away useless clutter, and starting again with an unencumbered life.

That's the way I decided to look at it. And strangely, in that moment I did feel better. I really did. And I knew what would make me feel even better.

I'd seen Streaky pull Sienna through her car window, so I knew that Savage meant to do her some real harm before he finally got rid of her. And that was another pile of garbage my mind would have to find a way to come to terms with. The only thing was, I don't think it could. Ever. It was a huge obstacle to my mental well-being, but there was simply no way I could clear the decks of something so burdensome. I wouldn't get any kind of invigoration from it.

I wouldn't be able to live with myself.

Unless…

"Do you know where Scholes is?"

"There's one in Bradford," he said, "and there's one in Leeds, love."

"The one in Leeds."

"Aye, I know it."

"Could you take us there?"

He turned again, a tissue in his hand. "You okay?"

I took it. "Thanks. I think I will be."

"It's gonna be another twenty-three quid, love," he said. "Sorry."

"What's your name?"

"Rudi."

"Hi, Rudi. I'm Becky. How do you feel about breaking speed limits?"

He looked at me in the mirror, the creases at the corners of his eyes deepening. "I've been known to brush the wrong side of them occasionally."

"This is one of those occasions."

"Husband trouble, is it?"

I nodded. "Something like that, yes."

Rudi turned the car around and roared back towards the Ring Road, making a left and heading in the direction of north-east Leeds, and Seacroft.

"I'm always a sucker for romance." He smiled.

Thankfully as we travelled, traffic was light, the lights were with us, and we saw no police. We cruised through Seacroft and headed away from the streetlights and into darkness, black fields speeding by on each side. A small cluster of orange streetlights up ahead, maybe half a mile away, signified the approach of the village of Scholes.

"Not far now, love."

"Have you ever had one of those passengers who offers a large amount of money to do something out of the ordinary?" I watched his eyebrows rise.

"Well, that's kind of you, love—"

"Becky," I said. "My name's Becky."

He slowed the car down. "Well now, Becky. I appreciate your offer, really I do, but I'm a happily married man." The car came to a halt. I could see the passenger side indicator lighting up the hedgerow to our left as it blinked on and off.

"No, no. Jesus, you got the wrong end of the stick!"

"I did?"

"Yes, you bloody did!"

"Ah, well," he said and then started to laugh.

I interrupted him though, no time for messing about. "I paid you one hundred to wait for me, and you did. It means I can trust you. And you, Rudi, can trust me. Can't you?"

He shrugged. "Yeah, suppose so, love."

"When we get to our destination I want you to wait for me again. I don't know how long I'll be gone, but I need to know you're going to be there when I come out."

I could see him nodding.

"I'm offering you a thousand. And I promise I'm good for it, right now."

He practically snapped his neck in his eagerness to turn around this time. "A thousand?"

"I'm your only fare for tonight though. No nipping off anywhere. I need you on standby."

"Lady, I'm yours all week for a thousand!"

"There's a petrol station, a sort of car repair garage in Scholes. Do you know it?"

"It won't be hard to find," he said. "If you blink you can miss Scholes altogether."

"That's where we're going."

His eyes screwed up. "Why, what's going on at a petrol station this time of night?"

"That is none of your business."

"I think you'll find it is. If I'm parked outside of it while you're doing funny business inside—"

"No funny business. I'm trying to help a—" I stared at Rudi's eyes. I saw the confusion there. I too was confused. "I'm trying to help a dear friend." I stared at him, my face straight, my moist eyes unblinking.

He turned front again, and cancelled the indicator. "I will call the police if anything dodgy goes down, love. I'm sorry, but I ain't getting into no funny business."

"Deal," I said. "No funny business."

Two things occurred to me then. Did Alison and Steve recognise Savage's men in Aire Street car park as they pulled Sienna from her car? If so, Savage's place in Scholes would be bursting with police, and Rudi and I needn't even slow the car down, let alone stop.

If there were no police when we arrived, it meant they hadn't recognised Savage's men, or they hadn't managed to pursue them as they fled. It could also mean that Savage was taking no chances, and had driven Sienna to an alternative destination.

Two minutes later, Rudi slowed to a walking pace, passing by a pair of padlocked chain-link gates across a gravel and compacted mud driveway.

No police.

No activity at all that I could see from here.

I could see a kind of forecourt beyond the gates, and behind them a small kiosk with a hangar-like building disappearing into the blackness at the edges. This was the place he'd brought me to while blindfolded, I was sure of it.

"Pull up there another twenty yards or so, Rudi."

He did, then cut the engine, turned off the headlights, and suddenly the whole scene went black. The streetlights ended behind us, in Scholes proper, maybe sixty or seventy yards away.

"Please wait for me. A thousand, remember?" I said, and climbed out. I closed the door and the darkness swept over me along with the chill of the night. I looked up and could see a rich blackness that was so intense that I could have had the blindfold on again. Pinpricks of light showed themselves when I became accustomed to the depth of that blackness, and then a wind blew my hair across my face, and I looked at the gates.

Here I was, as if taunting the devil. Here I was, dancing at the devil's door.

I heard Rudi's engine ticking as it cooled and I stepped up to the chain-link, and peered through. The hangar's roofline was shown in silhouette against the glow of artificial lights beyond it somewhere in the back yard. That was the back yard they'd driven me to the last time I was here. A shiver skittered up my back.

I held my breath and listened as the gates rattled in the breeze. I was sure I could hear a dim mixture of noise from there, but could make out nothing definite. Curling into the glow over the hangar's roof I saw grey smoke, something like exhaust smoke. And I heard a dog barking too, and that skitter became a full-blown shudder.

The taxi was still there. If I could reconcile my mind to giving up Sienna, I could climb aboard it right now, tell Rudi I'd changed my mind and we could leave, safely and in one piece. And still alive.

But my mind wouldn't rest. Forever it would think of this evening and of this wasted opportunity to put the things right that I still had control over. Even if my own forever was counted in minutes now rather than years.

I shrugged as if resolving the dilemma and searched the darkness out here looking for a way in. There was none, so I skirted left along the fence line, past Rudi's taxi and out into a blackness so dense that I couldn't see my hand before my eyes. The silence was crushing, just the sound of my feet hitting dusty ground, the noise of them bouncing off a low brick wall to my right.

In the distance, a pair of headlights grew silently larger, and within seconds they were dazzling and accompanied by the sound of an engine. I squinted, kept my head to the right so they wouldn't blind me, and it was they that showed me the gap in the wall another ten yards along. The vehicle passed by, the light gone as though someone flicked a switch, and all that was left was a receding sound of tyres on asphalt.

The gap in the wall turned out to be someone's garden path. No sooner had I stepped onto it did a security light over a green-painted door of an old detached house blitz the area with a brilliant white light. I took full advantage of it and marched up the path. It led to a shed in the back that looked as though it would fall over at any minute. The light went out and blackness fell upon me like a blindfold, and I was reduced to feeling my way along with green squares pinned to the backs of my retinas.

And then the obvious thought struck me.

I took out my phone, and switched on the torch. It had only a small light, but as under the foundations of Room 42, it was more than sufficient to guide me along this path that soon grew into a track.

The track was fifty yards long at best, and had succumbed at the far end to a tangle of brambles and nettles. It was wildly overgrown with thick moss and the treacherous remains of a long fallen dry-stone wall. Bushes overhead clawed at my face and the whole ensemble of nature crowded in on me until I was convinced this 'path' was a dead end and I'd have to navigate my way back and try to find another route in.

The torch died as something scurried across my foot, and I squealed and dropped the phone. My heart hammered again, and I could feel the adrenalin making my hands tremble as I searched the darkness. My fingertips grazed across the moss carpet, nudged the slugs and snails and God-knew what other creatures that lurked in wait.

I was beginning to fret, I could feel my surroundings closing in on me, and I began to panic, but I persevered and at last I found the phone. The torch had timed out, as it had under Room

42, but it took only seconds to bring illumination back to my surroundings and relief into my panicking mind.

Sienna screamed into the night, and my blood went cold. My pupils widened and I listened hard, but all I could hear was that sodding dog barking, and maybe men laughing – but even that could have been a trick of the breeze in the bushes above my head. But the scream – that fucker was real. I could see nothing to my right other than dense undergrowth, and my pummelling heart sank at the sight.

I bludgeoned on further. Goosebumps tingling, pushing aside the bushes, taking the kind of exaggerated steps you'd take to avoid being tripped by grabbing hands as I plodded on, crushing snails, through the snakes of brambles before me.

I was itching everywhere, had what felt like a thousand stinging cuts and grazes to my face and hands, prickles embedded in my jeans, and a pound of snail crud stuck to my trainers. The sleeves of my jacket were torn. My hair felt alive with insects and my cheeks ached because my eyes were permanently squinting to avoid stabbing branches and twigs.

Suddenly, I was out into nothingness again. I shone the tiny torch at the floor, and all it showed me was wheat. The air above it not cluttered with undergrowth any more, but black and impenetrable. To my right were more brambles but they seemed less hostile, more subdued. I was at the edge of a field, and before long the brambles and the bushes receded and I could see the back of Savage's premises.

Chapter Thirty-Nine

There was an array of vehicles, including Savage's black Range Rover and a black car, possibly the one I'd been picked up in on Garforth Main Street all those days ago, dumped in the centre of the yard. Along the back fence was a row of small trucks. They had refrigeration boxes above the cabs, and were sign written with something that ended in 'Logistics.' The floodlights didn't reach far enough for me to make out the rest of the words. They were a lot closer to the hangar, and pointing towards a centre-piece like candles on a table.

Two more trucks, similar to those parked against the back wall, were being slowly manoeuvred into the floodlit arena, smoke trailing into the night to be tugged away by the breeze.

Along the far fence were two or three rows of old vehicles; some stacked on the tops of others. Vehicle parts littered the floor, potholes and black oil spills visible everywhere the diffused light could reach. A pair of forklift trucks and a mound of rusting metal completed the montage.

It looked as though the men were getting ready for a party or a barbecue. I could make out crates of beer on a table, and then I saw Savage come from his shitty little office and unfold a metal-framed director's chair. He screamed something towards the offices, but I have no idea what, and then he lit up a cigarette. In the centre of the three mini floodlights was something like a bar stool, and the trucks were slowly reversing up to it, their annoying warning bleeps piercing the night air.

I swallowed, and wondered at how easily that chair could have been meant for me. And then I smiled, realising I was thinking in the past tense – that chair might *still* see my arse on it by the end

208

of this charade. I heard another scream, unmistakably Sienna's, and I wondered what the hell they were doing to her, but I forced myself not to dwell on it for too long; I was scared enough as it was.

I was getting cold, despite the warmth of the night, and I figured that was in part due to Sienna's predicament, the one I'd put her in, and partly because I was stupid enough to want to help her. A fraction of me countered that it wasn't stupid at all; that it was noble. I saw now that Sienna and I had been shafted by men – by Chris, by Savage, by the bully at school, by the smug arsehole at work who got promoted ahead of me – for our entire fucking lives. Women shafted by men – the oldest story in the book. Time to redress the balance.

A small but particularly toxic slice of my mind pointed a finger at me and screamed, 'Is the guilt setting in?' If I ever got out of this alive, I would work hard at banishing that slice to some unused basement room in my brain.

To my left, the field continued away into the darkness, well beyond the strength of my torch, and seeing as there was no way down into Savage's yard from here, I elected to travel with it and see what opportunity came my way. I knew I had to hurry though; no doubt they'd be bringing Sienna, the centre-piece – the entertainment – into the party soon, and I hadn't come all this way and got my sorry arse stung to bits just to witness her death.

There was a gap in the hedge, and through it I could see some feeble attempt at a demarcation with a rusted-through barbed wire fence standing before me. It literally fell apart the moment I touched it, and then I was technically inside Savage's property. I scooted down the slight incline, shielded from view by a thin line of saplings and long grass, so I had no need to worry about turning off the torch just yet. From the bottom of the embankment, it was an easy two-foot jump onto solid ground.

In front of me were more wrecked cars crammed tightly together, barely enough room to squeeze through, but when I had, I took stock of the situation. The three mobile flood lamps, standing about five feet tall on poles attached to large yellow batteries, faced a point in the centre where the bar stool stood.

The light died off pretty quickly against the darkness of the night, so from where Savage's fold-up chair was, he'd be able to see the circle of light only. He'd be able to see nothing beyond those lights at all, and that included me.

I stood upright, felt my back click, and then edged along to the front of the wrecked cars. I turned off the torch, hoping I wouldn't need it again; I didn't want Savage or any of his men, wherever they were, seeing it and coming to investigate. Hoping I was as invisible as I felt, I turned right, walked slowly and quietly over the rough ground in front of the four remaining refrigerated vans parked up against the wall.

Once I was at the far side of the compound, directly beneath the place I'd first heard Sienna scream, I turned and walked towards the back of Savage's chair, just me, feeling naked and vulnerable in front of a bare brick wall, relying on silence and their inability to see beyond the lamps' light.

The dogs leapt up from their dormancy outside some large wooden kennels in front of the offices, and near the rear entrance to the hangar. One of them ran in my direction only for a short chain to yank it to a violent halt, its claws tearing at the ground, saliva whipping from its frenzied barking mouth.

I had paused, petrified in fact, but as soon as I saw the chain snap taut, I continued edging my way closer to that chair. The other dog sniffed the air and then it too joined in with its companion and began to bark.

The industrial wheelie bins were a good twenty yards away, and I did my best to scuttle towards them silently but quickly. I tripped over some engine part and went sprawling into the oily mud that coated this end of the yard, ripping skin from my outstretched hands as I went down. I didn't scream or cry out, but I think the item I tripped over boomed. Luckily for me, the dogs' barking masked my clumsiness, and more or less on all-fours I finished my journey and squatted behind the bins trying to catch my breath and calm down, squeezing my stinging palms into my armpits.

I heard someone shout at the dogs, and shout again. One of them whimpered, and as I peered around the edge of the bin, I saw Streaky kick it. The other quietened also.

Savage grabbed a bottle of beer and sank into the director's chair again with a groan. "Come on," he shouted. "I got better things to be doing." He said something to Streaky that he must have then found funny because he coughed out a cloud of cigarette smoke.

Streaky downed a bottle, slammed it on the table, and grabbed another. He was laughing at the joke with Savage, and thrusting his groin at him. I was ten yards away, and I swear I could smell their combined sweat. It made me gag.

Behind the office, in the shade cast by it, the hangar's shutter door cracked, and then creaked up on spindles that could use some grease. They screamed as they rolled upward, drowning out even the sound of the nearby trucks, and I could make out a dim light inside.

Two men wearing green plastic aprons came out, dragging a black bin each. I watched them, even though Savage didn't look at all, and Streaky gave them only a cursory glance. Poking out from the top of one of the bins was a naked foot. It was splashed red.

I held my breath, and before I knew it, one of my bloodied palms was over my mouth. Was that Sienna? Was that her final scream I'd heard?

I didn't understand.

I looked back at the stool, confusion drowning out common sense. I suddenly realised that this whole thing was a trap. They'd seen me coming, they'd watched me enter the yard on CCTV; they knew I was behind a wheelie bin.

That stool was meant for me after all.

And now I didn't feel secure behind the bin any more. I felt exposed, and looked around for a way out, and for men approaching me. I saw no way out, but I didn't see anyone approaching either.

I looked back to the bins. As they dragged them over the rough ground, the foot wobbled about, twitching as though still alive. They passed from the shade into the light, and I saw how pale the foot was, how starkly the blood on it stood out – like it was an over-exposed photograph.

I also saw how big it was. That wasn't Sienna's foot at all.

I began to feel light-headed, and bile burned my throat. I looked away, closed my eyes for a minute and tried to breathe slowly and forget the horror I'd just seen. That foot must have belonged to Craig Gomersall. They called him Gummy.

I hate to admit it, but relief rushed through me like a cooling shower on a hot afternoon. And with it came gratitude.

Because of that list, and because of me, I had caused today to be his last. I wondered what he'd been doing when Savage's men had lifted him. Had they brought him here under false pretences, "come on, Savage has got a job for you," or had they just torn him from his girlfriend's arms and dragged him here screaming?

Chris's words shot across my mind: They're prepared to take the risk and take the money.

Still, I couldn't help feeling sorry for Gummy. Where had all that money got him?

A flash of light right across my face made me open my eyes again. Someone was reversing a van towards them. I saw the driver jump out; he left the motor running, and I could see its smoke snaking in the air in front of the headlights.

I couldn't see the bins any more because of the van, but I saw the back end of it drop slightly, heard the rear doors slam, and then the van trundled away, around the corner and out of sight.

I began trembling as the shutter doors closed again. And as it hit the bottom, the office door opened and two more men sidled out with Sienna between them.

I gasped. I couldn't help it, but no one took any notice of me. She was naked. Her head hung low and she was barely able to walk, so they dragged her to the arena. I could see the blood on her chest where it had run from wounds on her face still not visible to me.

I could feel the anger growing, and even though I tried to suppress it because I needed a clear mind, I couldn't help that hot surge. I almost cried out to her, I almost ran out to her, but if I'd done that, we'd both have died. Horribly.

I marvelled at the sickness of these men; that they could do this, and more, to a defenceless woman. I found myself biting the sleeve of my sweater to keep quiet.

They led her to the bar stool, and I heard her yelping. She tried to resist but she was already too weak and battered to do anything. She put up a token fight but all it did was make them laugh, and one of them stepped up and slapped her face. She stopped struggling then. They tied her arms around the back of the chair, and I looked on horrified as they helped themselves to her breasts, slapping them, kneading them. I almost looked away, but I forced myself to watch as some kind of penance for my own selfish retribution. You did this to her, you cow.

They'd parked the trucks only a few yards away from the stool, slender ropes hanging from a bar underneath the lamp clusters. They wasted no time placing her ankles in the loops and pulling them tight. I heard her groan.

"Hurry up!" Savage screamed again. One of the two men who'd tied Sienna down walked over to him, and I heard him ask, "When Streaky's finished with her could I—"

"No, you fucking can't. I wanna see this, and then I've people to hunt. So get on with it!"

The man, the same man Savage had brought to the train station with Streaky, grunted and trudged back to Sienna. Mick, that was his name. Her head still hung low, only now her legs were pulled out sideways as they took up the slack on the ropes. She managed a scream as they pulled too hard, and then Streaky was standing before her. The men in the trucks revved the engines, and Sienna screamed into the night. Savage laughed, slapping his leg like it was a comedy show. And to think, he'd had a relationship of sorts with her once.

It seemed cruel to leave her this long, but I needed to. I needed Streaky with his trousers down, and I'd needed one or both of the other men in their cabs, waiting for the all clear to drive off and pull the poor woman apart. I couldn't believe they were enjoying this, which they clearly were. I found the whole spectacle abhorrent, and I wish I'd had the nerve to call the police before I'd got this close.

I took the knife from my waistband, the one I'd nearly thrown from the taxi window as Rudi drove me to Horsforth. I stared at it, and saw that my hand was still trembling. I wondered if I'd be able to do this, or whether I'd mess it up and become the encore to Sienna's demise.

I remembered my resolve, I remembered that it didn't matter if I died this evening – though I'd prefer not to – that it was sufficient to try and put things right, which was the important thing. I found myself shaking my head, and I whispered, "What a load of bollocks."

Streaky stood before Sienna, and he massaged her breasts, and put his hand between her legs. That's when she began crying in huge gasping sobs, her head lolling around as the wailing began. Streaky slapped her across the face but it only made her cry worse. And then he fumbled with his trousers.

Savage sat back in his chair and I heard him laughing as the trucks continued to rev their engines.

That's when I could stand it no more.

Chapter Forty

My knees cracked as I crept forward, the knife in my right hand. I didn't wait, I didn't hesitate, and I'd told myself not to start thinking about it, but to just get on and do it. And that's what I did. I plunged the knife through the fabric of Savage's chair into his lower back, and before he could even scream, or stand, or fall out of the chair, I had my left arm around his neck and I pulled tight. "Do you know what the golden hour is?"

I was aware that he was struggling; his whole body was writhing in that chair to such an extent that I thought he'd fall out of it and drag me to the ground with him. I put the knife to his throat. "Do I have your attention?"

He was gasping, tiny little breaths, hands clutching at the arm rests. He nodded.

"I stabbed you in the kidney. You have a maximum of one hour to get into an operating theatre or die. Do you understand?"

He nodded again. "You stupid fucking cow!"

Streaky looked at us.

I pressed the tip of the knife into his neck, right where that big fat vein throbbed. "Want to turn that hour into fifteen seconds?"

His hands came off the chair in a gesture of compliance. I gritted my teeth and growled into his ear. "Tell Streaky to put his dick away and untie her."

Streaky, his fat head cocked to one side, walked towards us slowly, holding his trousers up, his dick shrinking by the second. I figured he couldn't clearly see me, just his boss who might have appeared to be having some kind of fit.

Meanwhile, I could feel the heat of Savage's blood as it trickled onto my right knee, and I could smell it as its steam wafted into the air.

"Dougie," Streaky said. "You okay?"

"Tell him," I hissed.

"Untie her."

"What?"

"I said fucking untie her!"

"I'm just about to get going on her!" But he stopped walking. He was squinting at Savage, shading his eyes from the lamp light, and he saw me or the blade, or both. "Fuck." He zipped up, and said, "You don't know how much fucking trouble you're in." He pointed his finger at me, and I went cold, and I almost shrieked as he came within touching range. "When I'm through with you, you'll pray for this." He cocked a thumb towards Sienna.

"Do it," Savage shrieked. "I'm bleeding to death, here!"

"And bring her clothes, you piece of shit," I added.

I didn't hear the footsteps behind me until it was too late.

Chapter Forty-One

I hit the floor at the side of Savage's director's chair. My head felt like it had been skewered right through from one side to the other. I winded myself as I went down too, but it was my consciousness that I was more worried about.

My blinks were getting longer, and I found myself sinking into the ocean, but instead of feeling scared, I felt relief trickle through me. I felt like the burden of life had finally got out of my way, and I began to go with it, just sinking serenely. The last time I encountered anything like this was when I got drunk on Jack Daniel's a couple of years ago, and I was watching the room spin vertically like a row of cherries on a fruit machine. I remember clinging onto the furniture trying to correct my faulty vision. But this time, I just relaxed and went with it, tumbling like a slow-motion cartwheel into the blackness of an oblivion I was unlikely to wake from.

Sienna's screaming brought me back to the surface again; and the burden of life hit me like a kick to the ribs. And it turns out, that's what had happened. The fruit machine's drums, cherries, the number sevens, the crowns, and all the other shit on them, slowly came to a halt, and I stared across at Mick.

Behind him, Savage had attempted to stand and failed, plopping back into his chair like a geriatric. "Get me to the fucking hospital, now," he screamed at them.

I looked at the knife. It was only a yard away, forgotten by Mick as he advanced on me again, ready to deliver another kick. That's when I pulled the gun from my jacket pocket.

Mick stopped dead.

Streaky stared down at me, and then Savage did too. I even saw Sienna look at me, her screaming put on hold for the time being. I was still on my back, gun in one hand, enjoying the fear this piece of black plastic invoked. They all put their hands in the air, suddenly taking a real and profound interest in me. I got to my feet and reeled, resting against Savage's chair. He didn't even have the energy to swear at me.

Mick backed away, licking his lips, and I bent down for my only real weapon, the knife. I was desperate for no one to call my bluff with the gun. I didn't want to fire it because all that fear I'd generated would disappear like a woman's scream into the night.

"Look, darling," Streaky said, approaching me slowly, palms extended, "ain't no need for guns, okay? Let us get him to a hospital, and we can sort—"

"Stop." I stared at him as I swapped the gun to my right hand, and grabbed the knife with my left. I pointed the gun at him as I approached Savage. "He won't need a hospital soon. And the longer you take to do what I say, the better the chance he has of needing an undertaker."

It all became a little bit crazy then. Everyone looked at everyone else, wondering what to do next. I broke the stalemate, and said to Streaky, "Go and get her fucking clothes, man!"

Savage tucked a hand behind him, I stepped up close, and dug the edge of the blade into his neck like it had never been away. He took a sharp breath and slowly pulled his hand away from his back, blood all over his fingertips. He looked at Streaky, and even from over his shoulder, I could see the agony in the creases of his face and his bared teeth. "Go on," he squeaked. "Quickly."

The dogs began barking again and pretty soon the two truck drivers had left their cabs and were hovering around us too, creeping ever closer. I kept my eyes front, my mouth horribly close to Savage's ear, and each time they got too close, I twitched that blade and listened to Savage gasp again. "Get away," he snarled. "Get the fuck away!"

Savage sighed as Streaky removed the ropes from Sienna's ankles. The ropes fell away from her wrists, and only then did Sienna look up. She couldn't see me because of the floodlight, but when she was free of the tethers, she screamed again, and tried to stand. The pain in her hips must have been dreadful for she could barely stand, relying on the bar stool to keep her from falling over.

She was wailing hard when Streaky threw her clothes at her. Sienna batted them away and went for him with claws and fists and feet, but he just shoved her away like she was nothing, and she skidded to the ground on her bare knees.

"Check those clothes for bugs, Sienna."

Streaky yelled at me, "I just pulled them out of the fucking bin! She wasn't going to need them again, you daft cow." He tried to laugh at me, to ridicule me, but I saw the concern he had for his boss written across his face, and perhaps a slice of regret at not getting to fulfil his fantasy this evening.

I felt a bit foolish then, but I soon regained the upper hand as I tweaked the blade at Savage's neck. Streaky's face soon straightened up, and he headed for us. I made Savage stand by pushing the blade a little deeper into his neck. Redness oozed out and ran inside his collar.

"Now we're going to walk out of here," I said, pointing the muzzle of the gun towards the gates. "No one's going to try anything. If they do, I swear I will push this blade through your neck. And what satisfaction will you get from killing us then?"

Streaky and the drivers encircled us, getting ever closer. I twitched the knife and Savage screamed, "Get back. Just get the fuck back!"

"Tell Streaky to unlock the back doors on one of the trucks." I could handle Savage, and I had Streaky more or less under control, but the others – four of them, maybe more, presented a real problem because I couldn't keep tabs on them.

"What?"

"Just do it. And get all your men inside."

Savage nodded at Streaky again, and I could see the anger eating away at Streaky as his face grew redder. His eyes became slits as he stared back at me. My nerve was holding for the time being, but I wasn't sure how much longer I could last. I felt like dropping the knife and the gun and yielding, just to get outside of the fear that ate at me just as the anger was eating at Streaky. I was pretty sure I was shaking so hard that my teeth would chatter if I didn't keep my jaw clenched as tightly as I did.

Mick swung the back door of a truck open, and he climbed inside, followed by another three men.

Streaky looked my way, and I shook my head at him. "Now the rest."

"That's it. Ain't no more."

"Would you like me and Mr Savage to go looking for them? Might take another twenty minutes, but I'm sure—"

"Streaky. Do it." The power had left Savage's voice, and it was ragged, barely above a whisper.

"Come out, lads!" Streaky turned in the centre of the floodlights, completely ignoring Sienna's yelps and groans as she struggled to dress. "Out. Now! All of you."

Two men came from the office, another from around the front of the truck that faced away from me, and astonishingly, another from the wheelie bin behind me.

"Get in," he told them. And when one of them questioned the order, Streaky punched him, and then kicked him towards the truck; and even through all the events of tonight, that punch and that kick yanked a gasp from me. It brought home to me the real danger I was in, and that it bubbled just below the surface, ready to pop any time. I reaffirmed my authority, tried to sound steady as I shouted, "Padlock it, and give the key to Sienna."

He knew that was the next order, and didn't question it; just did it, and tossed the key on the floor near her.

"There was another," Sienna said. "There was another man, I'm sure of it."

"That's all of us," Streaky countered.

I could try to call his bluff, but I was as desperate to be away from here as Savage was to get to the hospital. I took a chance. "All four of us are going around to the gate now." I glared at Streaky, daring any dissention. "He's becoming very weak now," I said, "he really needs urgent medical assistance."

"You'll need urgent medical assistance when I've finished with you."

"Very good," I said, "that's another twenty seconds of his life you've just wasted. Would you like to get into a more detailed argument, or should we just go?"

His tight lips disappeared from his crimson face, and I wouldn't have been surprised if steam had belched from his ears.

"Tell Streaky to unlock the gate and give the key to Sienna."

He did, and seeing the look on Streaky's face was the first bit of pleasure I'd had this evening, except stabbing Savage, that was pretty good too. His was a reaction that just kept giving. If I could have suppressed the fear, I could have grown to enjoy it.

We got to the gate very slowly. Savage was having problems walking now. A quick glance behind me told me why; there was a slim trail of blood all the way from the pool at his chair, right around the side of the hangar and the kiosk, and all the way out to the gate. I think the promise of an hour to live might have been a touch optimistic. I was devastated.

So long as this piece of crap still breathed, Sienna and I were safe. But if he *did* keel over, Streaky would snap our necks like match sticks. I licked my dry lips, and used my knife arm under Savage's to assist him. His head lolled, and he grew heavier, mumbled some shit about killing us slowly.

Sienna was still crying, but in between the sobs and the shrieks that still came from her intermittently, were the questions. "Why the hell did you wait so long?" And, "Why did you come back at all, you bitch?" But it was the last question that made me pause. It was only Savage struggling in my grip that got me moving again. She'd asked, "Why the hell did you kill Chris?"

That she'd spared the mental capacity to ask that question at a time like this told me it was prominent. I wish I could have drawn an inference from that knowledge, but I daren't go there and examine it just yet.

Right now, I felt disgusted with myself for putting her through this. But that sane part of my mind countered that she was the one who was shagging my husband. She was the one who'd forced me to kill him. She was the one who'd robbed me of my future with the man I was still in love with.

"Shut up, Sienna, or I'll tie you back in that bastard chair myself!"

We were through the gates – me, Sienna, and Savage. "Now close it," I told her. "Lock it again."

We could still hear the dogs in the background, but it was the man standing before us who snarled. He offered threats and curses as we slowly edged away, but I blanked my mind off and none of them got through. And then he stopped, and when I turned to look, he had gone.

We were twenty yards away when I took my arm from around Savage. It ached, and for a moment it wouldn't straighten back out. But when it did, I took the list of names from inside his jacket pocket.

Savage didn't make a move; I'd expected him to make a run for it, but he didn't, he couldn't. I could feel his strength deplete, I could feel him beginning to fold up. But before he did, I made Sienna search his pockets. I didn't want to let go of this piece of shit only for him to bring a gun out from somewhere and shoot us through the taxi window.

She asked, "Where's your car?"

"I got a taxi."

"You trusted a taxi driver who you've never met to meet us here?"

I glared at her over Savage's lolling head. "I trusted you, didn't I? And I've known you for twenty-five years!"

My fingers tingled, my eyes widened and I almost screamed with relief when I saw the red tail-lights come on some fifty yards away. That was the one thing I hadn't given any thought to other than seeking a reassurance from a man I didn't know – that he'd be here when we came out. And to think, he had two million pounds in his boot. Perhaps I suspected we wouldn't be coming out at all, and so would never encounter any trust issues.

But here we were; battered and bloodied, scarred inside and out. We'd made it. I had given us a very slim chance of success, maybe one or two percent. But we'd come through, and I allowed myself a little shriek of victory.

Rudi saw us coming and selected reverse. Those lights blinded us, but we struggled on until the taxi pulled up alongside.

I could hear the gates rattling again behind us. No doubt Streaky had found some bolt croppers and was busy working on the padlock right now. I didn't know how much time we had, but I kept that knife at Savage's throat until I could hear his breathing begin to suffer. He was croaking something but I couldn't tell what. Then Rudi stopped the car, and Savage sagged to the ground like a man made of shit. The gates behind us rattled again, and I could hear screaming and shouting coming from the yard.

I pushed Sienna towards the rear passenger side door, and she collapsed inside. I ran around to the other rear door, took a last glance at the gates, and then joined her on the back seat.

"Go, Rudi. Now!" When I slammed the door, panting, almost in tears with relief, I heard the doors lock. All of them. I looked at Rudi, and he turned in his seat. The lights from the dashboard shone on his face.

It wasn't Rudi.

Chapter Forty-two

He pointed a weapon at me. "Give me your gun." Sienna screamed at my side, "I told you there was another one!" She began beating at the driver's seat with her fists, kicking it. She was shrieking, shaking her head like she'd completely lost her mind.

"Gun!" he shouted.

"Sienna," I yelled, "what the hell—"

"Now. Gun!" But her madness distracted him when he really should have kept his eyes on me.

Sienna punched between the seats, knocking his weapon upwards. I pointed my air pistol in his face and pulled the trigger repeatedly. Black holes appeared, and then his left eye exploded. He dropped the weapon as both hands went to his face. And his scream was the loudest thing I'd ever heard. It filled the car, and he shook violently, until he collapsed against the side window. Sienna stopped immediately, and I jumped forward, reached for the central locking, and was out of the car in seconds.

I opened the driver's door and he fell out into the gutter, groaning, hands shaking before his bloodied face, fingers like crimson claws, rigid with fear. I left him lying on the pavement, rolling around slowly, pawing at the ground, whimpering. I got behind the wheel, pulled the seat forward, and slammed the door. When I turned on the headlights, I saw Rudi lying on the footpath twenty yards in front, outside the gateway to the old house with the green front door. I saw the pool of blood around his head, saw his wide-open eyes, and for a moment I was frozen there, hands on the wheel, just staring out at a man who I hardly knew but had liked. Dead for no reason at all.

Sienna screamed, "Go!"

I jumped. I slammed the car into gear and before I'd even let the clutch out, a pair of bolt croppers smashed my window, sending glass into my face. I screamed and revved the engine as Streaky yelled obscenities at me, and almost got a hand to my throat. And then we were off, roaring away into the night leaving behind carnage that looked like a film set.

* * *

I didn't think Streaky would follow. He had enough to keep him occupied back there; his priority would be to get Savage to a hospital. I had no idea if Savage would survive or not, but I really didn't care. If he was dead, I wouldn't mourn him; he needed to be off the streets and out of society once and for all. So, I guess I'd done what the police had failed to do.

I stopped five miles away, shook the glass from my hair and clothes, threw both guns and the knife into the River Aire, and made Sienna sit up front with me. It wasn't that I didn't trust her, it was just that… Well, yes, I suppose I didn't trust her. And why would I?

She cried for the next part of our journey, and I felt no inclination to disturb her. I thought briefly about reaching across and offering a comforting hand on her shoulder. But I talked myself out of it. I might have saved her from a horrible death – yes, one that I invoked – but it didn't mean we were friends. She deserved some suffering, and so I let her have it alone.

Once her crying stopped, the sniffling began, and I knew it wouldn't be long before the talking began too.

"Why did you change your mind?" she asked over the noise coming in through the smashed window.

"We're not friends," I said. "We're just travelling companions now, okay?"

"'Kay," she mumbled.

Eventually I turned to her, saw the blood from her nose and her split lip, saw her right eye swelling. She was shaking. I whispered, "If they were going to kill you by shooting you, or by simply stabbing you, then I wouldn't have come back for you."

"You couldn't live with the guilt, could you?"

"Listen, you're the guilty one here."

She half-laughed. "You think?"

"I know." I looked forward.

"I've been thinking about it, and I know you wanted to kill me right from the off. But you didn't; you kept me alive, you lied to me all the way until it was safe to give me up to Savage, so he could do your dirty work for you."

I found it difficult to tell whether she was sneering at me or whether it was just her damaged lip. "I can do my own dirty work. At the time, I just preferred his dirty work."

"But you changed—"

"Yes! I changed my mind. Now drop it."

I pulled up into an estate, just outside Horsforth, found a house with a line of washing hanging in the back garden. "Go get us a change of clothes."

"What?"

"How far into the airport do you think we'd get looking like this?"

"You'll drive away as soon as I get out of the car."

I switched off the engine, and handed over the keys. "Satisfied?"

She sniffled, took the keys, and climbed out.

I wouldn't have driven off without her. I had thought of it; of course I had. But I chose not to. She wasn't the friend I'd once considered as family, but she was Sienna, my longest and closest friend, and if anyone deserved a second chance, it was her. And me too, I deserved a second chance. I know that sounds like I changed my tune, but, I had nothing and no one else left. I didn't want to ruin the one last thing I had, irrespective of how selfish that sounded. I'm not saying I could ever forgive her, but I needed to know she would be okay.

While she was away, stealing us a new wardrobe, I dismantled my phone, took out the SIM, and when we had changed clothes, and got up to speed again, I threw it and the phone out of the window.

It was a twenty-five-minute drive to the airport, and my heart-rate had only just steadied itself as we pulled up outside. Once inside, we bought cosmetics and hid in the lavatories as we tried to clean up and cover our cuts and bruises.

"I've lied to you too," she said as we waited for tickets.

"I don't want to hear it."

"Why did you save me?"

I looked at her, and I nipped my armpit hard to keep the tears away. "Because I couldn't save my husband."

Chapter Forty-Three

We stayed the night in Paris because we were utterly shattered. We ate together and bought new clothes and lots of makeup. We would never be close friends again, but it seemed silly to be strangers alone in a new city. We would part company forever the next day.

I slept fitfully, was visited in the night by Chris, and even Sienna dared to put in an appearance. The bitch. I was horrified to see them both, but when my mind cottoned on to the fact that both of them had betrayed me, yet I had still retained my dignity, sleep came and repaired my damaged mind and body. I awoke feeling wonderful.

The next morning, I split off about five-hundred thousand and gave it to her. Call it severance pay, call it guilt money – it doesn't matter. It was both of those and more.

She hugged me, but I was cold to her. Even as she walked away and waved, I couldn't bring myself to acknowledge her. Yet, when she was gone from sight, my eyes welled up like I was sniffing whisky back home in my lounge with Chris at my side.

* * *

I took the train to Italy and was in Milan eight hours later.

The taxi took me to a hotel where I booked in for a couple of nights, just to get my feel for the place. And as I unpacked my few newly-acquired belongings, I found an envelope written on stationery from the Paris hotel. It simply said 'Becky' on the front.

I didn't open it, not right away, because I just wanted to forget the past, but now the past was tagging along for the ride. When I realised it wouldn't let go until I'd read the bastard thing, I put down my tea and tore open the envelope.

Becky,

I can't thank you enough for the change of heart. I'm so grateful that you risked your life to save mine, even though we've lost the friendship we had.

I wanted to clear something up though. I tried to tell you at the airport, but I guess you didn't want to hear it. So, I'm saying it now, because you have to know.

I am a one-man woman, and I lost him last year. I'm alone and intend on staying that way. Chris and I were not having an affair. I PROMISE. I told you we were just trying to protect you, and you were piling on the pressure, not prepared to believe the truth, and I thought it would just be easier to go along with it, rather than argue a point you wouldn't listen to. You won't know this, but he even bought me a plane ticket so I could get out of the country and away from Savage. I could choose where I was going to live. He died before he could give it to me though.

I hope you find happiness.

I still love you.

Sienna.

I didn't go out for the rest of the day. That short note struck me right at my core. At first, I chose not to believe her – it was easier. But then, I questioned my belief that they'd had an affair, and realised I had no firm basis. The wet patch in bed could have been Chris playing solo, but the air ticket? One ticket. For her. Where was Chris's? I didn't know any more. My mood sank to new depths as I read the letter over and over.

Back at Leeds train station, Savage had handed my passport to me in the small black leather folder that Chris always kept them in. I took it now, opened it, and saw my passport there, as it had been when I presented it to the hotel receptionist. But I looked in the zipped compartment at the back and Chris's passport fell out into my lap. Inside were two British Airways tickets. Mr Christopher Rose – dep London LHR – arr Shanghai PVG. Mrs Becky Rose – dep London LHR – arr Shanghai PVG. Both tickets were dated 27th of August, the date we had agreed upon.

I cried myself dry and drank myself into a stupor. Life was just too complicated, and I needed to be away from it.

* * *

Eventually, the news I'd been waiting to hear came my way as I scrolled through the English news on my new tablet. Savage had died in hospital – so I was a murderer again. His gang was dead too; most of his men jailed for years for crimes ranging from human trafficking to drugs offences, from murder to rape. I didn't like the word 'most,' though. No mention of Streaky.

I found a town outside Milan that I could settle in. Monza became my home, and within four weeks I had found a bank that I could exchange small amounts of sterling into euros each month without anyone asking awkward questions. It had a vault too, so my stash was safe there.

I rented a villa with a view to buying my own when the fancy took me. It wasn't by accident that I'd decided to learn Italian while at work in the library, since I had thought that's where Chris would take us. But he'd been cleverer than that. China had a fantastic standard of living and no extradition treaty with the UK.

I lived in a constant depression. But it was a new kind of depression, anchored to the past by my own irrational thoughts. My own guilt wouldn't allow me freedom from it – it was my penance to suffer.

And each time the doorbell rang or someone knocked, I would freeze. I would rush upstairs and peer down through the balcony rails to see who was there. After two months I'd stopped doing that, got used to the locals popping over to say hi, and even attracted some male attention. Stefano Rossi was his name, and he was a true gentleman; very courteous and stylish in that effortless Italian way.

He worked as an inspector in the local Polizia di Stato. I had a story prepared as I slowly sank into Italian society, and it didn't involve Chris, Sienna, or any of that bullshit I'd left behind.

I was clean, I was free of it, and I washed it from my mind at every opportunity. Lying had become so natural to me now.

Stefano and I were prepared to take it easy. That suited me just fine, especially since I couldn't ever see a time when Chris wouldn't visit me each night, and I would suffer the fresh pain of grief again every morning. Stefano didn't ask awkward questions and I'd become adept at deflecting all the rest. He was content to be with me for whom I was, and had little interest, yet, in pursuing my previous life.

My hair had grown back in the months since some English gangster had chopped it off, and I checked it in the hall mirror as a shadow appeared at the front door.

It was Tuesday, and I was getting ready to go out, had arranged for Stefano to collect me at eight, planning to eat at *Il Gusto della Vita*.

I eyed the shadow as it hesitated on my doorstep. I could see the colours of a bouquet mingling through the frosted glass. I wasn't surprised when the doorbell rang, but I was surprised that he was early. When Stefano said eight, he arrived at eight. Not a minute early, not a second late. I looked at the staircase, and decided there and then that I wasn't going to be afraid any longer.

So, Stefano was early, so what?

I checked my hair again and opened the door to him.

Only it wasn't him.

The flowers landed at my feet. "They're for your headstone." Alison looked at me through eyes that hadn't slept for a month. Her skin was grey, hair lank, and there was a constant tremor in her entire body.

I'd forgotten all about her, and the shock on my face at seeing her again caused the faintest of smiles on hers.

"We found Peter's car. Eventually found what was left of his body. One thing we didn't find was a direct link between him and you."

My heart screeched. "Then why are you here?" The moment I'd always feared had finally arrived. No more waiting, no more pretending.

"To give you this." She pointed a small handgun at me. I saw her index finger curl around the trigger, and she said, "Streaky sends his regards."

"You're the mole?"

I saw the muzzle flash. And in the very same instant, her head exploded into my face, and she fell forward onto the flowers, her hot blood pooling around my feet on the marble floor.

I felt no pain. Not initially anyway. But when I looked down, my own blood was running from my left side, just below the ribcage, pattering onto the floor in a steady stream. Stefano came into view, weapon in his hand, arm still outstretched; he looked past the body and up into my face.

But it wasn't Stefano's face at all. It was Chris's. It was my Chris.

His face was the last thing I saw, and we were on our way to a place far beyond China.

I love my Chris, always.

Acknowledgements

Writing is a solitary activity, but no one creates and publishes a book alone. Bloodhound Books have welcomed me into their fold and have been tremendously supportive from the outset.

I'm very grateful to them for their wisdom and their kindness. Sincere thanks go to Betsy Reavley, Sumaira Wilson, Sarah Hardy, my wonderful editor, Clare Law, and all those people behind the scenes at Bloodhound who've made this possible.

Thanks also to the other Bloodhound authors whose positivity knows no bounds. To Kath Middleton, my closest online friend, and to my Facebook friends in UK Crime Book Club, my Andrew Barrett page, and my Advance Reader's page – you're all awesome.

87157701R00143

Made in the USA
Columbia, SC
10 January 2018